NIGHTINGALE LANE PUBLISHING

The Curious Life of Lily Pond

Andrea Hicks

For the Whistling Man and his lovely lady...

CHAPTERS

LONDON 1889
Prologue

'Bloomin' cold tonight, Ruby,' said Nell, rubbing her hands together under her skimpy shawl. 'We must be bloody mad doin' what we do this weather. You wouldn't catch my 'usband walkin' the streets in the freezing cold. Nah, 'e's at 'ome in front of the fire, keepin' 'is eye on the kids.'

'You sure?' said Ruby, the older woman's eyes creasing at the corners with mirth. Her complexion was deathly pale, and her skin was as thin and dry as crinkled paper. Her cheeks were dark hollows, and underneath her eyes were dark half-moons where poverty had leached away her middle years and prematurely turned her into an old woman. Her claret-coloured skirt, frayed at the hem and stained with a lifetime of wear, brushed the snow and slush on the ordure covered pavements, soaking up the detritus so prevalent on London's streets. She pulled her shawl around her birdlike shoulders and tried to breathe the warmth of her breath into the palms of her hands.

'What d'yer mean, Ruby, am I sure?'

Ruby chuckled. 'I just seen 'im goin' into The Ship and Lamb wiv that bloke what 'e 'angs around wiv, er…Albert somefing, y'know, the one what's always in 'is cups and tryin' to sell somefing, usually a load a shit what no one wants. He'd sell 'is bloody gran'muvver if 'e could get rid of 'er and make a few bob.'

'She's dead, Ruby.'

'Is she? Well, e'd sell 'er bones then.'

Nell frowned. 'So, yer sayin' me 'usband ain't at 'ome.'

'That's what I'm sayin' gel. 'E's gorn to the pub wiv the money what you take 'ome of an evenin'.'

'For Chris' sake,' Nell cried, frustrated at what she'd suspected all along. 'Why do I do this? Gawd knows what I'm catchin' from them blokes from the docks and them dossers what lives in the slums in Dorset Street, and 'e's takin' me coin down the pub. If 'e's in the pub me kids are on their own, and it wouldn't be the first time neiver. 'E's such a lazy git. 'E don't do nuffin.' Won't even look for work no more cos 'e was turned down a few times at the factories and the docks. An' if I don't take enough coin 'ome 'e'll beat me 'til I'm black and blue.'

'Why don't yer leave 'im then? You're the one earning the coin not 'im. You'd manage wouldn't yer?'

'Yeah, well,' she cocked her head to one side and smiled a slow smile. 'I love 'im don't I?'

Ruby chuckled again. 'That's where they got us, girl. Can't do wiv 'em, can't do wiv out 'em.'

Nell smiled affectionately at the older woman. 'You should be 'at 'ome, Ruby, not walking these 'orrible streets looking for customers. You should 'ave your feet up at your age.'

Ruby shrugged. 'Old 'abits die 'ard, don't they? I got to selling a few bits and pieces what me son managed to get, but it don't bring in enough to feed the three of us. And then there's the rent, 'though what we pay it for I dunno. The 'ouse is fallin' ter bits. It's colder inside than what it is out 'ere. And we share wiv three other families what 'ave to use the same privy as us.' She shivered. 'Disgustin' an' all, they are.'

Nell sighed. 'Well. There ain't much doin,' is there? S'pose it's too cold for 'em to get their cocks out. Might get frostbite.' Both women threw back their heads and laughed, their breath turning into a pale vapour, a mist that surrounded them momentarily then floated away.

'Some of 'em don't 'ave enough down there to freeze into more than a skinny icicle,' chuckled Ruby. 'Not enough for us to feel it any 'ow.' They both laughed aloud again, shaking their heads, and wiping the tears from their eyes before they froze on their faces with bitter cold. 'Makes me laugh it do. They don't mind us 'avin' to lift our skirts and gettin' our kitties cold, do they?' They both howled with laughter again.

'I'm goin 'ome, Nell,' said Ruby, lifting her hand in a wave. 'If anyone comes down 'ere it's you they'll want. They only want the pretty ones these days. Reckon I'm getting' too old for this game.'

'I don't blame yer, Ruby. I ain't gonna be too much longer. Don't fink there's anythin' doin.' I'll just give it another arf an 'our. Then I'll go down the pub an' sort out that 'usband a mine, lazy git.'

Ruby lifted her hand in farewell. 'See yer tomorrow night, Nell?'

'That yer will, Ruby. Gotta make up fer tonight. Got nuffin in the cupboard to feed me kids wiv.' She shook her head. 'We could starve, and no one would care, would they?'

'Nah. Alright for them toffs what live in Westminster. They'll 'ave a Christmas all right. Bet they don't give the likes of us a second thought.' Nell nodded sadly and lowered her eyes to the pavement. 'And, Nell,' Nell looked up, 'don't be going down Dorset Street on yer own. Wait on the corner. Yer knows what it's like down there. Yer kids need yer…more than a few coins.'

Nell nodded and her pretty, red-cheeked face broke into a smile. 'I won't, Ruby, I promise. Thanks for caring about me.'

Ruby turned to shuffle down the street, her hand raised in a farewell. Nell watched her disappear into the fog as she blew onto her hands to warm them.

'Just another 'arf hour,' she said to herself. 'Then I'm off 'ome to me kids, and no doubt a blazing row with 'im.'

Andrea Hicks

Chapter 1
15th December 1889

The body lay on the corner of Dorset Street and Clay Street. A pool of slush around the body had turned black with the constant tramping of horses' feet, churning the mud and horse-dung into a fetid soup. The garments worn by the unfortunate deceased soaked up the foul odorous concoction like a sponge.

Across the body from shoulder to thigh lay a long piece of soot blackened timber, too heavy for anyone to move, and lying about the head were pieces of smashed brick and shards of glass, one of which had pierced an eye, cleaving it in two, the innards of which lay on a cold, dead cheek. I stood close by; my eyes trained with sorrow on the recumbent figure.

'Nasty night for you to be out, Mrs Pond,' said a police constable who was bending over the dead woman. 'Shouldn't you be at 'ome with your kiddies?' He glanced up at me through narrowed eyes, his hands on his knees.

'Constable Turner, you know perfectly well I'm a Miss and not a Mrs, and I certainly don't have any "kiddies" as you so eloquently put it.'

Constable Turner straightened up and sighed. 'Dunno what that means, but...'

'I know what *you* mean, Constable Turner. You mean this is no place for a woman.'

He sniffed. 'That's about the size of it.'

'The size of it is that a young woman has been slain on the streets of Spitalfields yet again. Not by that person who shall remain nameless and yet whose name has been on everyone's lips, but by a falling building, the consequences of which remain all around us. Something needs to be done, Constable Turner. Surely the people who live in these streets deserve better. Life is difficult enough for them and yet here we are, standing over a woman who has been killed by falling masonry, simply because those who had the responsibility of erecting these putrid buildings did not build them to the standard required to keep any inhabitants safe, or those standing outside it, it would seem.'

Constable Turner inhaled a breath and pushed his thumbs into the side pockets of his uniform jacket.

'I don't think that's anything to do with us, is it? And certainly nothing to do with the police force. We've got enough on our plates looking for that demon who slices up the women of this parish and then disappears into the fog. The building of 'ouses in these streets is up to the councillors, nothing to do with us constables.'

I shook my head in frustration. 'Just like a man?' I said under my breath, not caring if he heard me. 'All you care about is how much you can sink in the ale houses.'

'What was that you said, Miss Pond?'

'Oh, just that we'll see more sinking of these houses.' I took a notebook and silver-topped pencil from my carpet bag and jotted down my thoughts on the matter. 'They should be demolished, every single one of them.'

'And where will the people go who use them?' he asked me, frowning. 'In the meantime, I mean, before they build new ones. They 'ave to sleep somewhere, don't they? There's nowhere for 'em to go, Miss Pond, and frankly, I'm not sure you know what life's like for 'em, being the sort of woman you are and where you come from. Are you goin' ter invite 'em to stay at your gaff.'

I raised my eyes from my notebook and looked at him sharply, a little put out at his inference. 'And what kind of woman is that pray?'

He puffed out his chest and frowned. 'I didn't mean no offence, Miss Pond. You mean well, we all know that, and you've done some good things in the parish, making donations and suchlike, and making your rounds of the East End.' I nodded, waiting for him to damn me with faint praise. 'But you live in Harley Street, a much more salubrious manor, in a house that I believe was your father's until he sadly passed, a large accommodation which I've been led to believe is now yours. You and your sister, you've had...well,' he stroked his moustache thinking he might have gone too far, but then realised he had, and there was no going back so there was no choice but to go forward, 'what we, that is, people like me, would call a privileged life.'

I nodded and gritted my teeth. 'Yes, well, thank you so much for your summary of my life, Constable Turner, although how you've come by this information is a mystery to me, the contents of said information which simply shows you don't know me at all. I'm disappointed that your summation of me considers only what I own and my station in life and nothing more.' I stared at him for a long moment so he would understand the veracity of my rationale, then glanced down at the inert body soaking up the putrid mash underfoot. 'What will happen now? Will you not need to find the family of this poor girl?'

'My fellow constables are door-knocking at the lodging houses in Clay Street as we speak, in pairs or threes as is usual, although I doubt we'll find out who she is. I'm afraid no constable would venture into Dorset Street if they valued their life. My guess is that she didn't live here in these streets but was simply standing on the corner waiting for customers. You know what kind of girl she is of course?' I gave a swift nod. 'She was in the wrong place at the wrong time, Miss Pond, the same of which could be said for you. This is a dangerous place, a terrible place where bad things 'appen. We've 'ad all sorts goin' on 'ere this week. This is no place for the likes of you, or anyone else if the truth be told. Please go home, Miss Pond. Go back to the warmth of your hearth. If you've any sense, you'll stay there. I'll see to this young lady. There's no more pain for her to feel. She's past that, the poor lass.'

'Who will pay for her funeral?'

'A pauper's funeral and a pauper's grave, Miss Pond. That's what they get, these girls from the streets. There's no one to pay for the services of the vicar or the gravedigger, so they 'ave to 'ave what they're given.'

'Is any attempt made to find out who these girls are?' I asked him, my stomach churning with grief.

He shrugged. 'We do what we can, but often they don't have no one anyway, so there don't seem to be much point. And if they come from a brothel the madam will always deny knowledge of 'em 'cos they don't want ter pay for a funeral and such like. I've 'ad 'em close the door in me face more than once. Even if we find the families, they pretend not to know anything about 'em. Embarrassed see, but more importantly they don't want to 'ave to fork out for a gravedigger and whatnot.'

'And because they're the lowest of the low the police won't waste time on them?'

'I wouldn't put it quite like that…but, yes.'

'If her family are not found my sister and I will pay for the funeral and the gravedigger.'

'You sure, Miss Pond. You do a lot for these people already.'

I shrugged and sighed. If I were to tell him the truth, I would describe how helpless I felt, how much I grieved for the women and children who lived in the squalid streets who didn't have a future worth looking forward to. 'Not enough it would seem.'

'Well, even you can't build 'ouses, ma'am.'

'No, Constable Turner. I'm aware of that. I just pay for the funerals of the poor devils they fall on.'

'He said we were privileged, Violet. Constable Turner, the policeman who was on duty this evening. He said we live privileged lives.'

I sat on the settee in our sitting room and watched as Violet, my older sister, quietly lay her embroidery on her lap. She sighed as she took a moment to glance up at me, not without some sympathy. Her eyes were troubled. 'The point is, Lily, I suppose from where they view us, we do. We live in the home we were raised in and probably always will. We've never missed a meal in our lives, unless it was something we disliked so intensely we were allowed to slip it under the table to whichever dog was hiding there at the time, and I can honestly say I've never felt cold or unsafe here. As children we were surrounded by understanding and love, and our parents were always in residence until they passed. Do you think the inhabitants of Dorset Street, St Giles, and the streets about can say the same? And what about The Old Nichol in Shoreditch? Who would choose to live there, sister?'

'I'm not sure which is worse. They're all as degraded and rife with poverty as each other.'

Violet suddenly looked more interested. She pushed her embroidery aside and leant forward.

'Do you remember the wormery we were shown as girls by Farmer Daley's son, Joseph. We were fascinated, weren't we? Watching the worms as they forged their paths and tunnels through the earth as if they were living in a township.'

I shuddered; the memory clearly was not as popular with me as it was with Violet. 'I do remember it, Violet. I'm not sure I was as fascinated as you clearly were.'

'That's what The Old Nichol, and St Giles, and streets like Dorset Street remind me of. They're like wormeries. All the inhabitants pushing through the neglected streets creating their own paths in life.'

I nodded and pulled a face of regret. 'I won't disagree with that. They wade through their own filth on a daily basis. It saddens me terribly imagining what those places look like from the inside. The houses in The Old Nichol are more like rat's nests than wormeries, totally overrun with people from the terribly old to the just delivered. It's like hell on earth.'

'Have you been inside any of the houses? I thought you had been told it wasn't safe.'

'How am I expected to know how they live if I don't go into the homes. I must see it all for myself. One couldn't possibly have an informed opinion if one hadn't seen it.'

'You take too many risks, sister,' Violet said, shaking her head in exasperation, picking up her embroidery again. 'You've been warned on a number of occasions by the constables yet still you persist.'

I sat opposite Violet and leant forward, my elbows resting on my knees. I was ready for an in-depth discussion.

'But, Violet, I must. And who will persist if I don't? I wish you would come with me on one of my forays into the rookeries. You would be astonished…no…horrified at how those poor people live, and much of the time because of no fault of their own. It beggars belief to think we live in the same vicinity, not a handful of streets away. Why, I could walk there now if I had a mind to.'

'Yes, sister, but I could not!' She glanced down pointedly to her bath chair.

I pulled an apologetic smile. 'I'm sorry, Violet. I wasn't thinking. I was simply trying to make the point that the ones who need our help live a stone's throw from us. When I leave here and perambulate the streets I see them every day; *we* see them when we go out together, do we not? You see it as well as I do. The mothers dragging their poor children behind them, maybe five or six little individuals, sometimes more, all bedraggled, all malnourished. And the mother always looks ready to give up, to lie down on the pavement and well…die.' Violet tutted, but I continued with vehemence. It was a subject very dear to my heart. 'One can only wonder what they're going home to, that's if they have a home, a table with no food perhaps, nowhere to wash clothes…or even themselves. And their husbands, most who seem to have estranged themselves from their families, often in their cups and with no visible means of making life better for any of them.'

'Or any inclination,' Violet said, raising a sardonic eyebrow.

I nodded. 'That is true, but it's not the children's fault.'

Violet folded her embroidery and placed her silks carefully into her sewing basket with her usual efficiency. She gazed into the distance, deep in thought.

'Can you not find another way, Lily?'

I inclined my head. As usual Violet was going for the soft option, the too easy one people in our society thought was enough. Anything to keep me safe. 'You mean money, don't you?'

Violet nodded and picked up her embroidery again, peering at it closely before selecting a yellow silk from the small red and white basket. She inserted a fine needle into the centre of a flower to embroider the stamens. 'We can afford it.'

'Yes, we can, but the problem with simply giving money is it doesn't always go to where it's needed.'

'You mean the public houses of course.'

'Yes…and worse. Prostitutes do a roaring trade in these parts. It's a wonder they have time to bless themselves…and their madams take the largest part of what they earn. Some of those girls are barely finished with their lessons.' She frowned. 'No, Violet, if we're to help those who live in the rookeries and St Giles it must be hands on. We need to be where they are, to discover how they really live, who runs the gangs and organizes the prostitutes. Who takes care of the children and who doesn't.'

'There's always Peters and Levenshulme's.'

'Oh, no dear, that won't do. It's not a solution. It won't do at all.'

'Why not?' Violet looked exasperated, laying her embroidery on her lap with not a little force. 'It gets the children off the streets,' she said abruptly. 'They're properly clothed and given three meals a day, something some of them have never known. It must be better than running around the streets in filth, the snot running from their noses, sores on their faces and their bellies rumbling with starvation.'

'And leaves their parents to have more children. And those poor little dears are separated from their parents and sometimes from each other. The people who run the orphanages do their best but it's not an adequate substitute for family life, Violet. And when I visited there seemed to be no evidence of pastoral care. There were few toys and even less comforts.' I shook my head. 'No, Violet. We must begin at the beginning, find the source of the poverty and crime that rules the area.'

'And how do you propose to do that, sister?'

I took a deep breath, more than aware that if there were to be puzzling questions to answer, Violet would do the asking of them.

'I'm not sure yet, but I will find a way. Have no doubt.'

'And why, sister, must it be you who does so?'

I smiled and Violet returned it, affection in her eyes. 'Because there is no other like me, Violet. And I hope I have your full support.'

Violet widened her eyes. 'You always have my support, Lily. You try to do so much good, it's just that…'

I waited for my sister to finish her sentence. 'Just that, what exactly?'

'Sometimes it goes wrong. Meaning well and doing well seem to be two completely different things.'

I pursed my lips. Violet was astute and as sharp as a well-honed knife. It's why we got along so well. 'I'm well intentioned.'

Violet nodded. 'Yes, you are, but I feel strongly you must find another way to achieve whatever it is you're setting out to do. Your social conscience is to be admired, and of course, if there's anything I can do to help I will always assist you, but there have been incidents have there not? I'm reluctant to mention the time you went to The Old Nichol, but mention it I must. You offered to help with the children and the inhabitants thought you were from one of the workhouses, attempting to make off with their youngsters and ran you out of the streets. You were left dishevelled and panting, with a cut to your face.'

'I fell over and scraped my face on the wall. It was an accident.'

Violet sighed. 'I know, dear, but going to The Old Nichol dressed the way you were.'

I stared at my sister in astonishment. 'I was dressed how I usually dress, Violet, in a skirt, jacket and collared shirt. I wasn't wearing a tiara and an ermine trimmed cloak.'

'You stood out. The cut of your clothes, the newness of your boots when some of the children go barefoot. It was enough for the inhabitants to turn against you. They didn't trust your motives or your kindness, however well-intentioned. This is the very reason the constables warn you off when you go to the rookeries or perambulate the streets. They are worried for your safety, Lily.'

Violet sighed again and shook her head in frustration. She knew I was headstrong and well-intentioned, but this was a conversation we'd had many times before.

'And what would I do without you if anything should happen to you? Do you not think I worry when you go out on these odysseys of yours?' I felt chastened and Violet gazed at me with deep fondness. 'I understand, Lily, really I do. You're looking to make your life worthwhile, to live a commendable life, one that means something, but you take too many risks. The police constables think so. It's why they keep sending you home, back to your warm fire as they say. I don't think they understand your need to help those less fortunate.' She leant forward and placed a hand on my arm. 'Their behaviour and dismissal of you says everything about them, Lily. They don't care as you do, but you must care about yourself too. What would Truffle and I do without you?'

I chuckled and glanced across at our faithful fox terrier, Truffle, who had been with us for nearly ten years. He lay on the settee next to Violet, his head so close to her hand he was in danger of being stabbed with one of Violet's embroidery needles. I raised an eyebrow.

'A little dramatic don't you think?'

'I'm not being dramatic, Lily,' Violet said without looking at me, so intent was she on her embroidery. 'I'm being realistic. Mr Harrison says no person of sensibility would venture into such a place.'

'Mr Harrison is content to stay in front of his own hearth and pretend nothing untoward is going on outside his window.' I knew Violet was about to protest so I held up my hand to halt her. 'I know he is a good person, Violet,' I said softly, 'and a dear friend to you, but we're not all the same are we, dear?'

'Indeed, we are not,' she said looking up with a smile on her face. 'And thank the Lord for it. What a boring life it would be.'

'But much safer?'

'Yes, Lily, much, much safer.'

Chapter 2

I suddenly felt overwhelmingly tired and looked forward to sinking into the warmth of the plump eiderdown on my bed. I sighed as I made my way up the staircase. Violet was right of course. She always was in terms of sensible thinking. She was level-headed with a no-nonsense attitude to life, but knowing Violet as I did, I knew she was a romantic in her heart. Sometimes I wished she would allow that side of her personality to come to the fore, to break away from the shackles of what she deemed rational and wise. I had suspected that she harboured a hope that her friend, Mr Harrison, a man with a private income and a large, rambling house in Bayswater, would propose marriage to her. He was more than capable of keeping Violet in the circumstances in which she had been raised, and nothing would have given me greater pleasure than for her to find marital happiness with him.

A little niggle of thought came to me then, one I couldn't shake off. If he ever did propose, I hoped he would have the composure and surety to actually take part in his own marriage ceremony, unlike my fiancé, The Right Honourable Jonathan August-Trelawney, who for whatever reason, decided the day wasn't important enough for him to attend.

I opened the door to my room and felt a sense of comfort. This was the room I came to when I wanted solitude. After my defaulted wedding day I had spent a good deal of time here, its four walls providing me with safety on so many occasions, particularly when some of our associates wanted to collect the wedding presents that would never be used. Had those denizens of our society held back so as to soothe my sensibilities and allow me to settle gently into the life

I had assumed I would leave behind? No, they did not. Many of them could hardly wait until the church door had closed behind them before making their way to my home and picking over the remains like wolves picking over a carcass.

I sat at my dresser, staring into the mirror. I put my tongue out at my reflection, then laughed and shook my head at the ridiculousness of it all. Six months before I had been ready to leave this room, with its long windows looking out onto the large garden; the four-poster bed with its beautiful drapes and coverings in an intricate oriental design I adored. The detailed depiction of birds and trees and the ornate colours of the deepest red, luscious blues and greens spoke to my sense of style, and I had planned to repeat the sumptuous décor in what was to be my new home in Holland Park. But I had been left at the altar, waiting for my intended to join me so we could begin our new life together. He had not arrived and had not been seen since. The Right Honourable Jonathan August-Trelawney had disappeared from the face of the earth and proved himself to be not so honourable after all.

I thought I would never recover from the shame, the utter humiliation at being left standing at the altar alone in my beautiful wedding dress in the new fashion of white lace, a mode begun by Queen Victoria when she married Prince Albert, quietly crumbling from stunned devastation, while those around me, either embarrassed by the situation or excited by the amount of gossip with which it would provide them, had coughed nervously, or shuffled their hymn sheets, some using it as a fan, or tutted and shook their heads while smirking at their friends sitting in the pews as if to say, 'Well, she wasn't worthy of him. There is no surprise here.'

Then there was the whispering. Some behind their hands so I wouldn't hear the comments, some not caring if I heard. They were put out. *They*...had given up their afternoon to be present at the wedding, the one I, and Violet, had planned so meticulously. They had bought presents for the happy couple and expected them to be returned. I could hear them clearly; excruciating sympathy from some, derision from others. That unforgettable moment when I had need of comfort and succour in my life was when I learnt how cruel people could be.

I waited at the altar, praying the guests would leave so I would not have to turn and face their expressions of pity. When they had all abandoned me in the church, had gone out into the bright sunlight of a summers' afternoon to resume their lives, I lowered myself to the altar steps and sobbed, pushing my face into my bouquet of creamy pink roses and white lilies. The vicar had hovered for a time, then I heard him sigh, the hem of his cassock making a swishing sound against the terracotta tiles as he'd gone into the safety of the vestry.

'Lily?' A voice behind me said my name quietly, steadfastly. Violet had waited with me also, tears rolling down her face as she witnessed her beloved younger sister in her darkest hour. She had wheeled her bath chair up to the altar where I sat surrounded by yards of white satin and lace that glinted in the candlelight, while I tried to make herself as small as possible. 'Lily,' she whispered. 'Let's go home.'

We left the church together. Violet had gently wrapped her purple cloak around my shoulders to hide at least some of my wedding dress. I pulled the velvet hood over my hair to hide the flowers which had been woven into the lavish curls. We travelled home in our carriage, neither of us speaking, only my sobs punctuating the quiet darkness within the cab. Violet had pulled the leather curtains across the windows so I could have some privacy.

We both knew the news I had been jilted would be the talk of our society for at least a few days and would be a stain on our family. Both of us knew it would be forgotten by the gossips when other news came along for them to salivate over. And I envied them. How I wished I could get the awful memories of the day out of my mind. I will not forget so easily.

I did my best not to recall the way I had felt that day, but sometimes, when I was perhaps tired, or feeling life had let me down rather, a sense of abandonment flooded over me, making me shiver with anxiety as my eyes sparkled with unshed tears. At those times, moments I often found difficult to prevent, I would brush away the tears tutting to myself for allowing Jonathan's misdemeanour to further shadow my life.

But…I had to confess I was worried. Nothing had been heard from him since the evening before the wedding had been due to take place. He had previously been staying at his parents', Lord and Lady August-Trelawney who lived in Richmond, until the eve of the wedding where he was due to travel to the house of his grooms' man, The Right-Honourable Oliver Coombes. It transpired, after he had not arrived for the wedding, he hadn't arrived at his friend's home either. Oliver Coombes had not set eyes upon him.

I stared once more at the reflection in my mirror. I shook my head and lowered my chin to my chest, closing my eyes. Jonathan's handsome face loomed behind my eyelids. Not once had I contemplated a scenario where he would not be at the church to marry me. Never in my heart did I think he could be capable of such a malicious event; the possibility of his jilting me had never been considered, and deep down I still didn't believe it. I was certain something untoward had happened to Jonathan; that my being left standing alone at the altar had not been done out of his own free will and certainly not out of cruelty or amusement. I had said as much to Violet, but Violet had just sighed, shaken her head and said, 'I know you still love Jonathan, Lily, and I understand, really I do, my dear. You don't want to think badly of him. But he has disappeared from society, leaving not just your heart broken, but his parents' too. It would have been so much better if he'd said how he'd been feeling before the wedding was due to take place. It would have saved you, and his parents, so much heartache.'

I had gradually come to terms with the fact I would not end the year as a married woman. The plans I and Jonathan had made together would never bear fruit, and even if he suddenly appeared back in society, which Violet was almost certain of, I hoped we could be polite acquaintances rather than enemies.

Was he a cad? Had he successfully pulled the wool over my eyes? I had asked myself the question numerous times. I truly believed he was not, that something, or someone, had prevented Jonathan from attending his own wedding, and until I learnt otherwise, I would keep him in my heart...and my thoughts to myself.

Chapter 3

The following day, after a troubled sleep, I decided to continue my usual habit of choosing an area of London to investigate. This had been my raison d'etre for some months. It gave me a reason to get out of bed in the morning when I least felt like it and helped me to overcome my melancholy. The sights I saw in those places and the realisation of a necessity to act, and to act quickly, galvanised me to action. Yes, I had suffered a disappointment, and yes, my heart had been broken, but compared to the situations the inhabitants of the rookeries found themselves in, well…there *was* no comparison.

After breakfast, I bathed and dressed in my warmest worsted, tied on my bonnet, and made my way from our house in Harley Street where my Papa carried out his medical practice before he passed. My wonderful Mama was his nurse and I have always thought that Violet and my ability to care so deeply, and to empathise with people who lived a different life from the one we lived, came from them. My Papa was a wonderful man; so gentle with his patients, so kind and reassuring, and he was as sympathetic and benevolent as a parent.

I thought about what Constable Turner said to me the previous evening. He said that Violet and I were privileged, and of course when one sees how others live, he was correct. But Violet and I would not be judged solely on the accident of our birth. We were born to wealthy parents it is true, but both my sister and I felt we were not defined by it, and I for one was eager to put our seemingly elevated station in life to good use.

There were various places I could go, and as I reached the end of Harley Street I made up my mind to return to Dorset Street, the scene of the accident which took place the night before. I thought perhaps a visit to the police station in Agar Street first would provide me with more information. I made an attempt to hail a hansom cab on the corner of Harley Street and New Cavendish Street. Fortunately, one drew into the curb quite quickly for which I was grateful. It was still bitingly cold, and even though I was wearing my stoutest boots and warmest coat, the chill still managed to make its way through. For the first time since I had become a woman, I was thankful for my corset.

'Agar Street', I called up to the lone driver guiding the horses. He wore a huge, dark-brown woollen coat with a cape about his shoulders, and a top hat. His hands were encased in fingerless gloves and I wondered how he could possibly sit so long in the freezing air. 'The police station if you please.'

He touched the rim of his top hat and frowned. 'Everything alright, miss?

'Yes, thank you, driver. All is well.' He nodded and lifted the reins, shaking them so that the horses knew it was time to make way.

When the cab got to Agar Street the driver pulled the horses up outside the police station and I alighted the cab. The blue light outside shone into the mist which had begun to cling around the buildings, giving it a greyer hue. I sighed, wondering if we were due for a heavy fog, then went inside, thinking it was not the task one would wish to undertake as we neared Christmas; I should have been in the comfort of my own home as Constable Turner had suggested, rather than stepping inside a police station to discover the identity of a girl who had died under the bricks and mortar of a building so badly erected it tumbled to the street below.

I made my towards the desk where a young police officer sat shuffling papers.

'Madam?' he asked. 'How can I help?'

'I wish to speak with Constable Turner if you please.'

'Not 'ere, Madam. It's 'is day orf.'

'Oh,' I felt rather deflated. My plan to discover the girl's identity had stumbled before it had even begun.

'Is there anyone else who can 'elp you? Has a crime been committed that you wish to report?'

'Only a crime to humanity, officer,' I replied. 'I was present last evening when a young woman was killed by falling masonry on the corner of Dorset Street and Clay Street. I wanted to speak with Constable Turner regarding her identity.'

'I believe her identity was discovered, Madam. We have informed the young woman's family, but they requested we send her directly to the morgue and then to the paupers' cemetery as they do not have the wherewithal to pay for a funeral.'

I felt the hair on the back of my neck rise. I was angry. 'I informed Constable Turner that I would pay for the young woman's funeral.'

The officer stared at me. 'You'll need to 'urry then, Madam. She's due to be buried late this morning without the fanfare what is given to the rest of us,' he coughed, 'that's if we can afford it a' course.'

'Is there someone here I can speak to? I really think it would be pertinent for me to speak with someone with authority.'

'There's Chief Detective Stride, Madam. You are Miss Pond are you not? I believe you are acquainted with him.'

'Yes, officer. If he is here I would like to speak with him.'

'Perhaps you wouldn't mind waiting, Madam. I believe he is in conference with Detective Superintendent Welham.'

The officer went into an office behind the desk and spoke to someone inside. I heard the sound of someone pushing back a chair. Chief Detective Jeremiah Stride came to the door and invited me inside. He wore a smart mid-brown tweed waistcoat and trousers with a dark blue cravat, and a brown jacket. He looked harassed; his face was slightly pink.

'Miss Pond. I must confess you are the last person I expected to see today. You're usually on the streets of Whitechapel and beyond at this time of the year, giving alms to inhabitants of those places.'

'But I am here, Chief Detective, and with good reason.'

'And what might the reason be, Madam?' said a voice from inside the office. Chief Detective Stride directed me to sit in the chair opposite the desk, next to the Detective Superintendent who eyed me with some impatience.

'The young woman who was killed last night. She was a prostitute was she not, carrying out her usual habit of walking the streets of Dorset and Clay? She was killed on the corner of those streets by falling masonry. I came by this morning to ascertain whether her identity had been discovered and to offer to pay for her funeral. I understand she has been sent to the mortuary for dispatch to the paupers' cemetery.'

Welham glanced at me with unmistakable ire. He seemed offended by my presence. 'It is a police matter, Madam. I have heard your name in certain circles. I understand you would wish to do well by these people, but most of us would rather not highlight the obscenity of how the lower classes live. It brings all of us who reside in London into disrepute. Parker Street, St Giles and places like it need to be done away with.'

I glared at him, sensing Chief Detective Stride's discomfort at the conversation. 'And where should they go, sir? Would it not simply remove the problem somewhere else? Where would you have them live.'

Ignoring my question, he rose from his chair and addressed Chief Detective Stride. 'See that it's done, Chief Detective. It's what we pay you for.' Chief Detective Stride nodded. Detective Superintendent Welham glanced at me. 'And I suggest you leave policing to the police, Miss Pond. I understand you are concerned about the welfare of these people, but you must understand most of them are criminals; thieves, vagabonds, and prostitutes. And to answer your previous question, I'm not concerned where they go as long as it is as far away as is possible from my manor. They give the force more work to do than the rest of London, Madam, and we are overworked as it is.'

I looked away, seething at his inference the citizens of London should not have a say over their own futures. Could the man not see one's station in life was insignificant to one's hope for the future. They in the rookeries, more than anyone I surmised, had the right to wish for better.

Once Welham had left, the atmosphere in the room settled. Chief Detective Stride looked relieved we were alone. He shuffled the papers on his desk, turning some over so I couldn't see them, and took a deep breath.

'It is correct, Miss Pond. The burial has already been arranged. What with it being Christmas they want it done as soon as possible so as not to snarl things up in the New Year.'

'That's rather a harsh way of putting it, Chief Detective. They are human beings none the less.'

'I agree, Miss Pond, but it is how it is. In the cold light of day we deal with these people rather like ticking numbers off a list. It isn't right, and certainly distasteful, but the death toll from those streets and beyond is forever rising and there is usually no one to either organise or pay for a funeral. It is left to the town council to do both.'

'I have already offered to pay, Chief Detective. And I believe the poor woman's identity has been discovered.'

'It was, Madam. She was not a brothel whore, but worked the streets independently. She was married with five children.'

I gasped and not ashamed to say tears threatened. 'How did you discover who she was?'

He shuffled some papers on his desk and found what he was looking for. 'A Mrs Ruby Fletcher, another streetwalker. She came into the station first thing, saying her friend was missing, a Mrs Nell Thomas.' He threw the paper onto the desk and sighed, looking forlorn. 'She directed us to Nell Thomas's husband and he confirmed who she was. It goes without saying he is distraught and unsure how he's going to feed his family now that the breadwinner is no longer living.'

'She was the breadwinner?'

'Indeed.'

'Her husband had no work?'

'Couldn't get work, although he said he'd tried. Went to the factories and the docks every day, but things have slowed down over the festive season so there was nothing going.'

'So what will happen now?' Chief Detective Stride shrugged and a feeling of absolute melancholy overcame me. 'But the children, Chief Detective? What will happen to the children?'

'What happens to all of them who live in those environs. They'll likely end up on the street, scavenging, begging. It's the life they lead, Miss Pond. And there are many of them live the same life.'

'And the father?'

'Turns to the drink if he can get a coin. Strange isn't it? The public houses and taverns are always full to bursting point.'

I shook my head in frustration. 'Do you have their address, Chief Detective?'

He narrowed his eyes. 'Now, Miss Pond. You can't save all of them.'

'I appreciate that, Chief Detective Stride, but if I can help one poor family over Christmas, provide some sustenance for a short while and bring some joy into their lives, do you not think it would be a worthy undertaking?'

He pressed his lips together and inhaled a deep breath. I watched him as he did so. He was probably in his mid-thirties, not a man one could call handsome; his dark hair was wayward and much too long, reaching past his collar, yet he had an attractive manner. A little brusque perhaps but not unkind. I judged him young to be in such an elevated position in the police force, but I also knew he was intelligent, caring, and like myself, wanted to help those people whom he served in the rookeries and beyond, even though he was generally considered to be an unpopular visitor in those neighbourhoods.

'I'm not sure giving you their address is the right thing to do, Miss Pond,' he said, narrowing his eyes.

'Why ever not?'

He shuffled in his chair as though trying to find a better position, although I knew he was likely embarrassed and about to say something I would not like. 'You get involved.'

'Yes, Chief Detective. I do. Someone must, surely.'

'But why you, Ma'am?'

I admit he had taken the wind out of my sails. He had asked a question that Violet often asked me, one for which I could not find a reasonable answer.

'I...I don't know. Perhaps we could describe it as a calling, a need, selfish perhaps, to want to improve the lives of people who live a stone's throw away from my own home.' I shook my head again, agitated I could not put together an answer which would satisfy him or myself. 'It is all I can give you, Chief Detective. I am not trained as a member of the police force, or as a detectorist, but there is a need to shift the balance somewhat, to give the people who live in the rookeries, particularly the children, a chance of a better life.'

He nodded and smiled which transformed his face. It made his eyes sparkle and I noticed he had good teeth. He was clearly a man of hygienic habits.

'A very worthy calling, Miss Pond, one to which I subscribe.' He stood and walked to the window. 'Unfortunately, the process of making a difference to the lives of the inhabitants of the rookeries could best be described as trying to reach the bottom of a bottomless pit.' He turned to look at me. 'However, perhaps you could visit me again in the New Year. I have a proposition for you that might whet your appetite.'

I raised my eyebrows and widened my eyes. 'Will you not give me a clue, Chief Detective Stride?'

He shook his head. 'Best left until we can speak at length. I have somewhere else to be, and I am sure you have too, Miss Pond.' He returned to his desk and sat in the tufted leather captain's chair that had clearly seen better days. 'But in the meantime,' he pulled a small piece of paper towards him and reached for his pen, 'I will give you the Thomas's address.' He pushed the paper across the desk. 'All I ask is that you don't immerse yourself too deeply in that family's life, and please, please, on no account give them money. I can assure you those five children will not see a farthing of it. It will go down to the tavern which was where their father was when their mother was killed.'

I retrieved the paper without looking at it and pushed it into the top of my dolly-bag. 'He was drinking away her earnings.'

'Indeed.'

'So she was killed for nothing. The wrong place at the wrong time.' Chief Detective Stride nodded.

My heart sank, but I determined to help them. Our pantry in Harley Street was laden with good things I knew any child would be excited to see, and to eat, and if I could make those poor little mites' Christmas a better one after losing their mother, then I would.

'Another thing, Miss Pond.' I inclined my head, waiting for another instruction. 'I noticed you did not look at the address I gave you. When you do it may well give you pause.'

'I take it the house is in an insalubrious area, Chief Detective.'

'They're all insalubrious areas, Miss Pond, some worse than others, I grant you. That particular address resides in one of the worst. Do not go there at night, Miss Pond. Do not walk the streets as you would in Harley Street after five of the evening, particularly in the winter. Do not linger but walk steadfastly, and once you have found the address and carried out your ministrations leave promptly and walk sharply, and with purpose, to an area that is frequented by persons such as yourself. If you take a cab and ask the driver to wait for you, all to the good. In fact, I recommend it.'

I exhaled a breath and nodded. 'Anything else, Chief Detective Stride?'

'Keep safe, Miss Pond.'

Chapter 4

A smart rapping on my bedroom door pulled me out of my reverie and I turned on my dresser stool. I had been thinking about my visit to Nell Thomas's children, wondering with some apprehension about what I would find there. I had considered Chief Detective Stride's warnings which had shaken my resolve somewhat, but not being one to be frightened off I determined to grit my teeth and do what I had set out to do, which was visit the Thomas's. Whichever part of the rookeries they occupied one could be sure it would be neither salubrious or welcoming, but they were children, not vagabonds or thieves, and it broke my heart to think they had lost their mother at a time when one should be celebrating and putting cares aside.

'Come in.'

Meg, my maid, entered the room and bobbed a curtsey. 'Would you like me to help you dress for dinner, Miss Lily?'

'Yes, Meg, thank you.' I couldn't help sighing with anguish at the thought of the evening ahead. 'The Horrockses are dining with us this evening, aren't they?'

'Yes, Miss Lily. Mrs Horrocks is tryin' ter get you off with her son, Wilfred.'

My eyes widened involuntarily. 'Get me off with him? What does that mean?'

'Well, Miss Lily, now that you and Mr Jonathan are...sort of...well, not married, we think she's doin' 'er best ter get Mr Wilfred in your good books so to speak. Don't forget, Miss Lily, you're quite the catch.'

'Apparently not, Meg, as recent history would display bearing in mind I am still residing here. And we're not "sort of" not married. We're "definitely" not married.'

'I could kill 'im. Just like a man to go off on one when he's meant to be somewhere else. They get on my nerves they really do.'

Meg helped me out of my day dress, retied my corset so that my waist was little more than a hand's span, and chose an evening dress for that evening's dinner.

'You look so well in pink, Miss Lily. Brings out the blush on your cheeks and the sparkle in your eyes.'

'Mm.' I frowned, my thoughts elsewhere. 'Is Violet being taken care of?'

'Yes, Miss Lily. Mildred's looking after 'er since Rita left. That was a bit of a mystery an' all weren't it, 'er goin' off like that without sayin' why. The cook thinks she was in the family way and di'nt wanna tell anyone. Stupid girl.'

'We don't know that for certain.'

'No, we don't, but it do explain a lot. She was a bit flighty, Miss Lily, although it was a side to 'er you never saw.'

'I should hope not,' I answered, my mind continuing to flit elsewhere. 'When you said it was just like a man to go off on one when he was meant to be somewhere else, what did you mean? And what is 'on one'?'

I sat at my dresser again and allowed Meg to pin up my hair into barrel curls and fix them to the top of my head. It reminded me of the day I should have been married but I closed my eyes and tried not to think of it.

"E 'as to be somewhere don't 'e?'

I frowned. 'I don't know what you mean.'

Meg looked into the mirror and gazed at my reflection. 'It's a bit delicate, Miss Lily.'

'That doesn't matter. Tell me what's on your mind.'

'He weren't at the church where he was meant to be was 'e, so...'e must've been somewhere else.'

'And why d'you think he chose not to be at the church at the allotted time?'

Meg shrugged. 'Dunno. Got cold feet p'raps, or...,' Meg swallowed, 'or 'e got a better offer, or... 'e was in some sort 'a trouble.' I nodded. 'I dunno, Miss Lily,' she took some hairpins from Lily who was holding them up to her, 'but if I knew anything about Mr Jonathan, 'e loved you. We all said it, Me...and Cook, and the other maids. We was all so shocked when what 'appened, appened. You were the last person on earth to be jilted at the altar.' She bit her lip and curtseyed.

'Sorry, Miss Lily. I weren't thinkin'.'

I averted my eyes and inhaled deeply. 'Don't concern yourself, Meg. It was months ago. I feel much stronger now.' Meg smiled with contrition and nodded. 'And what do you think of Mr Wilfred?'

'Ugh, no, Miss Lily.' Meg screwed up her face into a look of disgust. "E looks like the back of an 'orses cart. No. Never in a million years.'

'And what are your plans, Miss Pond, now that....,' Mrs Horrocks pulled herself up before she finished the sentence in an embarrassing way, dabbed at her mouth with her napkin, and took a breath..., 'now that you are to remain at Pond House, which of course,' she waved her hand to emphasise her point, 'would not be a hardship. It is such a beautiful house. I'm sure anyone would be happy to own such a residence.'

Yes, I thought. And you would be extremely happy to see your son take ownership of it, wouldn't you? 'I have no immediate plans, Mrs Horrocks. Violet and I live very quietly as you see, and I think perhaps when one has had a disappointment one should take stock, as it were, before making any immediate decisions regarding the future.'

'But surely, my dear you would wish to marry eventually? One cannot always be sure that there will be suitors enough, and willing to marry...an older gel.'

'I am just twenty-two, Mrs Horrocks. Perhaps it was the fashion when you were young to marry much earlier, but I must say women today are more than happy not to marry the first suitor who offers them a means of engagement.'

Genevieve Horrocks looked horrified at my forward attitude. 'But what of the Right-Honourable August-Trelawney? You accepted him, and I would imagine you would not think quite so much of him as you did bearing in mind...well....'

It was at precisely that moment when I was made uncomfortably aware that Meg had pulled my corset too tight. Anger boiled in my chest and my stomach rolled at Genevieve Horrocks' assumption it was acceptable for her to question me about Jonathan. I glanced at Violet who almost imperceptibly shook her head.

'He was...is...an exceptional man,' I answered, pressing my napkin against my lips to prevent the bile I wished to exert against the inconsiderate woman from being put into words.

'There are many exceptional men, Miss Pond. Why, my own Wilfred is equally exceptional.' She flourished her hand towards her son. 'As you see he is quick-witted and has an intelligent turn of phrase,' she turned to her husband who had drunk so much port he was almost comatose, 'do you not think so, my dear.' She nudged him in the ribs and he sat up quickly, startled by the interruption to his sleep.

'What, what,' he blustered, his face red with alcohol, his mouth wet from where he'd drooled on his chest as he'd slept. 'Quite so, quite so.' He lowered his chin to his chest and closed his eyes.

'Does he take after Mr Horrocks?' I asked Mrs Horrocks. I glanced at Violet again who had pressed her lips together to stop herself from laughing. Wilfred Horrocks suddenly sat up as though he had been given instructions by his mother to arrive on stage when she mentioned his name. 'Pray tell, what is it that makes Wilfred so exceptional?'

Genevieve Horrocks' eyes narrowed, and she inhaled a breath. 'I would have thought it was obvious, Miss Pond. He is handsome is he not?'

Wilfred looked down at his plate and swallowed his embarrassment. 'Please, Mother. Don't go on so. Miss Pond will think us extremely rude.'

'But his good looks do not make him exceptional, Mrs Horrocks,' I said, recalling Meg's description of him. 'I am sure that Wilfred is a gentleman with perfect manners, but I must speak plainly. I do not wish for a husband. I intend to find an occupation that will elevate the poor of this city from the mire in which they live. Many of the children on our streets have no shoes, come rain or shine; most of them do not have a hot meal even once a day. I feel most strongly the balance of the population has been skewed, and someone should do something about it.'

Mrs Horrocks pushed her not inconsiderable chest forward and lifted her chin. 'And you think the someone is you? Why would you think such a thing, a girl who has had every advantage in life, who has been educated by the best tutors money can buy? Your parents believed in an education for girls, a belief to which I do not, and never have, subscribed. We women have a place in society, Miss Pond. There is no necessity for us to be educated to the same level as the other sex. They...make the decisions, the laws, and we...bear the children and make the home lives of our husbands and children comfortable and acceptable within the society in which they move. It is valuable work, Miss Pond.'

'But not to me, Mrs Horrocks. I would not decry another woman's choice. To be a wife and mother, I'm sure, would be a reward in itself...to some women...and I applaud them for it, but it is unlikely I will be one of those women. Jonathan August-Trelawney was well aware of my philosophies and ideals and he championed them. This is why I described him as an exceptional man. And while we discuss this subject I must impress upon you that I am no longer a girl, and therefore not expected to do as others bid me.'

'You have pert opinions, Miss Pond, many of which I'm sure most men would not appreciate, the point being of course, that Jonathan August-Trelawney is no longer here.'

Violet cleared her throat and rang a little bell she kept on the table to summon the servants.

'My, it has become quite late. Is your carriage waiting for you, Mrs Horrocks, or do you require to take ours?'

'We have our own carriage, thank you, Miss Pond. It has been an "interesting" evening.' She glanced at me, her eyebrows knotting together and her complexion darkening. 'I wish you well, Miss Pond. I hope your philosophies and ideals provide you with the diversion you are seemingly looking for.'

She rose from her chair which a servant pulled back at the right moment so she could leave the table. She turned and glanced at her husband, then her son.

'Wilfred, help your father, will you? I don't think he's feeling very well.'

Wilfred went across to his father who shrugged him off. 'I'm perfectly alright,' he said. He got up from the chair and staggered over to his wife. 'Come, my dear.' Mr and Mrs Horrocks went into the hall where the servants were waiting with their cloaks. Meg stared at me pointedly and rolled her eyes.

'I'm sorry, Miss Pond,' said Wilfred, who had lagged behind his parents. 'She means well.'

I nodded and made a small smile. 'I'm sure she does,' I replied quietly, wishing they would go.

'For what it's worth,' he continued, 'I think your idea is admirable, but I caution you. The rookeries are dangerous,' I glanced at Violet who raised her eyes in surprise. 'We see many a body who has fallen foul of some vagabond or miscreant who lives in the rookeries. My work in the apothecary and on the wards at the hospital brings me into that sphere I'm sorry to say.'

This news made me falter. 'You are a medic, sir?'

'Yes,' he sighed. 'I am. The hospital is where all life is. There are no secrets there and unfortunately too many deaths from that particular area inhabited by the very worst of our society it would seem. Please don't hesitate to call on me should you require my assistance in your work. I would always make myself available to you, after all, we should all do what we can for the disadvantaged of society.'

I smiled wider, bewildered by his friendliness towards me. 'Mr Horrocks...er, Wilfred, let me apologise...'

He held up a hand to halt me mid-sentence. 'There is no need for an apology. My mother put you in an impossible position, and I rather feel she should be apologising to you. You have been the perfect hostesses. She is not usually so bad mannered, but she feels I should marry soon and marry well.'

'And she has me in her sights.' I laughed to soften my words.

Wilfred nodded and chuckled. 'I'm afraid so. She seems to believe I'm incapable of making up my own mind.'

'Wilfred! Genevieve Horrocks's voice echoed around the hall. 'What are you doing? Your father is indisposed. We need to leave! What are you doing?'

He held up both hands. 'I should go. Thank you for dinner,' he bowed to Violet and then to me, 'and Miss Pond, Lily, please don't forget my offer of help.'

'Thank you, Wilfred. I can assure you I won't.'

I threw myself onto the settee and blew out a frustrated puff of breath.

'Thank goodness they've gone. I don't remember inviting them.'

'Nor me,' said Violet. 'Perhaps it was an invitation of long-standing we had forgotten.'

I frowned. 'Or none at all.' I sighed with frustration. 'Here we go again. It seems everyone we know wants to have me married to their damned sons. Honestly, Violet, it's getting rather tedious. Just the fact they need their Mamas to find them a wife says everything about them, and usually they're chinless wonders with no wit and a dearth of personality.'

Violet sighed as she wheeled herself closer to the chaise. 'Well, these young men you talk of are certainly not queuing up at my door, to be sure.'

I sat up looking contrite. 'Oh, Violet, darling,' I cried, reaching for her hand. 'I'm sorry. I wasn't thinking. So typical of me.' I shook my head and smiled at her. 'The ridiculous thing is you are by far the most beautiful and the most accomplished of us. They're utterly blind if you ask me.'

'They don't see any further than this,' Violet said, slapping her hand against the steering handle of her bath chair. 'A judgment is made as soon as their eyes fall upon it. I've seen it happen so often, the looks of pity, the comments made behind fans. There are times when I actually laugh because I can do no other.' She inhaled a wobbling breath which made my heart seize with sadness. 'Wilfred seemed nice though. It's a pity about his mother. She does him a disservice, absolutely no good at all. I would say he has the intelligence and wit to find his own wife if it's what he wants. Not everyone chooses marriage after all.'

'Yes, he was pleasant, and actually I think I would like him if he could get out from underneath his mother's apron.'

I kicked off my shoes and tucked my feet up on the chaise. 'Do you want to be married, Violet? You've never said.'

'I'm not sure, Lily. And I'm being utterly truthful. For me to marry I must find a man who will accept my disability will be with me all my life, and it will certainly affect our life together. He may want a family. I'm not sure I can have children...' she frowned slightly, '...I'm not even sure I want them. I envisage great difficulty ahead trying to raise a family from a bath chair.' She pulled a face. 'Plus, the gentleman would need to be a saint don't you think?'

'I do not. I think you do yourself down, Violet. You have so much to offer. You're stylish, beautiful and utterly intelligent. I think any man you chose would consider himself fortunate.'

Violet chuckled then wheeled herself across to the drinks console and poured two brandies. 'I have to meet this paragon of virtue first...' she returned to the chaise, two brandy glasses in one hand. She passed one to me, '...and as I rarely go anywhere in society, I think it's unlikely I'll ever meet my perfect gentleman.' She sipped from her brandy glass, eying me. 'What are your thoughts on Wilfred Horrocks?'

'Very different at the end of dinner from the beginning,' I answered her, grinning. 'He surprised me, I must admit. In fact, I thought he was rather nice. I do wish his horrible mother would let him be him. I think he would do so much better, don't you? He is clearly intelligent and has worked hard to become an apothecary...a position of responsibility. I really don't think he needs her meddling.'

'She's not the only one. How many mothers have inveigled themselves into our sphere simply to push their sons onto you since Jonathan...' Violet cringed. 'I'm so sorry, Lily. I shouldn't have mentioned him.'

'I leant my elbow on the arm of the settee and my head on my hand. 'Of course, you can mention him.'

'I just don't want to upset you. You've been through enough. This year has been...well, rather difficult shall we say.'

'The problem is, Violet, each time I meet an overly ambitious mother with her son I am reminded of Jonathan. Everything I do and everywhere I go is a constant reminder of the fact he did not attend our wedding, that he did not love me enough to participate in the most important day of our lives.' I took a sip from my glass of brandy. 'I was left floundering in floods of tears before the altar, something I'm still embarrassed about.'

Violet's mouth dropped open. 'Why should you be embarrassed? You were the one who kept the appointment.'

I shrugged. 'I know...' I sat up and stared at Violet. 'I still think something happened to him and I won't stop believing it until I'm proved otherwise.'

I brushed the tears from my eyes. I hated crying because I had always considered it such a weakness, but there were times when I didn't have the strength to prevent it.

'We loved each other. He understood my need for involvement within the society which is so far below our own. He championed everything I championed and actually wanted to be of help, which is precisely why I do not believe he left me at the altar for any motives of fear of being married, or feeling he was being coerced into marriage. We wanted to be together, Violet,' I looked lovingly at my sister, 'with you of course. We would have lived here or a new home chosen by the three of us, or even his house in Holland Park. You will always be with me...unless of course you choose not to be.'

Violet nodded. 'Do you mind my asking, Lily?' she asked quietly. 'Are you waiting for him to return?'

I felt my face flush and the skin at my hairline tingle with warmth. My eyes welled up again and I felt cross with myself that just the mention of his name could make my body react in such a way. 'I...I don't know if I'm waiting. There has been no news of him since our,' I hesitated, hardly sure if I could say the words, 'wedding day that should have been. It's so unfair that those around us think it was some discrepancy in my own personality that encouraged him to leave me standing at the altar, rather than any incongruity in his. The woman will always get the blame should something go wrong.'

'We live in a man's world, Lily. You should know it by now.'

'Oh, I do, I do. But Jonathan was different, which was why when he asked me to marry him I agreed readily. I could never marry a man who expected me to simply stay at home sewing or organising soirees for their husband's business associates.' I closed my eyes and shook my head, the thought of such a life sending shudders down my spine. 'Oh, no, it wouldn't do at all,' I opened my eyes, 'but it is precisely what these mothers who insist on pushing themselves into our sphere want for their sons.'

'So why, darling?' asked Violet, quietly. 'We've not really discussed it since it happened. Do you have any idea why he...left so suddenly?'

I shook my head, knowing my face was contorted with sorrow. 'No, no idea at all. I wish I could speak with him. I'm sure there's a reasonable explanation.'

Violet widened her eyes. 'It would need to be, although I can't imagine how reasonable it is to leave their fiancée at the altar.'

'Something happened to him, Violet, I'm sure of it. Meg said perhaps he'd got cold feet and I'm aware_some men do, but I don't believe it. We were looking forward to embarking on our life together. We were to travel, to see the world together. We had even spoken of beginning our own family, children we could teach on our travels. We were both extremely passionate about it. And he did not for one moment subscribe to the popular notion that women's brains were smaller than men's so therefore were not capable of logical thought. He often said the opposite was true, that women were far more practical and astute, and if the world was run with women at the helm life would be good for the many and not just the few.' I swallowed, my mouth and throat dry with unspent emotion. I could hardly prevent my voice from shaking. 'Something definitely happened to him.'

Violet's face darkened. 'Something untoward, you mean?' She lowered her voice to almost a whisper. 'Something final?'

I swallowed hard. I had to admit the thought had occurred to me. What other explanation could there be? 'I don't know, Violet. I know Jonathan, and his non-appearance seems so out of character. I know people always love to think the worst of a person's character, and I'm sure much has been said about him in a derogatory way, it's human nature, but they don't know him the way I do, and I am sure there is something more to it.'

Chapter 5

It wasn't until I hailed a cab the following morning that I was called to retrieve the piece of paper Chief Detective Stride had given me. The address he'd written was a house in Parker Street, Lincoln's Inn Fields. It was then I realised why he had warned me so vociferously regarding my safety.

Lincoln's Inn Fields was one of the most poverty-stricken areas of our fair city, and a blight on its reputation. There were many areas just like it, St. Giles on the edge of Fitzrovia for one, and of course the notorious Dorset Street, which was nothing more than a receptacle for all the human detritus one could imagine, a den of thieves, vagabonds, prostitutes, and murderers. Some of the inhabitants would kill a man for a penny or less. If you had coin you were fair game. No one with any sense would actually attempt to enter that environ; even the police would refuse to go into the street. Some officers would agree to go when a crime had been committed, but only if they were accompanied by many other officers, assuming there was safety in numbers, but I could assure them from my own investigations, numbers in no way would ensure their safety.

'Do you know that part of London, Madam?' the cab driver asked me. 'You appear to be alone. In my experience it ain't wise to consider goin' to such a place.'

'I know, driver. I am aware of its reputation, but I have an address I would visit, and I would be grateful if you would wait with your cab until I have finished my business.'

'I'll wait no more than ten minutes, Madam. Them blighters what live down there will have the cab out from underneath me and the 'orses roasting on their fires....and me in the gutter most likely.'

I nodded and tried to smile. 'I will pay double, sir, and I do not intend to linger at the address.' The cab driver gave a quick nod of the head. 'Fair enough, Madam.'

As we drove closer to Lincoln's Inn Fields I observed the changing scenery outside the cab window. The cab slowed as though the horses were reluctant to enter the area, the cab driver encouraging them to pick up speed.

I have to confess I wondered if I had been too hasty. I knew my own faults and shortcomings. I could be impetuous; my parents would often say so, but it was always said with affection and a chuckle. I was their precipitous daughter and therefore found myself in many scrapes, but my mother would say my heart was in the right place. I sincerely hoped it was true.

'This is it, Madam,' the driver called down to the cab from his position on the box seat behind the horses. 'We're in Lincoln's Inn Fields. Parker Street is just a couple of streets away.'

'Very well, driver,' I replied. 'Please pull up outside the address I gave you.'

'No longer than ten minutes, Madam,' he said as I climbed out of the cab. 'I'm sorry but I shall have to leave if you're any longer. I can't risk bein' 'ere longer than that.'

'Don't worry, driver. You have requested ten minutes and ten minutes is how long I shall be.'

'Yeah, well, I've 'eard it before. That's what my missus says when she goes to the market. An hour later an' I'm still waitin'. P'raps you could just let me know. I ain't got all day. And could you pay me afore yer go in, just as an assurance like?'

I nodded, paid him, then raised my hand in farewell and turned to the house, 71 Parker Street. 'Never fear, driver. I am a woman of my word...however, should there be a change in circumstances you will be the first to know.'

I heard him click his tongue which made me smile. 'And because you're a man and I merely a woman, you think you can tell me what to do even though you know me not at all,' I said under my breath.

The house in Parker Street looked the same as the others in the row, run down with shabby frontages and filthy windows, although only if the glass had actually been allowed to remain in the frame. The similarity of disrepair and neglect left one with a feeling of melancholy, but when I peered through the window of number seventy-one, I could see there was a fire in the grate in the small sitting room.

Five children sat in front of it warming their hands and toasting ragged pieces of bread on long-handled forks. This heartened me a little. They had a little to eat it seemed, but I guessed not too much more. A man came into the room with a tray and three tiny cups from which steam arose. Could this be soup? How I hoped it was. He lifted his face and we met eye to eye. I quickly pulled away from the window and went to the front door where I rapped on it with my gloved hand.

I held my breath. I was apprehensive. This poor family had lost their mother, the breadwinner if what Chief Detective Stride had said was correct. I wasn't sure what to expect, but I knew grief, and I could only assume the pall of sorrow at missing their mother hung over their little heads.

I heard a scuffle at the door and watched as the door handle was pulled downwards. Gradually the door was pulled open, scraping the lintel at the top and the doorstep at the bottom. An expletive was uttered on the other side of the door to which my mouth dropped open, but I managed to close it again before the door finally stood ajar. I leant slightly forward with a small smile.

'Mr Thomas?'

He nodded. 'That's me. Walter Thomas.' He was a big man, well-built with broad shoulders, but his cheeks were hollow, and there were dark circles under his eyes; I surmised from malnutrition and living in the circumstances in which he found himself.

'My name is Miss Pond. It was I who...' I looked down, unable to find the correct words. It seemed an impossible task.

'You found 'er, didn't yer? My Nell?'

'Yes, Mr Thomas. I decided to walk home from the shopping district,' I shook my head, 'a mistake I expect, but, yes it was I who found her. I keep a whistle in my reticule for such emergencies, and when I blew it, Constable Turner arrived. Thankfully he was on his beat.'

'I know 'im.'

'I'm afraid we didn't know who she was at first. It was Chief Detective Stride who informed me that sadly, it was your wife who had been hurt.'

He nodded, and then as if it had just occurred to him, invited me inside. I agreed, wondering if I'd made the most sensible decision, but I

I stepped over the threshold into the sitting room which led straight in from the mucky street. I tried to scrape the muck and slush off my boots before entering, but simply made more mess, so stepped inside.

It was warm in the room which I was eternally thankful for. At least the owners of five pairs of eyes which stared at me weren't shivering with cold. I smiled at them but they continued staring, and I assumed they had never seen a woman like me before. I turned to Mr Thomas.

'It's delightfully warm in here, Mr Thomas. It's such a comfort to get out of the cold.'

'It is that, but God knows what we're goin' ter do now.' He sat in a scruffy armchair and indicated for me to sit in the one opposite. I sat with some apprehension then scolded myself. The chair on which I was sitting was likely Nell Thomas's. She had sat with her five children, perhaps telling them stories or tending to them when one or other was unwell. I expect they climbed onto her knee when they needed a cuddle. The chair in which I sat had likely seen many of those moments.

'I don't want yer ter think I was 'appy about 'er goin' out at night, yer know, workin'. I was never 'appy about it but we 'ad no choice, Miss Pond. I couldn't get no work. I tried, every mornin', down at them factories, the tanners and the breweries, and on the docks. It's the only place a bloke like me can 'ope to get work.' He looked down at his children. 'Need it now, don't I, although only the good Lord knows what I'm ter do with me kids if I were to get any work. 'Ave to leave 'em on their own I s'pose.'

I frowned. 'They're rather young aren't they, Mr. Thomas, to be left by themselves?'

He shrugged. 'Not really. I was left on me own from the age of five. Used to go round the streets beggin' for food.' He chuckled at the memory. 'Nicked a bit an' all,' he said. 'A pie coolin' on a windowsill, an apple from the market.' He shrugged again. 'Ad to see, uvverwise I wouldn't 'ave got fed, and there was no guarantee I'd get anything off me Ma an' Pa neither when they got 'ome from work. We didn't 'ave much, and I 'ad a brother and sister what were younger 'an me.'

I gasped. 'So what happened to them?'

He frowned, looking bewildered. 'Came wiv me 'a course.'

'Oh my goodness.'

'It's 'ow we 'ad to live, Miss Pond.'

'And how will you live now? What will happen to the children?'

He inhaled then shook his head. 'Well...I 'ave to try and earn, don't I? No point in worryin' about 'em if I can't feed 'em.'

I frowned. 'I'm sorry, what do you mean?'

'If I can't feed 'em there's no point in 'em bein' 'ere is there. They'll likely starve.'

I gasped. 'Surely not, Mr Thomas. There must be someone who would take care of them for a coin while you work.'

'There's the rub, Miss Pond. There ain't no work lately, not for the likes of me anyways. No work, no coin. We can't win.'

I nodded and sat up straight. I could see this was a desperate situation for both him and his children. I was mindful of what Chief Inspector Stride had said to me about giving him money. This I would not do. I knew the frailties of men like Thomas, who when pushed to the limit would simply go to the public houses and spend what little money they had on alcohol to try and forget their troubles.

'My sister and I would like to help you, Mr Thomas.' I noticed his eyes widen, and I hoped he wasn't expecting a bag of coin. 'We would like to replenish your pantry so you and your little ones can eat over the Christmas period. I will also do my best to enquire about work for you so you will be self-sufficient in the following year. The children could go to the Ragged School. I see no reason why they should not be admitted...I will make enquiries myself.'

'Er, they've not never been to school, Ma'am. Not sure 'ow they would take it.'

'Sometimes we must do the right thing, Mr Thomas, and I strongly believe this is the right thing for you and your family.'

'And what about me missus's funeral?'

'That...will be paid for. A messenger will be sent to you to inform you of when the funeral will take place. Perhaps you could make sure your children are presented in a respectable manner,'... I glanced at their grubby faces, 'and a wash would not go amiss.'

Thomas nodded. 'Yes, ma'am.'

'I'll send some clothes for them.' He nodded again. 'And please, Mr Thomas, do not sell them, I beg you, at least before their mother's funeral. Perhaps they could wear them to the Ragged School.'

'Yes, ma'am.'

I stood and held out my hand to shake his, then withdrew it swiftly when I noticed his own hand. It was black with filth both on the skin and under the fingernails, where months of grime had gathered.

'I'll see myself out, Mr Thomas.' He nodded and I made my way to the front door, pulling my gloves on again before touching the handle.

'You might need some 'elp there, Ma'am, les' you want the door to fall on yer.'

'I'd rather it didn't, Mr Thomas.'

He rose from his chair languorously, as though he had all the troubles of the world on his shoulders, which I supposed, in his mind, was exactly what he had. 'You've got a cab, Miss Pond?'

'Indeed.'

'Good job an' all. Them's down the street'll probably 'ave a delivery comin'. You don't want ter get caught up in that.'

I frowned, wondering what he could mean. 'A delivery? Of what may I ask? How could anyone who lives here afford deliveries of anything?'

'Oh, it ain't for them. They sell 'em on. I was thinking of tryin' it meself. Means I can stay 'ere for the kiddies, like. Do it from 'ome. Just store stuff.'

'What...stuff exactly?'

'It comes from abroad I fink. From one of them far off continents. I saw one of the fings once, what they was takin' into the 'ouse. The cover'd come orf. It were like a big dog made of shiny stuff, all black and gold. They struggled to get it in the 'ouse, nearly dropped it which made 'em curse. Covered up me kid's ears as best I could. Must've cost a king's ransom that it must. Strange lookin' thing it were an' all. Wouldn't 'ave it in my 'ouse. It'd frighten the kids.' He frowned and scratched his chin. 'Some posh geezer was there an' all, tellin' the drivers where to put the stuff.' He sighed. 'Any'ow, nuffink to do with me I s'pose. Money goes to money so they say.' He smiled, revealing brown and broken teeth which made me wince and my stomach roll with queasiness.

I said nothing but slipped through the door into the street. In the time I had spent in the Thomas's house a fog had rolled in from the River Thames and was sweeping along the pavements. It was grey and opaque and hid everything in its wake. At first I thought it had hidden the cab I had left waiting outside the house, so dense was it, but I was mistaken. The cab had gone. In its place was the gutter, running with effluent and emitting a most evil odour, and likely a miasma. I withdrew my handkerchief from my reticule and covered my nose, but the odour had already made its way into my throat. I shuddered, praying the fumes would not cause me an illness.

'Your cab, Miss Pond?' Thomas said, standing at the open front door. 'Don't seem to be there.'

'It isn't.'

'What will yer do, Ma'am?'

My heart jumped with anxiety. I had never been in a situation such as this before and I felt at a disadvantage. I had of course heard much about the rookeries, and had visited them myself. They were a blight on our wonderful city, a vast putrid underbelly of swirling streets and alleyways, unlit by the gas lamps lining the streets circling Harley Street where Violet and I had spent our lives. No lamplighter would venture into the rookeries for fear of being attacked... or worse.

It was quite an amazement to me that one's imagination could render a body quite useless. I did not want to move from the Thomas's doorstep as covered in ordure as it was. I had read recently in one of our weekly newspapers, a young woman who had walked the streets close to Dorset Street had been abducted by a customer and taken to said street where she had been used, then thrown down a well. When found she had been mutilated almost beyond recognition. This was the thought that crossed my mind at that moment, and it was not helpful.

'Should I run for a cab, Ma'am?' Thomas asked.

'You could get a cab here?' I asked frowning. I knew from the conversation I'd had from the driver of the cab that had brought me to Parker Street it was doubtful.

'I'd have to go outside the area, Ma'am. Could take some time a course.'

I released a wobbling breath. 'No, thank you, Mr Thomas. I'll find my way out.'

'In the fog, Miss Pond?'

I nodded. For all the world I just wanted to be away from this dreadful place. 'I doubt that I shall see anyone, but they won't see me either. I can remember how we got here. Do not fear, Mr Thomas. I will return to my home at length.'

'If you say so, Ma'am.'

He shut the door, the sound of it sending a chill down my back. I looked left and right. We had entered Parker Street from the right so I began to make my way towards the corner. On the other side of the street was a woman with three children who were dressed in rags. One had no shoes, just rags wrapped around their feet. I could not discern whether it was a boy or girl. She hurried them along, clearly eager to get to her home which I assumed was much like the Thomas's. She glanced at me, her eyes cold and hard. I nodded but she did not return it, simply looked me up and down, taking in my green coat with astrakhan collar and my velvet bonnet. There was no connection to be had, and there never would be. I guessed that I, and those like me, were almost considered an enemy. It saddened me, but it was how it was, the reason why I had decided to offer help, even though at times I understood it was not wanted.

I wrapped my scarf around the lower half of my face and walked with purpose down Parker Street towards Drury Lane, or at least where I thought it was. When one travelled in a cab it very much distorted one's idea of how far a place was, but I felt if I could get to Drury Lane and then onto Museum Street, I would at least have more chance of seeing others who were trying to get home. Not many of us wanted to be out in the fog, particularly like the one which had descended upon London that morning. If they did, they were usually up to no good.

It was just as I was turning into Drury Lane that a horse and carriage pulling a covered cart passed me. I had hoped beyond all hope it was a cab looking for a fare. It was not. The cart made its way to two doors away from the Thomas's house. I heard a loud shout... 'slow down' or 'put down', something of that nature.

Through the fog I could make out three men. One had jumped onto the pavement from the seat at the front of the cart, the other from the back. The men standing on the pavement were dressed like costermongers. The man who alighted from the carriage was dressed in a much finer fashion. Even through the dense fog I could discern he wore a fitted coat and well-shod shoes. He did not wear a cap like the other men, but a well-polished high-topped hat that covered his hairline.

I watched for moment, then pressed myself against the wall hoping they would not see me. I was curious. These were surely the men that Walter Thomas had spoken of, the ones who expected a delivery of goods. I frowned. Surely the well-dressed gentleman did not reside in these streets, so what was his business there? It was then I remembered I was also there, hiding against a wall in the fog amongst the alleyways of a rookery, not the usual behaviour of a woman of my class. Should my peers discover where I had been, my reputation, such as it was after being jilted at the altar so publicly, would dissolve in a heartbeat. My mission in Parker Street had been beyond reproach, but I strongly felt the men who had alighted from the cart and were now standing on the pavement were on a mission that was most definitely not.

I pressed myself even flatter against the wall. My clothes were now sodden, not just with the dampness of the fog, but also with mucky water which was escaping from a gutter that had breached and was no longer fit for purpose. I shook my head and smiled to myself. I was used to getting myself into "situations" as my mother would so delicately put it. My father would simply laugh and say, 'what, again?' They would have approved of my mission I was sure of it.

The tarpaulin on the back of the cart was pulled back by both men as the front door of the house was opened and a women stepped out. She said nothing but stood on the pavement, watching them as they began to unload whatever it was they had delivered. I squinted into the fog. Walter Thomas said he had seen the men deliver a large dog previously, heavy enough for two men to lift. They were being directed by another man who he claimed was different from them in every way. This was the same man; I was in no doubt. He had used the term, "posh geezer" which even I knew meant someone from the same social class as myself.

The two men threw the tarpaulin onto the pavement when another man came out of the house. He almost barged the woman out of the way, then proceeded to unlock the flap at the back of the cart and pull himself up inside it. Once there he began to move the objects in the back, passing the smaller ones to the other two men who took them into the house. When the smaller pieces, which were all wrapped in what looked like rags and string, had been taken into the house, one of the other men jumped onto the back of the cart. Both men bent and began to push a large object towards the open flap.

'Careful, mate,' one of them called. 'This is the one 'e wants. Got ter be careful with it see. 'E's an important customer. Says 'e'll buy more if this lot is what 'e's 'opin' for.'

The man in the high-topped hat stood at the base of the cart, helping to gradually lower the huge piece onto the street below.

'I hope this thing is well-wrapped,' he said in a voice with an accent I was much more used to. 'If it gets covered in horse-shit and whatever else you people have in your streets we'll never sell it. He won't take it I promise you, and I'll be out of pocket. He won't stand for it, and neither will I bearing in mind it's my pocket that bears the danger.'

'Stop your mithering,' one of the men on the cart replied. 'It's wrapped as well as we could make it. They can't wait ter get their 'ands on it. This will take pride of place wherever it's aimed for.' He paused and eyed the man in the high-topped hat. 'And where *is* it going ter?' he asked with a smirk on his face.

'Mind your own bloody business, Smollett. You don't need to know where it's going just yet. You'll get the address when the customer is ready to receive it. Do your job, the one you're well-paid to do. And watch how you handle it. It's a perfect specimen.'

'Keep yer 'air on,' said Smollett, then he looked up and his face darkened. 'Who the 'ell's that.'

I startled. The one called Smollett had seen me. I turned and ran up Drury Lane, unsure of whereabouts in the street I was, or whether I would bump into someone coming in the other direction. I was quite sure I was close to Museum Street. I could hear footsteps behind me. Two sets of steps, one sounding like an echo of the other, were on my heels. I didn't stop to look round, but simply continued to run.

I was grateful for the fog as horrendous as it was. My chest began to seize and my breathing became laboured and painful in the filth laden mist. I needed to find somewhere to hide because I was quite sure I would not outrun them, not in my voluminous skirts and heeled boots. I decided to stop running because I gathered they had been following the sound of my footsteps which sounded hollow then muffled in equal measure. I tiptoed across the street, walking towards Museum Street until I found a narrow alleyway between two houses. I slipped down the alleyway, trying with difficulty to muffle my footsteps. All I could think about was the poor girl who had been thrown down a well, and I was certain, without any doubt whatsoever, what I had witnessed in Parker Street was an illegal endeavour which would therefore put me in danger.

I went down to where the walls of the alleyway curved in the direction of one of the house's yards and crouched down, squinting into the fog at the opening the other end. I held my breath, waiting for the men to pass on the other side of the street, praying they would not surmise where I had gone to escape them. Within seconds I heard them run past on the other side, both of them puffing with exertion.

'Where is she?' Smollett asked, bending over with his hands on his knees.

'Blowed if I know,' said the other. 'Who is she any 'ow? Why was she there?'

'Got ter be one of 'is lot,' said Smollett. 'She weren't like no one what lives round 'ere. D'int yer see 'er, all decked out in velvet and whatnot.'

'P'raps she wants to buy somethin'.'

'So why did she run then? Nah, she weren't lookin' fer somethin' to buy. Dunno what she wanted but it weren't that.' He stood and put his hands on his hips, still puffing. 'We'll just tell 'is nibs we lost 'er,' he said. 'What's he gonna do? He d'int exactly try an' 'elp did 'e. Them sort don't run anywhere. They get their servants to do it.'

The other one nodded. 'Yeah, alright. I can't run no more any 'ow. I'm sick of doin' 'is biddin'. It's not like 'e 'as to take much of the risk is it? We're the ones what'll get the book thrown at us.'

Smollett shrugged. 'We need 'is pocketbook.'

'Maybe we need ter get our own pocketbook.'

'We will...in time. Just got ter sell a bit more stuff then we can get rid of 'im,' said Smollett.

'What, yer mean...yer know...get *rid* of 'im?'

'That's exactly what I mean,' replied Smollett. I nearly gasped, pressing my hand over my mouth to prevent myself from crying out.

The other man rubbed his hands together. 'Yeah, good idea. I'll enjoy that.'

I waited. It was getting colder, and even with the fog obliterating the sky I could tell it was at least an hour past lunchtime. It was only when I heard a noise behind me in one of the yards I decided to move out of the alleyway and make my way to a busier thoroughfare. At the entrance to the alleyway I looked out, peering both left and right to make sure Smollett and his cohort were not waiting for me to appear, but the street seemed empty and I could hear nothing, the fog muffling any sound.

I crossed Shaftesbury Avenue and walked with some difficulty towards Oxford Street. My knees and hips seemed to have fused into numbness whilst being crouched in the same position for so long, not helped by the increasing cold. The fog had begun to clear a little and I breathed a sigh of relief. I could make out lights from shop windows, and for the first time that morning I felt safe.

I made my way into Little Russell Street, and then into Great Russell Street, willing myself forward, picturing in my mind's eye the welcome sight of the front door of my home. At Bedford Square Gardens I managed to hail a cab. My feet were sore, and although I knew I was more than capable of walking the rest of the way down Tottenham

Court Road, Howland Street, and Cavendish Street, I craved the safety and anonymity the inside of a cab would give me. Within fifteen minutes we had pulled up outside our home in Harley Street. I gave a huge sigh and was surprised when tears threatened.

'There's no place like home,' I whispered to myself as I climbed out of the carriage.

It had been an experience, one I did not want to repeat, but at least now I knew just how dangerous life was in the rookeries. I had to acknowledge perhaps my gung-ho confidence at how much help I could give the poor families in the rookeries had over-shadowed my understanding of how much caution I should take when dealing with some of the inhabitants.

The girl who had been thrown into the well had not been far from my thoughts. It was she who had made me guarded, she, losing her life at the hands of a criminal in the Dorset Street tenements who had made me more circumspect. Before I had read about her and her demise, I would have confronted those men and asked them what they were doing, threatened them with the police and more, which I realised now would have put me in grave danger. It was quite likely I would have joined her in the well. She had saved my life.

Chapter 6

'Lily! Violet's hand flew to her mouth in dismay when she saw me.

I had gone into the drawing room with our steward, Foote, his gaze following me with some consternation and not a little surprise.

'What on earth happened to you?' asked Violet, her eyebrows knotting in alarm.

I went across to the huge, gilded mirror over the fireplace and stared at my reflection. I decided it was just as well I had hailed the services of a cab. My appearance resembled that of a mad woman. Making my way down Tottenham Court Road may have elicited some comment, even questions, from those who shopped or worked there.

'The morning didn't turn out quite as I expected, sister,' I answered.

Violet wheeled herself towards where I stood and looked up at me. 'You look as though you've been in a fight. Your bonnet is a shapeless pile, and your coat...soaked through and covered in who knows what. And what is that smell?' She covered the lower half of her face with her hands, then wheeled herself over to the other side of the room and held up a hand to halt my answer. 'No, don't tell me. I'm quite sure I don't want to know. That coat is finished surely. You've rolled in something?'

I removed the offending garment and asked Foote to send for Meg. Foote turned on his heel as though relieved to get away. When Meg entered the drawing room, she immediately wrinkled her nose.

'Ugh, Madam, what *is* that smell?'

'Can this be cleaned, Meg, or should it be got rid of?'

'Oh, Miss Lily. 'Ow on earth did that 'appen. Reckon it can be cleaned. I'll leave it outside to get rid of the smell. A good soak in soda crystals should fix it.' She held it by the collar between finger and thumb and held her nose with her other hand. 'Did someone push you over, Ma'am?'

'Not quite, Meg. I'll tell you about it later.'

'Fair enough,' she said, holding the garment as far away from her as she could as she left the room.

'And the hat?' asked Violet.

I unpinned my bonnet and threw it on the fire where it sizzled before bursting into flames. 'That's the only place for it I think. I need to wash, Violet. The odour of the tenements has clung to me. I can still smell it and it's making me feel quite sick.'

I left the drawing room and went upstairs to my room where I requested a bath of hot water. Foote and the gardener, Mason, brought the bath up to my room, and once it had been filled with hot water and my favourite unguents, washed my hair and bathed. I could not prevent a wave of melancholy go through me as I dressed. Meg had laid out a white linen blouse and a wine-coloured skirt. I pinned up my hair into a plain chignon. Meg was better at it than I, but I was sure she had other things on her mind at that moment.

I returned to the drawing room where Violet sat patiently with her embroidery. She looked up as I sat on the settee.

'Well?' she said. 'Something untoward clearly happened, Lily.'

I nodded, then sat and regaled her with all the happenings of the morning; the situation in which Mr Thomas found himself, and the men who were clearly undertaking something illegal. When I told her about the chase she was beside herself.

'Oh, my goodness, Lily. You could have been attacked, or...' she stared off into the distance, 'even killed.'

I swallowed hard at the memory of it. 'I believe you're right, Violet. The man called Smollett alluded to killing the man in the high-hat. It sounded as though they wanted rid of him so they could take the proceeds of their illegal doings for themselves, although I believe he was a gentleman and the person financing their operation.'

'Not much of a gentleman. What gentleman would behave in such a way?'

'Not all gentlemen are good, Violet. They are not good just because they are gentlemen. Some are as evilly intended as those from the rookeries.'

'So what will you do?'

'This afternoon I will go back to the Agar Street police station and speak with Chief Detective Stride. He should know about it. Then I will at least feel I have done as much as I can do. I hope never to return to Parker Street.'

Violet frowned. 'But Lily, you have been to some of the others, St. Giles for instance. You went there last Christmas did you not, to administer alms. You even went into one of the courts,' she gave me a sideways look, 'where the inhabitants assumed you were from the workhouse and were there to take their children.' She pursed her lips. I was reminded of her disapproval.

'Yes, but it felt different. I went there for the families, to acquaint myself with exactly what is needed to make their lives better.'

'But not the children of Parker Street?'

I sighed feeling not a little guilty. 'It's a dreadful place. In the courts of St Giles, and even The Old Nichol as awful as it is, there is a sense of community, at least in the daytime. Only the Good Lord knows what it must be like during the night hours.'

'A den of iniquity no doubt,' said Violet, sucking the tip of her finger where she had pierced it with her embroidery needle. 'You heard what Wilfred Horrocks said about the people who are admitted to his infirmary, mostly vagabonds, or thieves, or those who have been attacked in their own homes.' Violet shook her head. 'No good goes on there, and no good can come of it.

'You know what you saw when you went there; the rooms dark and damp, each room housing a separate family, some with six children...or more. Why...one of the houses, if they could ever be worthy of the name, had forty-eight people living in it. Water is supplied for only ten minutes every day from a stream which is then stopped when the landlord decides. If they need water they must go elsewhere. And this only runs until Sunday. If they're fortunate one of the buildings might have an outside tap. And as for bathing and...well, their ablutions, it takes place in whatever place they can find which results in a disgusting and surely medically dangerous ordure underfoot and a miasma which would fell a horse, unless there is an outhouse, which is not guaranteed by any means. For their homes they pay two shillings per week to a landlord who clearly does not have a care except for the coin in his pocket. And you wish to change all this, sister. You wish to change the living conditions of those people unfortunate enough to live there but who have nowhere else to go. My darling girl, I think you need a better, more solid plan.'

I knew Violet was right in what she said. The task was almost impossible, but I used the word 'almost' advisedly. There were others like me who wished to change the landscape of these people's lives; I was quite certain I was not the only one who felt as I did. Jonathan had been one of those people, which was why I had considered him my soulmate and agreed to marry him. Happily, I had found a helpmeet in Wilfred Horrocks, who had promised assistance should I need it. And if past experience of the rookeries was anything to go by, I'm sure I would.

Chapter 7

Chief Detective Stride raised his eyebrows when he saw me enter the Agar Street police station, clearly surprised I was visiting again so soon.

'Miss Pond? Can't keep away from us I see.'

'I hope you have time to speak with me, Chief Detective. I have some information you may find interesting.'

He nodded and showed me into his office and closed the door, but not before asking one of his constables to deliver some refreshment. I was glad. I was sorely in need of a cup of tea, and a slice of cake would not have gone amiss, as I had had, what one would define, a rather skimpy lunch.

Indicating for me to sit in the chair opposite his desk, he went around to the other side and sat in what one could perhaps describe as a captain's chair, a tufted leather monstrosity which had seen better days but looked extremely comfortable. He leant his elbows on the desk and clasped his hands together. I noticed he was wearing a rather ornate wedding ring, yet it was on his right hand. I hoped he hadn't noticed my staring at it.

'So, Miss Pond. What is it you think I will find interesting?'

'I have had a day of it quite frankly, Chief Detective.'

He chuckled and leant back in his carbuncle of a chair. 'Really? How so?'

'I went to 71 Parker Street and spoke with Mr Thomas. I was pleased to see his children were being fed, even if it was simply bread and some rather thin gruel, but it was hot and seemed to fill their bellies. He alluded to the notion he thought they would be better off dead because he didn't know how he would feed them...he has no work, and because Christmas is on the horizon is unlikely to get any.'

Stride frowned. 'Did he actually say that?'

'No, but it was what he meant. He also said if he could find work he would need to leave them during the day, the youngest is no more than two I would say, and they would have to beg in the streets, or steal, to feed themselves.'

Chief Detective Stride shrugged. 'It's not uncommon, Miss Pond.'

'I realise that. He said he was forced to do the very same thing himself when he was a child, but it doesn't make it acceptable.'

'Have you given them anything?'

'I sent two members of our staff this afternoon, with a selection of food from our personal pantry; a ham, two chickens, vegetables, and some sweet treats for the children. Even a bottle of porter. It should see them through the Christmas festivities. I also suggested he send the children to the Ragged School while he is searching for work. I offered to make enquiries myself on the matter. If he cleaned himself up he could get a job in service, although it wouldn't be inside the house, perhaps gardening or animal husbandry. The children will also need clothes if they are to go to the Ragged School. Ragged implies the children are destitute as many are, but the school will expect a level of cleanliness, I'm sure.'

'And you will provide the clothes?'

'Of course. I know families with children. They will be hand-me-downs but they'll be in perfect condition.'

'He'll sell them.'

'Perhaps. I will have them delivered in time for their mother's funeral, and they can be worn again at the Ragged School. I had a rather unfortunate experience this morning, which is the reason I'm here.'

At that moment a constable knocked on the office door and entered, at Chief Detective Stride's command, carrying a tray on which there were two cups of tea and a plate of the longed-for cake. I fell unconsciously into the role of all women by handing him a cup of tea and a plate on which he could place his slice of cake.

'What happened, Miss Pond? Please tell me you didn't go into the rookeries again. You know what occurred last time.'

'You, and my sister, Violet, seem to take great pleasure in not allowing me to forget, Chief Detective Stride. No, I did not go into the rookeries, although it hardly seemed a necessity. Parker Street is equally as bad if not worse. At least in the rookeries there is a sense of community; that is, of course, until someone oversteps the mark and is the recipient of a sliced through throat. Parker Street is devoid of even the smallest sense of community.' I shook my head at the memory. 'It seems there is more going on in Parker Street than downtrodden families.'

Chief Detective Stride frowned; his cup held in mid-air as he digested what I'd said.

'In what way?'

'When I was with the Thomas family, and more than ready to leave I can assure you, Mr Thomas said there had been regular deliveries to a house in Parker Street just two doors away from his home. I was astonished at this because one could not envisage such a poor address as having deliveries of anything.' I took a sip of tea and a bite of cake before I continued. The cake was rather dry with the expected frosting almost non-existent. I made a mental note to bring one of Cook's cakes with me next time I had occasion to visit. 'As luck would have it, and in the event, it turned out to be not so lucky, the cab I had hired to wait for me in Parker Street decided it was too dangerous for him to remain and made off.' I glanced at Chief Detective Stride for a change in demeanour. He sighed heavily with exasperation as I knew he would. 'A fog had covered Parker Street and the surrounding area and I wondered how I should get home, but while I considered my options of which there seemed to be none other than walking, a carriage pulled up pulling a covered cart of all things, outside the house Mr Thomas had mentioned.

'The carriage was driven by two men, who sat on the box seat. When the carriage stopped a man alighted from it. He was extremely well-dressed; his clothes were clearly of the finest quality. He wore a brushed high-hat and his shoes were buffed to a mirror shine. He began to give instructions to the men who had driven the carriage, telling them to unload whatever it was in the back of the cart and take it into the house in Parker Street.'

'And what was in the cart?'

'That I do not know, but Mr Thomas said previously he had seen them unloading what looked like a rather large sculpted black dog, enhanced somewhat with gold paint, which had been wrapped badly in rags. He said the head was protruding from the rags. He also said it was a hideous thing he would not want his children to see.'

Chief Inspector Stride shook his head and gazed into the distance. 'A black dog.' His gaze settled on me. 'What kind of a dog? Children like dogs unless they're the scavenging kind.'

'Again, I don't know, but the fog allowed me to watch from the corner of the street as they unloaded the cart. There were many smaller items, but then a much larger one which the well-dressed gentleman seemed to be most concerned about. He entreated the men to be careful with it as it was a special...what was the word,' I searched my brain and found it, 'specimen.'

'Specimen? Specimen of what?' I shrugged and took another bite of cake, deciding to leave the rest on the plate. It was almost inedible.

'What happened next?'

This was the question I'd hoped Jeremiah Stride would not ask. 'They saw me watching them and gave chase.'

Chief Detective Stride looked startled and near choked on a piece of cake that had lodged in his throat. I went around to his side of the desk and thumped him rather vociferously on the back between the shoulder blades. The offending piece of cake flew out of his mouth and landed on the papers on the desk. I went around to my side of the desk, took my seat and continued.

'Although the arrival of the fog had given me pause and caused some anxiety, the smell from it was repulsive and I was worried it would cause some disgusting illness or other, it served me rather well. I ran as fast as one can in a capacious skirt, but because I had let vanity get the better of me this morning by donning my new heeled boots, the decision to wear them did not help in my quest to outrun them.'

Chief Detective Stride cleared his throat and took long gulp of tea, supposedly because his throat was rather sore. 'But you're here, Miss Pond,' he said, rubbing his eyes which were still watering from coughing and my banging him on the back.

'I hid.'

'You hid?'

'Down an alleyway between two houses. It was quite disgusting. So much detritus around the buildings, even a dead cat which had obviously lain on the ground for weeks and had been pulled apart by rats. How do people live this way?'

'Yet here you are, Miss Pond, sitting in front of me, unless you are an apparition, so I surmise you managed to get away.'

'Well, of course. I waited and held my breath for as long as I could, mostly because of the stink, the miasma of which I was sure would cause me to catch a deadly illness. The two men ran by the opening then back again when they realised they had lost me. But here is the interesting bit.' Chief Detective Stride leant forward. 'They stood in front of the opening and discussed what they were doing. I heard them perfectly clearly, Chief Detective. They were discussing the man who had arrived in the carriage, the well-dressed man. They said they needed him at present because they needed his pocketbook, but when they had a pocketbook of their own they would get rid of him.'

Chief Detective Stride's eyes widened. 'Get rid of him? As in...kill him?'

'I believe entirely it is what they meant. They also mentioned St Giles and someone called Dines. I do believe they have contacts there who are likely involved in the same venture, whatever it may be.'

Stride took a deep breath, then took another bite of the cake that had nearly been the death of him. He chewed thoughtfully. 'Any more names?'

'Smollett. He was one of the men who chased me. I heard the gentleman call him by that name.'

He smiled. 'Smollett,' he said then nodded. 'A name I'm familiar with. And clearly you got to Harley Street safely or you wouldn't be here. Did they see you leave?'

'They did not. And as for my getting home safely, I can assure you I arrived nothing in comparison to how I left my home this morning. My coat was soaked in God knows what where I had been squatting near to the ground and my hat I threw onto the fire, but yes. I arrived home by hansom after quite a walk.'

'What do you think is going on?'

'I've no idea, Chief Detective Stride, but I would put my house on the event of it not being legal. It seemed rather cloak and dagger to me, and one does not kill one's business associates simply to get them out of the way. I fully believe the gentleman from the carriage will be done away with unless someone steps in to stop it.'

'We would need a warrant to search the premises, and a good reason to obtain a warrant. They don't give them out like sweets.'

'Why can't you just turn up unannounced? It's the best way to catch them at it, surely.'

He shook his head. 'Not allowed, Miss Pond. We can call on them, ask a few questions to which they won't have any answers, or simply make answers up to satisfy us, and deny having any knowledge of any deliveries. A pointless exercise I'm afraid, one which will cost me money and eat into my budget which gets smaller every year. We need proof...to obtain a warrant and arrest them of wrongdoing...if they are doing wrong.'

'I would say it is a given. There is no question I assure you.'

'It may well be, but we need more.'

'What do you suggest?'

He stared at me as though taking my measure.

'I mentioned to you I had something in mind.' I nodded. 'It is an idea I read about in The Police Review. It is called under-cover policing.' I nodded, wondering what on earth under-cover policing had to do with me. 'However, I would prefer not to discuss it here. Walls have ears as I'm sure you are aware, Miss Pond. One should be circumspect about how much is discussed within close proximity to staff.'

'Are you referring to *my* staff, Chief Detective Stride?' He nodded. 'Well, I must agree downstairs staff often know what I'm thinking before do.' I inclined my head to one side. 'Is it this you refer to?'

'In a manner of speaking. I wonder if we could meet somewhere less obtrusive, a public house perhaps, near Harley Street. I would prefer to discuss my idea there if you have no objection.'

I widened my eyes. 'Should I bring a chaperone?'

'I'd rather you didn't, Miss Pond. I would prefer for this to stay between us. At least then if there are any leaks, we'll know it's either you...or me who has leaked the information.'

I must confess I was astonished Chief Detective Stride asked to meet me in a public house, and without a chaperone too. It was unheard of in my circle of society. And the talk of leaks had me almost hypnotised. I was quite sure I had never leaked anything in my life. I'd never had cause to, but I was also fascinated by what it was he wanted me to do, so I readily agreed.

'Would this evening, suit, Miss Pond? I'll wait outside for you if I arrive first.'

'This evening suits very well, Chief Detective Stride. I have no other engagements. Where should we meet?'

'I understand The Lamb and Anchor is quite near to your home.'

'Indeed it is. What time?'

'Shall we say half past seven. The after-work drinkers will have gone by then and we should be sure to get a table.'

I rose from my seat and made a small bow of my head, clutching my dolly bag in front of me. 'Until half past seven, Chief Detective Stride. And please don't be late.'

He chuckled. 'I wouldn't dream of it.'

Chapter 8

I had never ventured into a public house by myself. It was something women of my class just did not do, simply because public houses were considered rather low-class. On my journey back in a hansom from the Agar Street police station I thought about it very carefully. Had I been rather too eager to agree to meeting Chief Detective Stride in The Lamb and Anchor?

I considered myself a forward-thinking woman and was willing to undertake a task so out of my range of comfort, but I knew it would be frowned upon by those in my society if they should ever discover what I had done. My standing in the world had already been shaken by my being jilted at the altar in front of influential guests. Also, I wondered what Violet would make of it. Then I had an idea. I would take her with me.

I bit my lip in consternation, because although I considered Violet to be as forward thinking as myself, she may well draw the line at meeting a man she had never met before in a public house. Or, she could very well relish the idea and view it as an adventure. I hoped it was the latter rather than the former. Violet was astute and sensible, far more level-headed than I could ever hope to be.

I alighted the hansom in Harley Street. The clock in the hall chimed the hour of three o'clock and with it being so close to Christmas the afternoon had closed in.

How I loved our house...our home, which had been our home for ever. As soon as I returned to Harley Street and ran up the stone steps to the black front door with the brass knocker I felt myself relax, as though I was in the place I was meant to be. My sanctuary if you will.

Violet had said the same and I had joked with her that perhaps neither of us would marry, simply because we would not want to leave Harley Street. Or we would expect our spouses to move into our house and we would all live together. We had laughed at the idea, but I'm quite sure privately Violet was concerned I would marry, and she would be left alone. It would never happen. Wherever I went Violet would come too. And if there was any objection, I would simply stay with her. She was my best friend, my helpmeet, and my confidant.

'You've done what?'

'I've agreed to meet Chief Detective Stride in The Lamb and Anchor Public House at half past seven this evening.'

Violet's eyes widened and she shook her head. 'Whatever next?' She wheeled herself over to the window and drew the curtains to a close, something Meg or one of the other maids would have done, but it was rather like Violet was trying to keep out prying eyes...and ears from observing and listening to our conversation.

'You seem determined to cause a scandal, Lily,' she said sotto voce, as though she really believed walls had ears. 'And why are you meeting this man? And why would you agree to meet him in a public house of all places, and without a chaperone?'

'Do you think I need a chaperone?'

'Of course you should have a chaperone. You're not a streetwalker.'

'I thought perhaps you could come with me.'

Violet's mouth dropped open, and then she burst into laughter. 'Oh, Lily,' she cried, wiping her eyes with a fine, lawn handkerchief. 'If anyone else had said that to me I would have taken offence, but...well, it's you isn't it? Your ideas are simply outrageous. Such a joke, even from your lips.'

I sat on the chaise beside her bath chair and put my arm around her shoulders. 'It wasn't a joke,' I said quietly. 'You can come with me. If you want to see yourself as my chaperone then so be it, but I would rather you came because you are interested in what Chief Detective Stride has to say.'

'Why would I be interested in what he has to say? What have you got yourself involved in, Lily?'

'Nothing as yet, but I think he has a job for me.'

'A job!' Violet reached for my hand and squeezed it. 'Darling, you don't need a job. Working women need a job to pay for...things. We don't need to work. Mama and Papa left us extremely well provided for.'

'It's not about money, Violet. It's about doing something worthwhile, something that means ...something. I want to change people's lives for the better.' I took a deep breath, hoping I was explaining myself properly. 'I'd like to change at least one person's life, a child perhaps who never has enough to eat, who washes perhaps once in a blue moon because there is never enough water, and who shares a bed with a dozen others.

'If you had only seen the Thomas children this morning. They were toasting pieces of stale bread in front of the living room fire. Mr Thomas gave them bowls of gruel so they could dip their bread into it to soften it, but there weren't enough bowls to go round. There were three small bowls and five children. This was breakfast for them and he admitted it was all he had. No kidneys, or chops, or eggs for *them*. Five children, Violet! Can you imagine?'

I saw Violet swallow and she closed her eyes momentarily. She turned to me, her beautiful grey eyes soft and kind. I detected the threat of tears beginning at her eyelashes. 'You let your heart rule your head,' she said softly. 'You always have.'

I nodded, knowing deep inside she understood my need to redress the balance. 'You're right, but my heart is in the right place. It's not just money these people need, Violet. They need care and guidance. It occurred to me when I was at the Thomas's. Those children had scabs on their faces. Their hair was overtaken by lice. They were filthy and so were their clothes. How would they ever fight off infection or illness should it come their way? They need health care, particularly the children. I thought I might recruit Wilfred Horrocks to offer free healthcare to those who really need it.'

Violet nodded. 'Well, that is a good idea. I'm sure he would help. He seemed ready to.'

'Please come with me, Violet. I need your opinion and your advice. And yes, it would be better for me to meet a gentleman with another woman with me. I'm more than capable of meeting him alone, but society demands we are chaperoned. I don't want to damage our marriage prospects even further than I already have.'

'You didn't damage them, Lily.'

I blew out a sigh. 'I wish everyone saw it that way.'

Chapter 9

We left the house at a quarter past the hour. Dreyfus, our footman, carried first the bath chair to the pavement, then Violet to the bath chair. It was something we had done many times before, but the journey we were about to undertake was new to both of us. Highlighted in the street gas lamps was a fall of sleet which had been threatening all day. It was bitterly cold.

'Are you warm enough, Violet,' I asked her. I was always worried Violet might catch a chill. She was prone to ailments, and whenever she succumbed to a chill she seemed to suffer far more than I, should I catch a cold.

'Yes, I'm warm, perhaps a little too warm. Mildred worries so much about me she has piled on the coats and scarves. And look at this damned hat she chose for me. It's monstrous.'

'Monstrous it may be,' I said as I wheeled her toward The Lamb and Anchor, 'but I dare any illness to come for you. It would never get past all those layers.'

Violet chuckled. 'All they'll find is a puddle of water where I've melted.'

'You can cast them off once we're inside, but for now, I'm with Mildred on the matter.'

Chief Detective Stride was waiting for us outside The Lamb and Anchor Public House, although I could tell by his expression he was rather surprised when he saw it was "us" rather than "me". His shoulders and the brim of his bowler hat were covered in tiny flecks of snow. For some reason this amused me. He looked rather like a Christmas ornament I thought, which had been left standing outside the public house. He made a short bow to us both, looking at me with widened eyes as if to say, 'I thought you were coming alone.'

He found a table in the centre of the room, one where Violet could safely keep her bath chair out of everyone's way. The room wasn't as large as I had expected and was not in good repair. The chairs and tables were scuffed and covered with beer stains. The ceiling, which I'm sure was white some years ago, was now a sickly yellow, a veneer of nicotine and other substances changing its appearance. There was also an odour, a nauseating, cloying smell that got stuck in one's throat. I felt I could actually taste it which made my stomach roll with disgust.

The bar from where the barkeep served drinks had surely once been a beautiful piece of furniture, but years of misuse and lack of cleaning had turned it into an object which would not have looked out of place in one of the houses in the rookeries. Clearly many of the men who used the public house on their journey home from work came from the lower orders and had thankfully left which meant there were few patrons.

'A drink, ladies,' said Chief Detective Stride. 'A sherry perhaps.'

'A sherry will do very nicely thank you,' I answered. 'And for Violet?' I glanced at my sister and she nodded her agreement. Chief Detective Stride went to the bar to speak to the barkeep and my sister began to divest herself of the wrappings Mildred had insisted she wear.

'So, this is a public house,' she said under her breath. 'What a place.'

'One wonders why these places are so popular, but I'm guessing when someone is in their cups their surroundings mean little to them.'

'And why do those men keep knocking their knuckles on the table?' She inclined her head towards a corner table where five men were sitting with their jars of ale, playing a game of some kind.

'Dominoes,' said Stride as he joined us at the table. 'They're knocking to let the other players know they can't lay a domino, a card if you will.' He glanced at Violet who looked comely in a claret velvet gown enhanced by a sparkling white lace fichu. His eyes rested on her for some moments as though fully taking in her countenance.

Violet was a beautiful woman. Mildred had curled her blonde hair into large curls and pinned them to the top of her head making her neck look elongated and rather swanlike. Her grey eyes sparkled in the light from the chandeliers which, although had likely not seen a duster in years, emitted an attractive glow. He watched her as she picked up her glass of sherry and took a sip, seemingly entranced.

'Er.' He cleared his throat. 'They play until none of the players can take a turn then count up the remaining dominoes. The player with the least dominoes in his hand is the winner.'

I smiled at Chief Detective Stride's expression. This man was not so short sighted as some of our acquaintance. I truly believed all he could see was Violet, and not her cumbersome bath chair.

'So, Chief Detective.' I decided it was time for him to take his attention off my lovely sister and get to the point. He had asked to meet me and I had agreed. Now I needed to know why. 'What is all this about?'

He took a swig from his glass of stout and nodded. 'First of all I would appreciate it if you did not speak of my rank while we are here. You may call me Mr Stride or...Jeremiah.'

I pressed my lips together to prevent myself from laughing. 'Oh, I think it should be Jeremiah,' I said. 'So much friendlier. And we are Lily,' I said, laying a hand against my chest to indicate myself, 'and Violet, my sister.'

Jeremiah bowed his head towards us. 'It's a pleasure to meet you, ladies,' he replied, more to Violet than to me. 'I take it your parents were fond of flowers.'

'Indeed, sir, they were. We had another sister who unfortunately did not survive babyhood. She was Artemisia.'

'I'm sorry for your loss, and that of your parents.'

'Thank you.'

'I'm aware it seems a trifle familiar to address each other by our Christian names, but it would be dangerous to allow the patrons here to think we are anything other than friends who have met for a cordial discussion.'

I nodded. 'And if we are not friends, what are we?'

Violet stared at him, clearly as interested as I was about exactly what our relationship was, and why we had been summoned to The Lamb and Anchor, a place we had never set foot in before.

Jeremiah took another gulp of stout then rubbed his hands together. 'You have demonstrated you have an interest in the lives of the poor souls who inhabit the rookeries,' he said, directing his question to me. 'And whatever I or anyone else says you will not be warned off. I understand that Constable Turner had a quiet word with you about the questionable safety of your activities.'

'As have I,' said Violet, taking another sip of sherry so she didn't have to make eye contact with me.

'He is concerned you will not stop doing your rounds of the rookeries, that you seemingly have no fear. This is either because you have courage, or you're naïve of the dangers awaiting you in such places. I believe you're brave, Lily,' he continued, 'particularly after your last escapade in Parker Street. Most women would have had an attack of the vapours should they have been placed in the same position, but you are self-aware and self-protecting which I believe saved you. I can assure you had those men caught up with you it's quite likely you would have gone missing and we would have found your body floating in the Thames.'

Violet gasped and I felt rather chastised, but I was determined to fight my corner. 'The strange thing is, Jeremiah, I did not at any moment feel I was in any real danger. The fog, which I first thought would bring about my downfall, acted as my saviour. They could not see me, only hear my footsteps because I was wearing those blasted heeled boots.'

Violet looked scandalised by my language. 'Lily!'

'I stopped running and tiptoed the rest of the way, or until I came to the alleyway between the houses which provided a hiding place. It was because I didn't try to run all the way to Museum Street, I was in the fortunate position of being able to hear them speak and hear them I did. Every word.'

'We have a file on a Jim Smollett.'

I grinned. 'You do?'

'I got one of the constables to go through our files. The name Smollett comes up quite often, but it's probably not just the man you saw in Parker Street.'

I frowned. 'What do you mean, Jeremiah? Are you saying there's more than one Smollett?'

'I am indeed. The family lives at Seven Dials, not far from Covent Garden.'

'Not far from us then,' said Violet.

'Indeed,' I replied. 'As I mentioned before, the courts and alleyways such as St Giles which are inhabited by gangs, prostitutes and temporary gin palaces are within walking distance of our own front door.'

'It leaves one cold to think of it.'

I glanced at her and put a hand on one of hers. 'You're perfectly safe, Violet. We are but two minutes' walk from home. We will not stay long

I glanced at Chief Inspector Stride. 'Jeremiah is about to tell me why we needed to have this meeting here.'

He nodded, understanding my intimation I wished to return Violet home as soon as maybe.

'As I said, Lily, you are a brave woman. One might say reckless. In fact, Constable Turner used that very word.'

'Constable Turner is a misogynist. He told me to go home to my hearth.'

'And with good reason. But I, unlike Constable Turner, think you are a woman to be reckoned with and I'm fairly sure, if I have summed up your personality correctly, that you will do whatever you think needs to be done.'

I nodded, thinking it was a fair assessment of my character. 'I am aware of what needs to be done, Jeremiah. I have been to the rookeries as you well know. I may be reckless but in my opinion it will take a certain amount of recklessness to change those environs. I am also fully aware the reason so much undetected and unsolved crime goes on there is because there is no one brave enough to regulate them. Not even the police. They steal, maim, and kill at will. They literally get away with murder. This criminal behaviour impacts on the families who are forced to live in places such as St Giles, The Old Nichol, Dean Street and Dorset Street.

'Dorset Street in particular has a dreadful reputation and is fully worthy of it. The poverty and lack of decent housing means those with little money are forced to find shelter in the doss houses. The men who live there work in the tanneries, the foundries, or the breweries. It is the only work available to them. Then, after a day's work of filth and goodness knows what, they must find a bed in a doss house owned by a middle-class gentleman, I use the term loosely, who charges a third of the man's pay for a bed which has been vacated perhaps only minutes before by a complete stranger. There are often two to a bed, one up one down, sometimes more. These are grown men, Jeremiah, not criminals, but men who have a desire to work, but unfortunately are treated the same as the lowest common denominator, the brawlers, the criminals and the madams.'

My diatribe finished, I took a deep breath and a long sip of sherry. I could feel Violet's eyes on my face. My voice had wobbled and I'm sure she felt I would burst into tears, but thankfully I had not been brought so low. I was angry; frustrated at the injustice of it all. Seeing the condition of the five children of the Thomas family had sickened me. I had pushed it to the back of my mind because of the illegal activity I was sure was going on there, but when I considered those poor wee mite's pale faces, their sunken eyes and lice riddled hair, it made my heart drop to the very soles of my feet.

'You are a passionate soul, Lily,' Jeremiah said after a few moments, 'which is why I would like to offer you a position as an undercover agent.'

I gasped and Violet began to cough. She cleared her throat and wiped her lips with a lace-edged handkerchief. 'A what?'

'An undercover agent, Miss Pond.' I couldn't help but notice he did not address her by her Christian name but instead showed deference.

'Which is?'

'I'd like Lily to go into the rookeries and live as one of them. She will need to keep her wits about her and her ear to the ground. She will then be expected to report back to me any criminal activity being undertaken or planned.'

Violet turned to look at me, aghast at Chief Detective Stride's suggestion.

'And what does my sister think of this idea?' she asked. 'To become an agent for the police, a person who infiltrates the rookeries and lives as they do in all the filth and detritus they endure every day? And how exactly is she meant to be accepted by these people who are suspicious of everyone, who would kill a man for a penny or the shoes on his feet.' She turned to Stride and I knew I could rely on my sister to ask the most pertinent question of all. 'Would you do it...Jeremiah?' Her question was laced with irony.

Chief Detective Stride shifted in his chair, then took a swig of stout. 'I'm not sure I'd be very convincing, Miss Pond. Plus, many of the criminals around these parts know me. They don't know Lily.'

'I suppose you're saying, no, you would not do it. What will my sister gain from it?'

I felt I had to intervene. 'I'm not sure it's about gain, Violet. It sounds like an idea I should seriously consider. I've wanted to do more to help for many a year, but one is taking one's life in one's hands if there is no support. This way I'll have the support of the police,' I glanced at Stride, 'will I not, Stride.' I decided to call him Stride. I had begun to feel increasingly uncomfortable calling him Jeremiah. Too familiar. Everyone knows familiarity breeds contempt.

He raised his eyebrows but then seemed to submit to my will. 'There will be some support.'

'But you won't be there all the time, will you.' This was a statement from Violet rather than a question. 'No, of course you won't,' she continued, answering her own question and gripping her hands resolutely in front of her. 'Because if it was your intention to be, you'd either do it yourself, or get one of your constables to do it. And that leads me to another question, Jeremiah. Why couldn't one of your colleagues do it?'

'We never have enough constables on the beat, Miss Pond. We are unable to release them from their duties. I should tell you we have someone there already, a woman.'

My mouth dropped open. 'An undercover agent?'

He nodded and lit a cigarette from a packet he had purchased from the barkeep. 'She will be your passage into the rookery. She'll introduce you, make up some story or other about you being a friend with nowhere to stay. That's how you'll get in.'

'Who is this woman,' asked Violet. 'And why is she working for you?'

'She's a private detective who has worked with us before. She helped us catch one of the biggest confidence trickster and coin changer gangs in the East End, simply by befriending them and finding out about them, playing a part if you like. She was previously an actress.'

'And you wish for me to do the same?' He nodded and took a long draw on the cigarette then puffed out a stream of smoke which was presumably why the ceiling in the public house was so yellow. 'But your role will be different.'

I frowned. 'In what way?'

'We want you to dress as a young man, be...a young man.'

Violet snorted a laugh. 'That's not very flattering. Why do you think Lily could pass herself off as a man? She looks nothing like a man.'

'She's tall and slender. And strong if I'm not mistaken. Certainly strong in constitution. And she'll be given the right clothes to wear.' He turned his attention to me. Of course, you'll have to practise speaking differently. Get rid of your rounded vowels, drop your aitches. To convince them you'll have to become one of them.'

My head was spinning and I could barely think along one train of thought. 'Which rookery will I be expected to live in?'

'St Giles.'

'Oh, my God,' cried Violet, which drew the attention of the men playing dominoes at the corner table. She spoke sotto voce. 'Surely not. Apart from Dorset Street it is the worst area of London. You are not serious, Chief Detective.' Violet had lost the willingness to be friendly to Stride. She was appalled. 'If they discover her duplicity, they will kill her. And what is the need for her to be there? I think I may have missed something.'

'You discovered something quite by chance this morning, Miss Pond. Lily. We know something big is happening in the rookeries. We've known for a while. We know it's something illegal but we haven't been able to catch the tail of it. What you witnessed was one of the most important pieces of information we've received so far. We've got snouts on the streets who would sell their own grandmothers for a penny. We give them a shilling and they're willing to spill the beans. Thus far, we know they're receiving stolen goods from someone in the know, and we know they're getting rid of the goods to people who should know better.'

I frowned. 'You mean from our society, don't you? You mean the upper echelon.'

'I'm afraid so.'

'And these goods. Do you know what they are?'

He shook his head. 'Sadly not. But with your help, and Bessie Clacket's, not only will we find out, but we'll also catch them in the act.'

'Bessie Clacket? She's the private investigator already in St. Giles?'

'She is?'

'Is she not frightened of being found out?'

'If she is she's not mentioned it to me.'

'Does she get paid?' asked Violet, ever the bookkeeper. She always kept the books at home for the running of our house. Nothing untoward ever got past her.

'She is paid. Yes, of course.'

'And will Lily be paid?'

I smiled a little, thinking if Violet had all her faculties, she would be just the sort of person Chief Detective Stride was looking for. She was as strong and robust as I could ever be, but an illness as a child had robbed her of the use of her legs. A sudden sadness overwhelmed me and I put my hand on her arm.

'I'm not worried about payment, Violet,' I said softly.

She stared hard at me. 'Well, you should be. You want to help people, don't you? Any recompense you receive for this utterly ridiculous undertaking could be used to provide alms for those very people you want to help, although I can't for one moment think you're going to agree to this travesty.' I don't remember Violet blinking once during her diatribe. She was incensed, *that* I could see, and Stride looked embarrassed. It was quiet for a moment until she turned her attention to poor Chief Detective Stride who, if I remember correctly, flinched. 'And you, Jeremiah. Will you take responsibility for whatever befalls my sister? Will it make you culpable should we find her body floating in the Thames? The term "manslaughter" springs to mind, although even your loss of reputation and subsequent prison sentence or hanging will not bring my sister back.'

Stride swallowed and then took another gulp of stout, emptying his glass.

'I'm not anticipating anything so dire to happen, Miss Pond. Bessie Clacket has been at St Giles for three months. She knows what to do, and she will instruct Lily on how to behave, what to do and what not to do, what to say and what not to say. She is an expert.'

'And what makes her such an expert?'

'She worked in a circus as a bareback horse rider, doing tricks and suchlike. She's a contortionist who performs her contortions on the back of a horse. She told me living in the circus was as dangerous as living in a rookery. The prospect of living in St Giles didn't deter her at all. She still does contortions. Her spider is something to behold, quite unnerving truth be told, but she has certainly seen some life, perhaps things you or I would prefer not to see.'

'And how do you know her, Jeremiah?'

Stride went a rather unfetching shade of pink. 'We were...well, sweethearts once, I s'pose. Yes, we were. After my wife died I took my son and daughter to the circus. They were entranced by her and wanted to meet her backstage, so to speak. She did her spider contortion for them. My son tried to be brave and kept a stoical countenance, but my daughter screamed like blue blazes. Bessie, er, Miss Clacket, changed behind a screen and returned without her strange cosmetics and black attire so they could see she was an ordinary person after all. We got talking. She said she was intent on leaving the circus because she wasn't getting any younger and the contortions were inflaming her joints.' He shrugged. 'I asked her if she would have dinner with me, and she agreed.'

He looked down at the empty glass in his hand and a wave of sorrow went through me. We didn't know what was happening in other people's lives. It was so easy for one to spring to a quick judgement. I'd had no idea he'd been widowed, or he had children. It was unspoken, but I believed he was lonely.

'But you're not together any longer, Stride?' I asked him gently.

'We're friends, Lily. Just friends. The children are fond of her, as am I. When the intelligence was passed to us by one of our snouts regarding what was going on at St. Giles, she jumped at the chance of infiltrating the courts and alleyways. She seemingly had no fear of it whatsoever. I beseeched her to think on it long and hard but she was insistent. She left the circus and immediately went to work.' He looked up at me. 'I think you'll like her, Lily.'

There was clearly something I needed to ask him. 'Why is Miss Clacket not playing the part of a man?' Violet nodded with anticipation and leant towards him waiting for his answer. Stride faltered but seemingly decided to be honest. 'She has a different build. I don't think she would pass as a male.'

'Do you mean...womanly?' I asked him. He had the grace to look slightly embarrassed. 'And I am not?'

'You're more...boyish. A leaner figure. And younger,' he added enthusiastically, I'm sure with an intention to smooth my ruffled feathers.

I chuckled. 'Does Miss Clacket know about me?'

'She does. She thinks it's an excellent idea. She can only learn so much from the women at St Giles. She knows the men, but if she tried to befriend any of them it would damage the rapport she has built with the women. They accepted her when she told them her story. She simply told them the truth about her life in the circus and was readily accepted.

'She immediately set about trying to find a job. She works in a laundry, meaning she is able to take the other women's clothes, surreptitiously of course, have them washed, and be paid for it. It means on occasion, the inhabitants of the court where she lives acquire cleaner clothes and she is able to put money in the pot. She has made herself indispensable. What we really need is for an agent to befriend the men. They won't allow anyone into their inner circle unless they're a man. The men will have more information about what is going on and what criminal dealings they are either in the middle of, or are planning.

'It is why I wanted us to meet here at the public house rather than in your home. This is the sort of place you'll be expected to frequent on a regular basis I should imagine. The public houses are where deals are made and money is paid. The men from the rookeries spend half their lives in the pubs, but women are rarely seen there. And I should say the public houses in, and near, St. Giles are a different prospect to this one. This one is positively salubrious in comparison.'

I inhaled a deep breath and glanced at Violet who looked less than happy. What Stride was asking me to undertake was dangerous. I had been to the rookeries, had gone into one of the courts and seen the gloomy mean streets and the common lodging houses.

If Stride had suggested I infiltrate Dorset Street, or Dean Street, or Flower Street, I would have refused immediately. Those streets were like nests of vermin, and no one should ever attempt to infiltrate them or to befriend anyone who used the lodging houses. Anyone who went there was in danger of being attacked and killed. Some of the inhabitants would strip a man of his clothes and leave him for dead in the streets, simply because the attacker wanted his jacket or his boots. Dorset Street was indeed the worst street in London.

'I'm not expecting you to give me an answer immediately, Lily,' Stride said as he got up and went to the bar where the barkeep was wiping the beer-sticky top with a filthy rag. Violet leant toward me and spoke in a low voice, presumably Stride couldn't hear.

'Lily,' she almost hissed. 'You cannot be considering it. What would our parents think?'

I stared at her; my eyes wide. 'Our parents, Violet? What did they ever say?'

She sat back in her bath chair and shook her head. 'You'll do it no matter what I say.'

'Not yet, sister. I haven't said yes. And if you want to know what our parents would say, then I think you know as well as I do. They would encourage me to follow my heart.'

'Not your head?' she said in a frustrated voice.

'No, Violet. Not my head. My head would have a good long conversation with me about how filthy the rookeries are, and how in danger I will be of catching something from the miasma which permeates those environs. My head would remind me of the girl who was taken to one of the courts and thrown down an unused well in Dorset Street after being raped. My head would tell me I am an idiot for even considering an idea which may see me murdered by a vagrant and left on the street to be torn apart by rats and dogs. I'm well aware of what my head would tell me, Violet. But if everyone listened to what went on in their heads nothing would ever get done. If I do it, I do it for the Thomas children, and all the other children who go to bed tonight with no food in their bellies or love in their hearts.'

Violet looked down at her hands in her lap and I thought she would cry. Stride returned from the bar and placed another sherry on the table for each of us. He resumed his seat as the barkeep came out from behind the bar and brought over a stout for him.

'Miss Pond,' he whispered. 'Your sister will be cared for I promise you. If I may, and you have no objection, I will visit you at your home from time to time to give you a progress report. I have my snouts on the streets as well as Bessie. They are not as inveigling as Bessie; she is a consummate actress, but I have contact with them, more to protect Bessie than anything else. If they think either Lily or Bessie are in danger, they will tell the police immediately and we will get them out, one way or the other, even if it causes a turf war.'

Violet breathed in and made a small smile. 'Do I have your word on it, Jeremiah?'

'You have my word, Miss Pond,' he said solemnly. Violet glanced at me and shrugged her slight shoulders.

By the time we'd left the Lamb and Anchor and bid Stride good night, the fall of sleet had developed into a snowfall. It brightened the street, and the gas lamps picked out individual flakes as they fell past the flame. It felt festive and my heart leapt. I wrapped Violet's cape around her as tightly as I could and made sure her scarf covered the lower half of her face. I was relieved we only had a short way to walk; we could see the lights shining in the drawing room window from the pavement outside The Lamb and Anchor.

'I do trust you, you know, Lily. I know you think I won't support your decision, but I promise you I will. If truth be told I wish I could come with you.'

I rubbed her shoulder as I steered her towards the house. 'I know you would, darling, but honestly, Violet, you would never pass as a man. I thought Detective Inspector Stride would have an attack of the vapours when you took off your coat and bonnet. His expression gave him away. He was entranced.'

'Lily! You're embarrassing me,' she cried, but there was a smile in her voice.

Back at the house Dreyfus had been waiting in the hall for a sign of our return. He ran down the steps and lifted Violet from the bath chair, taking her out of the snowfall and into the warmth of the house where he placed her on a chaise. The bath chair followed. Meg and Mildred were waiting in the drawing room to help remove our outer garments and take them into the drying room. I settled on the opposite settee and kicked off my boots. Meg returned to the drawing room with two hot toddies.

'Thought these would go down well, Madams, just lemon, a little whiskey, cloves, and some brown sugar. They'll help yer sleep if nothing else.'

I smiled up at her. 'Thank you, Meg, you're so thoughtful.' She nodded and made a small curtsey, then left Violet and I to discuss our evening.

'You should make the most of that,' said Violet, blowing on her toddy. 'You won't be getting anything like it where you're going.'

'I'm not going until after Christmas, Violet. I want to spend Christmas with you and the staff, help decorate the tree and hang the bunting, just like always.'

'Do you think you'll be back for the next one?'

'I intend to be back a long time before next Christmas I can assure you. Bessie Clacket might be inured to life in St Giles, but I am not. It is going to be a huge shock to the system, and yes, a little dangerous, but I will be careful. If I haven't made any headway after two weeks have gone by, I will return home. If I don't hear anything about criminal activity, I would say it's because the men in St Giles don't trust me enough to speak of it around me, and however long I stay it won't make a difference.'

'Perhaps you could make something up, like a stay in Pentonville, allow them to think you are a seasoned villain.'

'I think it's an excellent idea. Thank you. Perhaps you could help me come up with something.'

'Do you think it's acceptable for Chief Detective Stride to visit me here? After all, I won't have a chaperone.'

I nodded and understood her concern. 'If it gives you unease, ask Meg to be your chaperone. I trust her implicitly.'

'What will you tell her?'

'The truth.'

'But Chief Detective Stride said...'

'I know what he said, but I won't lie to Meg. She has been with me for years. We almost grew up together. And she will need to know if she's to chaperone you. I'm sure you'll want to know how it's all going and I'm still in the land of the living, and she's the person I want to be by your side if you can't have me.'

Violet shivered. 'Please don't say that Lily.' Her beautiful grey eyes fixed on me and I knew what she was about to say. 'You're all I have.'

'And you're all I have. We have each other and we always will, no matter what happens.'

Chapter 10

'But, Madam,' cried Meg. 'Is this a joke or one of them stories in a penny dreadful. You ain't an actress are yer, not like the other woman.' She shook her head, wringing her hands in front of her as she sat on the window seat in my bedroom. 'What does Miss Violet say?'

'Miss Violet has given me her support, although I must say it was given rather grudgingly. She's not happy, of course, and I understand why, but I must do this. There must be a reason for my existence, a purpose. I can't sit about all day like a pampered pet.'

We were in my bedroom. Meg had come up to help me get undressed and brush my hair. It was something she had been doing since I was a child and my thoughts had instantly gone to the rookeries. Did they own hairbrushes? I thought not. Did they bathe regularly? Of course not. This was the life I would need to get used to if I were to be successful in my quest. And what of the men. Looking, dressing, and behaving like a man would certainly help me in one aspect and for that I was grateful. I wondered how Bessie Clacket managed to stave off men who would use women for whatever they wanted. Surely it wasn't part of her remit to sleep with men simply because they demanded it. I shuddered and gritted my teeth. What sort of hell had I exposed myself to?'

'And you want me to take care of Miss Violet, Madam, while you're away?'

I nodded, meeting her eyes with my own in the dresser mirror. 'Chief Detective Stride will be visiting Violet from time to time to inform her of my progress. She will need a chaperone and of course I suggested you will be the perfect person. I know how much you care for her, and I expect you and Mildred to reassure Violet and take the very best care of her while I'm away.'

'And how long do you think it will be for?'

I shrugged. 'I have no idea, Meg. How long is a piece of string? I suppose it will be until the job is done, until Chief Detective Stride has caught the men who are profiteering from the current criminal activity going on in St Giles. Apparently, they are making hundreds, if not thousands, of pounds from stealing and selling these objects, whatever they are.'

Meg gasped. 'They're not goin' ter like it when someone stops 'em.'

'Well, it won't be me, have no fear of that. I'll simply be providing information to Chief Detective Stride's', the name escaped me momentarily, 'oh, yes...snouts.'

'And then you can come 'ome?'

'And then I'll return home. Believe me, Meg, this is not an experience I will relish, but there will be some payment which will immediately provide alms for children of the rookeries. I'm thinking of starting some sort of charity for them, and I'm hoping Violet will want to be involved. And you, perhaps, if you would like to help.'

'I'll always 'elp you, Madam, you know that, but at the moment I need you ter come 'ome safe and sound. That's what's most important to me, and I'm sure I'm right when I say it's what Miss Violet wants too.'

After two more meetings with Chief Detective Stride, it was agreed I would meet Bessie Clacket on New Year's Day. I was to go to The Bushel Public House on the edge of Fitzrovia, plainly dressed, with Meg by my side as my companion. I had made a point of telling Stride I had furnished Meg with the details of my new occupation as I felt there should be no secrets between us. He was less than pleased, but I insisted she was as loyal a servant as one could wish for, and we were as much friends as mistress and lady's maid. He had grudgingly accepted her involvement. I knew he could sense that unless he had accepted it, I would not be willing to help him.

'You know her better than I,' he said. 'You're sure she has no association with the rookeries? One wrong word in the right ear could be very harmful for you, and Bessie.'

'Let me reassure you, Stride. She knows no one from the rookeries. She has been with my family since she was a child. You can have no fear on that score.'

On Christmas Eve I decided to make an unannounced visit to The Bloomsbury Dispensary for the Sick Poor in Great Russell Street. I decided to walk even though the snow lay thick on the ground. I liked being outdoors. When snow had fallen it made even the most derelict of places look salubrious. Yes, it was a façade of sorts, but as my footsteps crunched against the snowfall I felt quite merry.

Christmas Day was the following day, and Violet, Meg, Mildred and Cook had joined me in making our house in Harley Street look beautifully festive, festooning the tree with glittering garlands and lighting the candles. It would have been nice to curl up in front of the fire with Dickens's last book, Our Mutual Friend, and some sweetmeats, but I felt, bearing in mind I had an important task in front of me in the new year, I would delay my own pleasure.

I left Harley Street and made my way to Warren Street. Warren Street would take me to Gower Street which in turn led to Great Russell Street. I was sorely tempted to make a detour to the British Museum Library in Montague Place, but decided my visit to the Bloomsbury Dispensary was more important. I had spent many a happy hour with Violet in the quiet surroundings of the library, sitting in comfort where one could read the news of the day or retrieve a book one had read in childhood which had become a favourite. It was a place where one felt as though one were alone, where only the rustling of someone turning pages in a book would provide the only interruption.

I passed Bedford Square which looked like a Christmas card, then slowly made my way towards Great Russell Street. The streets were crowded with people, either those hurrying as fast as they could as they made their way to work, or, those who could afford it, shopping for last minute presents for their loved ones. The snow underfoot was quickly turning into a mucky slush; easier to walk through than impacted snow but, when mixed with mud from the dray carts and horse dung, left an ordure which was extremely unpleasant. I was glad I had worn my sturdier boots although they were covered in the slimy soup of goodness knows what by the time I got to the entrance of the dispensary in Great Russell Street.

The street was as busy as other streets I had walked that morning. There were many dray carts delivering to the restaurants and cafés in Great Russell Street. Through their windows one could see many were taking advantage of the season to fill up on mince pies and hot tea, and I must admit it made my mouth water at the spicy fragrance leaving the premises each time someone opened a door. It was certainly preferable to the stink emanating from underfoot.

The Bloomsbury Dispensary for the Sick Poor was an imposing building, double fronted with an impressive entrance. As I stepped over the threshold, I realised the façade was just that. Inside was a plethora of illness and poverty, the odour sickly and cloying. Men, women, and children lined up to receive the medicines they needed to get them through the Christmas season.

The front hall was assaulted by sneezes, hacking coughs, and crying babies. Mothers looked harassed and worried. Some men were almost bent double with chest infections and phlegmy coughs, likely brought about by smoking which some of them were still doing as they coughed their germs into the space. I put my gloved hand across the lower half of my face and went to the desk. A young nurse was busy taking the names and addresses of people seeking medicine. She looked up when she sensed my presence and instantly frowned when she saw my appearance.

'Madam?'

'I'd like to see Wilfred Horrocks please. Is he here today?'

'Yes, Madam. Mr Horrocks is always here. Today is our busiest day of the year.' I nodded, hoping Wilfred would at least be permitted to have Christmas Day with his family, although if he were spending it with Genevieve Horrocks, one would forgive him for wanting to be at the dispensary. 'Would you like to come this way, Madam, and I'll tell him you're here.'

She led me toward a door behind her and guided me into a small room at the back. It was a waiting room of sorts, although not one put together with comfort in mind.

'May I take your name, Madam?'

'Miss Lily Pond. I'm afraid I don't have an appointment.'

She smiled. 'Not to worry. Mr Horrocks is due a break. Been on duty since six this morning. It 'asn't stopped and won't any time soon. This is always the busiest time of year for us 'cos people are frightened of being ill over Christmas Day. We only close for one day though.' I returned her smile and nodded, hoping I wasn't about to overstep the mark with Wilfred Horrocks.

The door flew open and Wilfred entered the room in a flurry. His white coat was stained at the front and his rather wayward red hair stood up on end. His cheeks were red, with exertion it seemed. He pushed his glasses up his nose and smiled when he saw me, making a quick bow in my direction.

'Lily,' he cried. 'It's wonderful to see you of course, but I'm surprised you've come here of all places, particularly on Christmas Eve.' He sat on one of the uncomfortable chairs. 'How can I be of help.'

'You look as though you've been running, Wilfred.'

He chuckled. 'Well, I suppose I have in a way. We must move fast in the apothecary. If we don't, those queues of people waiting in the hall will get longer and longer and I'll be here until midnight. We do our best to get medicines to those who need it as quickly as possible, and it does feel rather as though one is on a treadmill.'

'Are you the only apothecary here?'

'Oh, no, I have two colleagues who move as fast as I do. It's almost like a dance. We note the affliction, make out a prescription, then dance around each other, reaching up to the shelves for what we need to make up the medicines. Time goes very quickly here.'

I couldn't help but smile. 'I can't help thinking you rather enjoy it, Wilfred.'

'Oh, I do, apart from the obvious. The influenza has taken hold this year. One can't imagine how it must be to leave the outside where it is cold and has been snowing, to enter an uninhabitable abode where it is just as cold and very likely has no fire to ease one's aches and pains. Unimaginable actually.'

'What else do you see here?'

The pox is a favourite.' I chuckled at his words. 'More in the summer than in the winter. I expect you can guess why.' I nodded. 'Bronchitis. We see the same people time and time again. We advise them to reduce the number of cigarettes they smoke, but of course for some of the people who come here it is their only pleasure...apart from drinking of course. We see many who clearly have sclerosis but there's nothing we can do. We give them an infusion of milk thistle but,' he shrugged, 'it's usually short-term for those patients.'

'And what of those who've been stabbed or...worse.'

'They will go to the infirmary, and if they survive will come here for laudanum for the pain. The problem is they become addicted to it and either pretend they have pain just to get a bottle or will go on to take even more addictive medicines, like opium. That's what I meant when I said we try to provide medicines for those who need it. Some simply come here for a bottle of laudanum, and they'll make up any story to get it.'

'And the children?'

'Lots of them. Too many. It's quite heart-breaking. Mostly from the rookeries. There's no urgent care for them, and of course the parents will leave it before coming here or going to the hospital. Some leave it far too long resulting in dire consequences because they have no money for medicines. We had a case recently of a girl about twelve whose appendix had burst. She had been left for seven days. Didn't make it of course. Peritonitis set in and took her.'

'Do they have to pay for medicines?'

'If they can. A few pence only. Some don't even have that, even though the costs are kept low. Some give false names so they can't be found and be asked to pay. We rely on donations.'

'I'd like to make a donation.'

Wilfred frowned. 'Is it why you came here?'

I shook my head and decided to get straight to the point. 'I know of a family of five children in Parker Street who have recently lost their mother. Their father still lives but they have nothing. I think they could use some of your help. I noticed terrible sores around their mouths which I'm sure will not heal without interference, and they are alive with lice. Could you help, do you think?'

He pulled a face. 'Parker Street?'

'You know it.'

'Unfortunately, yes.'

I rose from the hard chair with some relief and held my hand out to him. 'I don't blame you if you choose not to go there, but they are greatly in need of help, particularly now their mother has gone.'

'What happened?'

'She was hit by falling masonry on the corner of Dorset Street.' Wilfred sighed and shook his head. 'A prostitute?'

I nodded and opened my reticule, taking out an envelope which I gave him. 'My donation, Wilfred. If you feel you would rather not go to Parker Street I understand completely. My donations to the dispensary do not rely upon it I assure you. The family lives at number seventy-one. If you do decide to visit them, please don't go alone. I made the mistake of doing so.' His eyes widened and I grinned. 'Please make sure you take someone with you, two someone's if possible.' He nodded and said nothing. 'Have a wonderful Christmas, Wilfred. You do a sterling job here. One wonders what would happen to these people if it were not for you.'

We shook hands and I opened the door to the waiting room. The line of the sick was longer than when I had arrived, and when I stepped over the threshold the queue continued out of the door and up Great Russell Street; a dichotomy when one observed many of the people strolling down the street were well-heeled. I doubted they gave the sick poor a second thought. My heart sank with sorrow. What terrible lives these people lived. I could have wept but I knew tears would do them no good. I prayed my donation would help those who were so in need of it.

Chapter 11

It was a bitterly cold day and I shivered even though I wore my warmest coat. Meg glanced up at me as I wrapped my shawl tightly around my shoulders.

'I didn't think it could get any colder, Madam,' she said, her voice almost mumbling as she pushed her chin further down into her muffler.

'I agree. Christmas was bitter, but the temperature seems to have dropped even further. It doesn't bode well for those living in the rookeries, does it?'

I looked down at her and made a small smile. 'Couldn't you go in the summer, Miss Lily? It might not smell as nice but at least it'll be warmer.'

'And full of diseases and pestilence.' I couldn't help sighing as I wondered about the wisdom of my decision. 'I don't think any season is a good season in the rookeries. One wonders how Miss Clacket has survived it.'

'Who's Miss Clacket?'

The woman we're meeting today. She's been living in the rookeries for months at the behest of Chief Detective Stride. She'll be waiting in The Bushel Public House.'

'What for?'

'So she can tell me what I need to do to fit in. I've been practising how to speak for days, and I'm grateful for your help in that, Meg. When one has spoken in a certain way all one's life, it's so very difficult to change. I just hope I'm up to what will be expected of me.'

I'd dressed appropriately of course, nothing like my usual dress when leaving the house. I'd refused to eschew my coat because of the weather, but my boots had been expertly scuffed up by Meg who had worn them into the garden and scraped them along the garden wall and the gravel paths. My hat was an old one on which I'd had great pleasure stamping on, rendering the crown flat, the flowers limp, and the brim worse for wear. Another one to throw on the fire. Violet had shaken her head when she'd seen it.

'I hope you don't meet anyone you know. Genevieve Horrocks would have a blue fit if she saw you in that hat.'

'And all to the good I say,' I'd replied. 'Perhaps she'll have second thoughts about me marrying her son.'

'I thought you liked him.'

'I do...very much, but not in the way one would need to like a man if one were to consider marrying him.'

The Bushel was full to bursting. As soon as we came upon the entrance reservations began to crowd out my other thoughts, but it was too late. Bessie Clacket had waited outside and had recognised me immediately. I assumed Chief Detective Stride had given her a description.

'Lily?' she asked as Meg and I stopped in front of her. This put me in rather a conundrum. Should I speak in my normal voice, or should I adopt the one I'd been practising. I decided to try out the latter. At least if she thought it inauthentic she would let me know.

'Bessie?' I answered. I glanced at Meg who bit her lip and lowered her gaze.

'In we go then,' Bessie said in a determined voice. She eyed us suspiciously giving me the impression she thought perhaps I wasn't up to the job. I swallowed hard wondering if she was right. I could see Bessie was the sort of person who took no nonsense and my stomach rolled. Meg and I followed Bessie into The Bushel Public House.

When Chief Detective Stride said the public houses near St Giles would be even less salubrious than The Lamb and Anchor, he wasn't wrong. The gloom inside was much like one would expect in a cave. There were cobwebs hanging from the ceiling and around the walls like ghostly bunting. In the cobweb bunting were dead flies which had been captured, very likely years before, and held in a state of infinite death.

The walls and ceiling were the colour of brimstone from the endless swathes of nicotine laden smoke that wafted upwards and stayed just below the ceiling in a perpetual cloud. There were a great many patrons if one could call them that. To my untrained eye they all looked suspicious. These were the men who came from the rookeries, the ones who leant cockily on the bar with a foot on a brass foot rail inches from the floor, hardened criminals no doubt, although some of the men, those sitting at the tables, looked down at heel, their eyes lowered as they quietly supped a glass of ale, looking neither right or left.

'There's a table there,' said Bessie, pointing to a small table in the middle of the room. 'Take it quick before anyone else gets it. It'll really start filling up soon seein' as it's dinner.'

Meg and I went across to the table. Bessie went to the bar and came back with two sherries and a pint of beer on a tray.

'Didn't think you'd want beer,' she said. Meg and I thanked her but said nothing more.

Bessie sat at the table and took a long swig from the ale. She looked about thirty-years-of-age, although could have been younger, and wore a scarf wound around her head, gypsy style. Her jacket was tweed, once good I thought, but was covered in dust and dirt. Her skirt was cotton, dark blue with a fringe around the bottom. I realised later it wasn't a fringe, but where the fabric had frayed. She wore grey fingerless gloves, and underneath her skirt, much to my surprise, a pair of trousers. Scuffed boots with frayed laces finished the convincing ensemble.

'So,' she said, placing her knuckles on her knees. 'You want to work with me.'

I breathed in. 'I think the word "want" stretches the point too far, Miss Clacket. Stride offered me the position because I'm interested in the welfare of the children in the rookeries, particularly St Giles. I understand from him something is going on that he would like to explore.'

Bessie nodded. 'That's true, but you can forget the 'earts and flowers stuff. This is serious.' She lowered her voice. 'It's dangerous, Miss Pond, I won't pretend otherwise. If you've a mind to, you can change your decision right now. No one would think any the less of yer. Living in the rookeries ain't for the faint 'earted. And you'll need to fit in. I've done what I can but the women are often kept in the dark. It's the men what we need to speak ter. They're the ones what 'ave got all the information and they're the ones you'll need to win over.'

'So why didn't Stride simply find a man to do it.'

Bessie made a sardonic smile. 'Are you kiddin'? 'Cos they got more sense that's why. They know if they're caught out they'll 'ave their throats cut. Like I said you 'ave to be tough to live in the rookeries.' She looked me up and down. 'And I reckon it ain't the life you're used to.'

I heard Meg gasp and a swirl of anger went through me threatening to choke me. I know Bessie was simply being honest about the trials that lay in front of me, but she didn't know me. She was making an assumption based on the way I looked and how I dressed and not on anything I was capable of. It simply made me even more determined.

I took a sip of sherry before I spoke.

'Please don't judge me, Miss Clacket. You are unaware of what I am capable of and I'm more than willing to take instruction from you. Let's put any doubts aside and get on with it. You simply need to tell me what you want from me and I'll deliver. I will follow your lead which is what Stride has asked of me. I have visited the rookeries in the past. I know how they're run and what goes on there. I also know women have no importance in any of the rookeries and surrounding streets unless they're lying on their backs with their legs open.' I heard Meg gasp again. 'I sincerely hope you haven't found yourself in such a position.'

I took a gulp of sherry and allowed it to warm my insides as it went down to my stomach.

'In my opinion a judgement made on sight alone *is* dangerous, and I am capable of taking care of myself when the occasion calls for it. Tell me what you want me to do.'

Bessie made a tight-lipped grin. 'E said you were a fiery miss. I'm glad of it, and so will you need ter be. Fair enough, Lily. You'll be known as Edwin Smith and my cousin. They won't let you in otherwise. And less of the Miss Clacket. No one there speaks of my family name and I want it kept that way. Most of the women just go by their first names. If you're not asked anything then you don't tell, it's as simple as that. Don't give anything away for free. D'yer get me?'

I nodded once. 'Of course. I understand the English language and I have absorbed what you've said.'

'And your voice. It won't work, Edwin. I'll be calling you Edwin from now on. We don't want no slip ups. You'll 'ave to practise a bit, get used to dropping yer aitches and that sort of thing, and more. You'll need to change everythin', voice, look, appearance. Everythin'. You can be a quiet sort, only speak when you're spoken to. That way it'll lessen the danger of you bein' found out. And while we're on the subject...if yer get yourself in ter trouble you'll 'ave to get yerself out of it. Don't expect me to come runnin' if the heats on 'cause I won't. I need to keep up the pretence and I won't be 'elpin you out so don't expect it.' She pushed her glass towards me. 'You can get the next one.'

'You want me to go to the bar?'

Bessie chuckled. 'And why not, Edwin? You'll be doin' a lot of that let me tell yer. If you're to find anythin' out it'll be in the pubs and taverns. The men get loose lipped and might let something slip.' She nodded towards the glass and I glanced at Meg.

'Do you want another, Meg?' I asked her.

'No thank you,' she replied, looking unhappy. 'I've got to work later.'

I went to the bar and ordered another drink for Bessie. I heard her ask Meg, 'You 'er maid?'

Meg nodded then looked down at her hands.

'She's a good person, Bessie, and I 'ope you'll treat 'er as such. I've known 'er since we was kids and she's never said a cross word to me in all that time. She wants to 'elp people. She didn't ask fer this job. Chief Detective Stride offered it to 'er and she agreed. I 'ope you'll treat 'er with a bit of respect and kindness. It's all any of us need, ain't it, and she'll do a good job. She's already practising the voice and I'll find 'er the right clothes, but if you leave her to snuff out in them stew pots you'll 'ave me to answer to.'

Meg and I walked back to Harley Street after our meeting with Bessie Clacket. I suddenly had the urge to slip my arm through hers and she gazed up at me in surprise. We had always been close, but always in a verbal way rather than physical. I'd always thought of her as more of a friend than a maid. She was easy to speak with and didn't appear to judge anyone on face value. To me she was the best of women, head and shoulders above some of the women I knew in my own society. One wasn't encouraged to hug a retainer or maid, and if any of our society had seen me slip my arm through Meg's they would have been scandalised. Suddenly I didn't care.

'Thank you, Meg.'

'What for, Miss Lily.'

I smiled at her. 'I heard what you said to Bessie Clacket. Thank you for being on my side.'

'I know it ain't my place, Miss Lily, but I think she needs to be on yer side an' all. You'll need a friend in there 'specially as you're meant to be a man. She needs to step up and give you some protection and some 'elp to fit in with the people what live there.'

'Did you like her?'

'Not much, but she's 'ard. She's got an 'ard face and an 'ard mouth and I s'pose it's what happens when someone's lived in St Giles for any length of time. But she ain't like you, Miss.' She shook her head. 'No, she's nothin' like you.' She looked up at me again. 'If you get into trouble, Miss Lily, I'll come to yer aid. I always would. You know that. And I ain't the only one. All the staff love you and Miss Violet.' She turned away, blushing slightly. 'And my young man. 'E'd do anything for yer too.'

I smiled at her and she returned it. 'You have a young man? Who? He must work for us if he knows me.'

'Dreyfus, Miss Lily. The footman. We've been stepping out for a little while now, a few months, Miss Lily. Six months about.'

'But it's wonderful, Meg. Has he mentioned marriage?'

'We have talked about it, but I don't want to say yet. It'll mean I'll 'ave to leave you won't it, and I'm not sure I'm ready for it.'

I stared at her in astonishment. 'Why will you have to leave me? I'm afraid I don't understand.'

Meg glanced up at me looking sad. 'Don't married women 'ave to leave their employment? I thought it was 'ow it worked.'

'Oh, Meg, please don't let that thought deter you from marrying Dreyfus. You leave when you're ready to leave. Violet and I would be thrilled for you. Dreyfus won't have to leave so why should you?'

Meg shrugged. 'Cook says it's 'ow it works.'

'It may have done in Cook's day, but not in ours. You stay as long as you like.' She smiled looking much happier. 'Anyway, I said, squeezing her arm. 'What would I do without you?'

'Forget your appointments and forget to ask for your clothes to be pressed.'

'Exactly.'

Chapter 12

I waited on the corner of Museum Street for Bessie to meet me. The snow had all but gone and all that was left was a slimy broth of horse dung, slush, and mud from the dray carts. It was a bit too near to The Museum Library for comfort. I dreaded seeing any of my acquaintances, particularly Wilfred Horrocks who I knew often went there to study and research medicines new and old, but when I examined my thoughts sensibly, I realised it was likely they would not recognise me, would see me as just another layabout standing on a corner, leaning against a wall with my hands in my pockets.

Meg had coached me in how to speak and how to stand, and put her hands on the correct clothing. I'm not sure how I would have found everything I needed if it hadn't been for her. Even Dreyfus had helped, although she assured me he had no idea why I wanted the clothing, apart from the fact it was to go to a man with no work who lived in the rookeries. It was the truth I suppose, except I was the man.

Meg had me walking up and down the drawing room with a much different gait to the one I was used to. I was to walk with my legs further apart and my hands in my pockets, looking down at the pretend pavement. By the end of the sessions my hips ached so much I could barely sleep. She said I should try smoking because she felt it was fairly certain every man would smoke, and even some of the women. She and I were quite certain Bessie did. Her fingers had the tell-tale signs on them; the brown nails and the yellow fingers on one hand. I thought it was a disgusting habit, cigars even more so, although at times the smell of a good cigar was quite pleasant after dinner. I doubted I would see many cigars where I was headed. Or many dinners come to that. And then there was my hair.

'What will you do about your hair,' asked Violet. My hand flew immediately to my tresses which Meg had pinned into a chignon that morning. I had always thought my hair was my best asset. It was chestnut in colour, long and thick. I closed my eyes realising I would have to make the sacrifice. I didn't know any men who had their hair dressed in a chignon.

'I suppose it will have to come off.'

Violet shook her head. 'Oh, Lily,' she sighed, tears threatening. 'You love your hair. We all love your hair.'

'It'll grow back again. My hair grows quickly. I can't go into a rookery with an expertly coiffed chignon. I don't think it will work.'

That evening Meg took the shears to my hair. She cut it to just below my ears, roughly shorn, like a man who couldn't afford a barber. She stood back to admire her handiwork while I looked to the floor to see my beautiful hair lying in thick strands on the carpet.

'It looks real, Miss Lily. Once you've got yer hands and face scruffed up, you'll be just like a young bloke from the rookeries.

I nodded. 'Thank you, Meg.' I stared at her in the mirror. 'What does scruffed up mean?'

'Dirt, Miss. I doubt you'll find a clean face or pair of 'ands in the rookeries. They don't have anywhere to wash. Didn't you notice Bessie's 'ands?' I always notice 'ands. A pair of 'ands can tell you a lot about a person, whether they've never done a days' work in their lives, a bit like yours if you don't mind me sayin', or whether they worked in the foundries or the breweries. Or pickin' hops. It's easy really to read 'ands. Yours need to be roughed up and dirty, with grime under the fingernails what needs to be there at all times. Don't worry, Miss Lily. I'll sort you out.'

'Thank you, Meg. I'm very grateful.'

Before I left for St Giles, I went to say goodbye to Violet. I was dressed as my alter-ego, an appearance of which Truffle did not approve. When I went into the dining room after lunch in my scruffy clothes and my face and hands soiled with mud he barked furiously as though I was a complete stranger. It upset me rather, but it proved one thing; he didn't recognise me.

'Truffle isn't happy,' said Violet, putting a hand on Truffle's head to quiet him. 'You look completely different, Lily.'

'Would you recognise me, Violet?'

She shook her head. 'I'm not sure I would. Everything about you has changed; your walk, your stance, your appearance. And your lovely hair. There no more.'

'I have to leave now, Violet. Bessie will be waiting for me. I don't think she's the sort to hold back if I'm late.'

She nodded sadly 'I know,' she said in a small voice. 'The time has gone round too quickly. I hope your stay at St Giles will be short lived and you will return to us soon.'

Meg joined us in the dining room. She glanced at Violet looking worried, then turned and smiled. 'I know you'll be alright, Miss Lily. If anyone can do this, you can.'

I left the house by the garden door and went across the frosty flower beds, climbing over the wall at the back. If the neighbours had seen an itinerant man leave the house they would have certainly called the police. This was the beginning of my new life and I prayed to all that was Holy I had made the right decision.

'Oi.' I was startled out of my reverie by Bessie Clacket, her voice low and gravelly as she walked towards me.

'Edwin,' she cried, elbowing me in my side. 'Ow are yer, mate?'

'I'm alright, Bessie,' I said, keeping my voice low and gruff, and wincing at the pointed elbow she'd shoved between my ribs. 'How...'Ow are you?'

'Not bad, not bad.' She frowned at me. 'Yer looking a bit rough if yer don't mind me sayin'. What ails yer?' I baulked at this but hoped it was because she was simply playing her role.

'Ain't got nowhere to stay 'ave I? Need a bed for the night. You know of anywhere?'

Bessie shrugged. 'Yer can come back wiv me if yer like. Might 'ave somethin' there for yer. No promises mind.'

I shrugged and lowered my gaze. 'Fair enough.'

I followed Bessie at a trudge down Drury Lane, trying to keep my head down while at the same time taking in my surroundings. My cap was pulled low over my eyes which meant I couldn't see very much of anything, but I did notice a sign announcing the Hampshire Hog Yard. I had a memory of that place, but I couldn't think why and my mind was on other things. I sensed our surroundings, although not particularly salubrious during my wait for Bessie Clacket, was becoming increasingly worse. The buildings seemed to be closing in on us and the closer they became the more claustrophobic I felt.

Up and down the street were makeshift stalls selling everything from items found on the edge of the Thames by the mudlarks; old clay pipes, pieces of metal, and the odd piece of costume jewellery made from glass to watercress filched from the edge of the river where it grew wild. This was something no one would eat if they could do without it.

Girls of no more than ten years would hawk watercress around the rough-and-ready market, offering it to all comers at a penny a bunch, and one could only wonder what damage it did to the people who ate it. The Thames was full of detritus, muck from the inhabitants of London, sewage, horse dung, and bodies. The smell coming from the Thames's waters was worse than putrid, but it wasn't too different from the odours coming from the filthy streets in the rookeries. The air was heavy with it.

I stared down at the offensive soup beneath our feet, remembering the last time I had entered the obscene environs. I had been unceremoniously chased out by a band of men and women, and I had wished my skirts and petticoats had been less voluminous, my stays looser, and my boots made for running.

'You've been 'ere before 'aven't you?' asked Bessie.

I nodded. 'A while back. I doubt they'll recognise me. They were too busy chasing me out of the courts.'

Bessie lifted her eyebrows. 'They chased yer? Why?'

'I was there on a mission to help the children. I brought in some baked goods and sweetmeats, but their parents thought I was from the workhouse; that I was trying to steal the children away. They formed a group and chased me until I got to Great Russell Street where I became hidden in the crowd, a saving grace. It seems I get chased quite often.'

'Well, you'd better make sure yer don't make 'em want ter chase you this time. I'm tellin' you they'll wait until you're a'kip and slit your throat while you're snoring. I doubt they'll give you the chance to run.'

I inhaled a deep breath and nodded. Was I frightened? Yes, I cannot lie. I had taken on a task of mammoth proportions and knew I could be in danger, but what was the alternative? My heart was still feeling the effects of my jilting, and of course had Jonathan and I married I would not be walking into the entrance of St Giles, and to who knew what.

'Where will I stay?'

'I'll try to get you into our 'ouse. It's full to burstin' as it is but one more won't make no difference.' She shook her head. 'God knows 'ow you'll manage, Edwin. If yer lucky, you'll sleep on a palliasse. If you ain't lucky, you'll sleep on the floor. You 'ave ter grab what yer can, and if the biggest bloke in the 'ouse wants the bed you've got, or the palliasse you've got in yer 'and', she turned to look at me, 'give it to 'im.' I nodded and swallowed hard.

As we turned into the parish, I saw we had entered Tiborn Road, the beginning of the west end of St Giles. I followed Bessie into St Giles High Street. As we walked down the High Street, I lifted my head and glanced into the gloomy courts. The smell was overwhelming and I was shaken by the fact I could almost taste it. Would I survive the illnesses held within the miasma? And when the fogs came, would any of the people in the stew pot of filth and criminality survive?

None of the courts were empty. All were full of people; dirty, down and out, most standing around a fire lit in the middle of the courts. Their clothes were ragged, most hadn't a coat on their backs even though the weather was as bitter as I had ever known it. Some fires were so close to the buildings a rogue spark would have taken them up in a flash, but when I raised my eyes and saw the buildings in which the inhabitants lived it may well have been a mercy.

A road, New Oxford Street, had been constructed directly through the middle of the parish. It had been hailed in the newspapers as the answer to the many problems of the parish of St Giles in the Fields and the Seven Dials, yet all it had achieved was to push those who had lived in the buildings which had been demolished to the north and south of the parish.

The families who had been living in the demolished buildings had been made homeless. The place of which they were familiar was St Giles. Their families were there, their friends, if one could have a friend in such a place, lived there. Where else were they to go but to the streets, courts, and alleyways which had been left standing. They had nowhere to go. It had been noted that in some of the remaining streets one hundred people resided in just a few small houses. The building of New Oxford Street had failed. All it had achieved was to push criminals, itinerants, vagabonds, thieves, and prostitutes together, where they could plan even more illegal activity.

I had never seen anywhere quite so ramshackle. I had visited there before of course, but the cold weather and the lack of maintenance had rendered the buildings uninhabitable. Yet here we were, observing structures that looked as though they were held together by pieces of string, still being lived in by men, women and children of all ages.

There was so much chatter and noise I could barely think. Dogs were running around the courts, their coats matted and filthy. Emaciated children played games in the muck on the ground, as feral as the dogs which were of indeterminate breeds. There were myriad rats; dead and mutilated bodies lying around the courts and alleyways where children played, and dogs pulling the decaying vermin bodies apart.

Sewage ran through the courts, and the smell from the cesspools was unendurable. But endure it I must if I were to do the job I had been sent to do. I was determined to see it to the end. I could only hope it would not be the end of my life I would be made to see, should things go horribly wrong.

'Oi, Bessie.'

I glanced towards where the voice had come from. In front of one of the houses was a young woman, dressed much the same as every other woman in the court, but who seemed fresher faced, and dare I say a mite healthier than those with whom she lived. She had long, red, curly hair which she'd covered with a brightly coloured scarf. It stood out like a sore thumb amongst the brown clothes and the gloom surrounding her.

'That's Sylvie,' murmured Bessie. 'She works with me in the laundry. She'll want to know who you are. She's got an eye for the men.' She waved to Sylvie and made her way towards her. 'Hello, Sylvie. Not so cold today is it?' I widened my eyes wondering how much colder it could get.

'Nah, lost that bite what we 'ad yesterday.' She peered around Bessie, smiling. 'Who's this then? Ain't seen 'im 'round 'ere before.'

'This is Edwin, Sylvie,' Bess said, grinning at me. 'Me cousin from Spitalfields. Just done a spell in Pentonville. Been chucked out of 'is lodging 'ouse. Got crowded and 'e was too late to get a place. Needs somewhere to stay. I said we'd find a place for 'im 'ere for a time. That alright?'

Sylvie nodded. 'Yeah, I should fink so. We'll find room for him. Skinny one ain't 'e? 'E won't take up much room.'

Bessie smiled at her and gave her a hug. 'I knew you'd say that, me girl. Kind 'earted you are.' She thumbed behind her shoulder to indicate me. 'He's a quiet one an' all. Bit...' she touched the side of her head with her finger then twirled it round, 'yer know, simple like. Don't say much. Came from the daft side of the family.'

'They don't need to say much, do they ducks,' Sylvie answered and they both roared with laughter. 'Long as they've got what it takes it's all what matters.' She glanced at me again. 'Got any coin as 'e? If 'e wants fed 'e'll need to pay. There ain't no spongers 'ere.'

Bessie turned to me, her eyes wide. 'You got any coin, Edwin? Her eyes widened still further and I nodded. She had told me to take some money with me. 'Money talks,' she'd said. 'Bring some coin and they won't turn you away.'

I reached into the pocket of the baggy trousers Meg had procured for me and found the coins I'd placed there, holding them out in my filthy hand. I'd made sure to go into the garden at our house in Harley Street and rub my fingernails into the freezing earth. The dirt had instantly transformed my hands from those which were soft and well-cared for to a pair with ingrained filth. I'd rubbed some onto my face and through my hair, rendering it spikey with icy muck. I remembered hoping our neighbours weren't looking out of their windows. They would have thought I'd gone completely mad and needed to go to the asylum.

'Let's 'ave a look then,' said Sylvie, barging Bessie out of the way to stand in front of me. She peered into my palm and then smiled up at me, her teeth cleaner than I thought they'd be. 'That's a tidy sum,' she said. Her hand moved like the strike of a snake, whipping the money out of my hand in one startlingly fast movement. 'How d'yer get yer coin then?' she asked.

Bessie moved next to me. 'Does a bit a coining and ringing, don't yer, Edwin. And a spot of pickpocketing.' She stared at me, and I nodded. 'Sometimes works in the tannery if they got anyfing for 'im. He might be quiet, but he does a lot of fings, don't yer, Edwin?' I nodded compliantly, but I would have felt more confident if I'd known what coining and ringing were. I made a mental note to ask Bessie what they were. All I needed was for someone to ask me about it and I would have been lost.

Sylvie nodded. 'That's interesting, that is. Might be able to put 'im to good use.' She narrowed her eyes. 'Where do yer do your pickpocketing? I 'ere there's a lot to be made round some of them 'otels in Park Lane, 'though you 'ave to be careful.'

I nodded. 'Yeah,' I said in my gruffest voice. 'I do alright there though there's uvvers what are doin' it as well. I lay on the ground and pretend to be ill. Lots of the toffs ignore me thinkin' I'm drunk, but there's always some soft sod what'll come over to see what's 'appened. Then I take 'em. Wait for 'em to bend down to me then go for the inside of the jacket. Run like the blazes I do. I can run I can. Covent Garden ain't bad niver.'

Sylvie turned to look at Bessie, nodding. 'Yeah, 'e ain't as daft as you said, Bessie. 'E knows what's what alright. I like that in a man.'

I glanced at Bessie thinking she'd be pleased with my performance, but her expression didn't change. Her eyes did though, and she looked rather displeased.

'Told yer, didn't I,' she said to Sylvie. 'E'll be an asset to us 'e will, specially wiv the fings what are goin' on, Sylvie. The blokes might be able to use 'im.'

'Mm, we'll 'ave to wait and see about that, Bessie. Got ter test him out first. Don't know 'im do we. 'E could be anyone.'

'E is anyone. 'E's me cousin, Edwin Smith from Spitalfields. I'm vouching for 'im. Known 'im since I was a kid.' She linked her arm through one of Sylvie's and turned her away from me, whispering in her ear. 'E ain't got the nous to do anyfink off 'is own back, Sylvie. 'E's a bit slow. Always 'as bin, but 'e'll work for yer. Promise yer that. Specially if yer nice to 'im. He's like a kid. Got the mind of a kid see. Always 'as 'ad.'

I saw Sylvie nod. 'Yeah, yeah, alright. 'E seems alright, but still. We'll see, Bessie.' She changed the subject. 'You working tonight?'

Bessie shook her head. 'Nah, got another girl in fer tonight. I'm on first fing tomorrow mornin'. What about you?'

'Yeah, same. Got ter do somethin' about them bitches what is takin' our work. I need the coin. They come from over on the Seven Dials and they can bloody well stay there. Might 'ave ter do somethin' about it. A blade to the throat should see 'em off.' She glanced over to me with a sly smile on her face. 'Although now we got another earner it'll make life easier.' She nodded and glanced back at Bessie. 'I reckon e'll do, but e'll 'ave to prove 'imself. I want ter see 'is coin before I introduce 'im to the blokes.' She sauntered off, swaying cockily as she went, then looked back at me and winked.

'What the 'ell was all that about?' Bessie hissed at me when Sylvie was out of earshot. 'All that pretendin' to be ill and whatnot. I told yer not to say anythin'. Don't give anythin' up unless yer asked.'

'I thought I *was* asked,' I answered, more than a little peeved she'd told Sylvie I was slow in the head and had the mind of a child. 'I can't be dumb all the time. I have to say something surely.'

She sighed and nodded, then pulled a quick smile. 'Yer did alright, Edwin.'

Chapter 13

Late that afternoon the gathering of people in the courtyard dispersed a little and I felt awkward. I knew I must get into the swing of life in the rookery, but I was unsure of how to make myself look part of it.

'What now?' I asked Bessie who had just returned from the laundry. As she entered the court in Charlotte Street, I heard her complaining to one of the women her hours had been cut and she wasn't earning as much as she'd been used to.

'Make sure you don't 'ang about the court all day. They need to see yer doin' somethin'. If you've got coin and you ain't earnin' it some'ow they'll start asking questions. The men 'ave gone to the Whistle and Flute on the corner of Drury Lane. It wouldn't 'urt to go there in a bit and get familiarised. You don't 'ave to speak to 'em, just look and listen. Yer don't know what you might 'ear.'

I looked at her dolefully. 'I don't have any money left, Bessie. I gave it to Sylvie.'

She rolled her eyes. 'Well, there's yer first lesson. Yer don't give 'em everythin', understand? Make sure you keep some back fer yourself, just in case.'

'Just in case of what?'

'I dunno. Anythin'.'

'Do I have to go on my...me own?'

She rested her hands on her ample hips and sighed. 'Come on, I'll walk yer to the pub, but you'll 'ave to go in by yerself. They don't like us women in there of an evenin'.'

'What about money, I mean coin?'

'Ere,' she said, pulling a few pennies out of her apron pocket and pouring them into my hand. 'Take this. And for Chris' sake don't go buying sherry. They'll think you're a molly. An 'arf pint of ale, that's what you ask for, then get a seat by yerself but just near enough to 'ear what they're sayin'. You don't 'ave to stay long 'cause the sensible talk will only last about 'alf an hour. By then they'll be in their cups an' anythin' they say won't make no sense anyhow. Make your way back to the court. Are yer watching where we're goin'?'

It was then I realised we were going a different way.

'Never use the same way in and out of St Giles two days in a row. It's the best way to get clobbered. People a watchin' yer even though you might not see 'em. Keep your eye on where yer goin'.'

I looked around. The alleyways and labyrinthian streets all looked the same to my naïve eye. All were run down; all were occupied by the same sort of people, thin, with sunken eyes, and ravaged by poverty. There were lines of grey washing running from one side of the street to the other, the garments mostly frozen solid.

I shook my head, then shrugged and nodded. I knew I must get used to this new life and I hoped and prayed it wouldn't be for long. In my mind's eye I could see Harley Street with its line of beautifully rendered houses and shiny black wrought iron gates, the windows sparkling with tilly lamps, or a Christmas tree not yet taken down after the Christmas festivities.

By now the gas lamps lining the street would have been lit. I loved sitting at the drawing room window watching the world go by, observing the street as the light faded until it became dusk. I glanced at Bessie, wondering what her other life was like and whether she had ever regretted agreeing to living in the rookeries. I dearly wanted to ask her, but I felt I didn't know her well enough to ask her something so personal. Perhaps when I knew her better, when I had become used to this nightmare I had willingly entered she would allow me to remind her of the time before. Until then, I would be entirely alone.

Bessie left me on the corner of Kemble Street and Drury Lane, pointing me in the direction of the Whistle and Flute. I thanked her and took a deep breath. God knows what den of thieves I was about to enter, and my stomach rolled with anticipation. I put the coins Bessie had given me in my pocket and I heard them jingle as I walked along the street the way Meg had taught me. I hunched my shoulders feeling an instant pull in my back, and widened my stance as I walked which gave me a broad gait. I hoped I looked like any of hundreds of other men from the rookeries making their way to the public houses around St Giles. It was busy; people were rushing past, knocking into me as I went, meaning I had to concentrate on my gait once again so I would not draw enquiring eyes. Some of them moved swiftly, dodging those in front of them, as though their lives depended on it. Perhaps they did. How was I to know how they lived their lives? I imagined if I lived in the rookery for any length of time I would soon find out.

The Whistle and Flute was a rather ramshackle building, three stories high, with double doors that opened out onto the street. The doors were painted brown as were the window frames. Some of the glass in the windows had been shaded out so one could not see the patrons as one walked by. I guessed this was a boon to many of the men inside.

The floors above looked well enough; some had been dressed with curtains, one with lace. I assumed it was where the landlord and his family resided and the mistress had made it home.

As I got closer to the public house the noise from inside got louder then abated each time one of the doors was opened and someone else went inside. The sound of dozens of voices, mostly male although I discerned some were female in the mix, blared out onto the street, along with the odour of stale beer and the smoke from years of cigarette detritus. It was a most sickly smell, one of stickiness and decay, and a feeling of dread came over me. I soldiered on and pulled on one of the doors to give myself entry into The Whistle and Flute. The crescendo of voices swept over me. Some patrons stopped and eyed me as though I were an oddity, and I assumed it was simply because no one knew who I was. A new face in a familiar crowd.

I kept my head down and went to the bar, pushing my boot onto the once shiny brass railing around the bottom, and leant on the top of the bar which reflected the glow from the gas lamps in puddles of spilt beer. I moved my arm to the edge of the bar to ensure I wouldn't lean in the stickiness. I glanced to the end of the bar where men were practically lying across it, in their cups and almost insensible.

'What can I get yer, mate?' The barkeep approached me, polishing a glass on a filthy cloth.

'An ale please, barkeep,' I said gruffly.

He nodded and went to a pump, pulling the handle towards him as he filled the glass with frothing ale. 'You're new 'ere ain't yer?' I nodded as he pushed the glass of ale towards me. 'That'll be tuppence.' I passed tuppence across to him, thinking perhaps if beer and spirits were somewhat more expensive there wouldn't be so many drunks. 'What do we call yer then?'

I took a small sip of the beer, the froth landing on my theatrical moustache. 'Edwin. Edwin Smith.'

'Where'd yer come from?'

'Spitalfields doss houses. They're full to burstin'. Couldn't get a bed.'

'So you've come 'ere? Why?'

I realised this line of questioning was because he didn't trust me and I could have told him to mind his own business, but I needed to make connections in the community, so I honoured him with an answer.

'Me cousin lives in St Giles. She found me a place.'

He nodded and pursed his lips. 'Right.' He proceeded to wipe the top of the bar with the cloth he'd used to polish the glass which he'd filled with beer. I wondered what manner of diseases I would pick up simply by drinking the ale. 'And who's yer cousin?'

'Bessie.' I remembered Bessie telling me she didn't like her second name to be bandied about, but I had a feeling the barkeep would ask me anyway and I would be expected to divulge it.

'Bessie who?'

'Bessie Clacket.'

A smile crossed his face. 'Oh, right, yeah, I know Bessie. She's a good 'un she is.' He inclined his head towards the glass in my hand. 'Beer alright?'

I lifted my glass in salute to him. 'The best.'

This seemed to please him and he pointed to the corner of the room. 'Table come free over there, Edwin. Take the weight of yer feet, mate.' I lifted my glass in salute again and made my way to where he'd directed me, relieved I was to be released from the inquisition.

I sat at the small, filthy table where the last occupant had left a pool of beer and the remains of his cigarette. I lowered my head hoping I would not be joined by any of the other patrons. To be drawn into a conversation with any of these men could mean danger. I had not perfected my voice and there were terms and phrases they used I had never once heard of in my life. I thought listening to some of the random conversations taking place around me would give me an idea of the subjects the men liked discussing.

The other tables were taken up with men playing dominoes, the game explained to me by Stride, but these men weren't playing for matches. They were gambling with money. I refrained from shaking my head with frustration, but it was how I felt. Frustrated and incensed. This cavalier attitude towards the coin in their pocket was precisely what had brought families like the Thomas's so low, the drinking and gambling with money which should have been putting food on the table. I had a sinking feeling in my stomach.

I sipped at my beer, inwardly wincing at the thought of the germs floating in it when an argument broke out between two of the men. One I recognised, a huge man with a neck like a bull who had been warming himself by the fire in the courtyard. I believed his name was Ronnie. I had been aware of his eyes, restless, twitching with uncertainty and very likely mistrust of those who stood around him. The other man was also large but not as stockily built. The larger man had grabbed the smaller one by the neck and pushed one of his arms up his back which had made him holler in pain. The barkeep rolled his eyes and slammed the cloth down on top of the bar.

'Come on, Ronnie, leave him be. Yer know what 'e's like. Yer should do bein' he's yer brother.'

'I'll sodding kill 'im,' shouted Ronnie. 'Called me a dunder'ead. I ain't no bloody dunder'ead.' The men around them burst into laughter, then pushed their faces into their beer as Ronnie's expression turned thunderous. 'I'll 'ave you lot an' all,' he cried, shaking a finger at them with his other hand. His arm was still around his brother's throat. 'You'll be wiping the smiles off your chaunting faces by the time I've done wiv yer.'

'Ronnie,' cried the barkeep who had been joined by a woman behind the bar, presumably to see what all the commotion was about. Ronnie tightened his hold on his brother.

'Ronnie. Come on now, ducks,' she said. 'Let 'im go.'

'I will not. I was the one what found the fings. I was the one what told you about 'em...and I'm the one what should be in charge, not you lot. 'Ow come Smollett's taken over any'ow. He ain't even livin' in St Giles so 'ow did 'e find out about it? Must a bin one a you lot. And that posh geezer? Who the feckin' ell is 'e?' A mumble of disquiet went through the other men and some turned away.

'You might not be a dunder'ead, Ronnie, but you got a big mouth,' one of them said.

I couldn't believe my luck. My ears instantly tuned in to what Ronnie had said. I said a quiet thank you to Bessie whose idea it was for me to visit The Whistle and Flute. Perhaps this meant my stay in St Giles wouldn't be so long after all. Ronnie had said Smollett, so clearly I was in the right place at the right time.

'Keep yer bloody voice down,' hissed one of the men whose eyes suddenly became glassily sharp, and it wasn't with drink. He glanced about him looking angry and I lowered my eyes, pretending not to have heard any of the conversation going on at the bar.

I spotted a newspaper on one of the chairs at a vacant table and went across to retrieve it, thinking it would make me somewhat anonymous. I could pretend I was reading instead of listening. My plan was flawed, as I soon discovered.

'Oi!'

A voice from the bar stilled my hand.

'What d'yer fink yer doin' mate. That's my rag.'

I glanced up to see a weasel of a man glaring at me with narrowed eyes. I glanced down at the offending article, thinking it had had the opposite effect to the one I had been hoping for. I held the newspaper up in one hand, partially to cover my face.

'Sorry, mate. Fought it 'ad been left. D'int know it were yourn. I'll put it back.' I got up from my table and slipped the newspaper back on the chair.

'What d'yer want wiv a bleedin' newspaper, Stinky Ralph,' someone called from the bar. 'Yer can't read.' The gathering at the bar burst into shouts of laughter, including Ronnie who seemed to have forgotten his anger. His brother leant against the bar rubbing his neck, frowning up at the big man.

'I can bloody read,' answered the man they called Stinky Ralph. I wondered why they had given him such a name. They all stank. 'Got me learnin' from the Ragged School, din't I.'

One of the men cruelly mocked him. 'Aww...'e learnt at the Ragged School, din't 'e?'

There was another round of raucous laughter. Stinky Ralph slunk over to the table where he'd left his newspaper. He picked it up and slung it in my direction.

'Ere, you 'ave it. Them bastards are al'us taking the piss out a me.' I nodded my thanks, hoping he'd either leave or go back to his mates. I'd heard the name Smollett mentioned and I felt sure it was the best information I would get that evening. Stinky Ralph had other ideas.

'Who're you then?' he called to me, then sat at my table without being invited. 'Ain't seen you 'ere afore.'

I regarded him as he sat in the chair next to me. He wore a cap pulled down to just below his eyebrows. His jacket was made of a material with a velvet-like sheen. It had huge pockets at the front. The jacket reached his knees under which had been tied pieces of frayed and filthy string. From there onwards his trousers were stiff with muck as were his boots. I discovered why his mates called him Stinky Ralph. The smell coming off him was vomit inducing.

'Don't sit next to him, mate,' someone called from the bar. I glanced up towards the men. Some were so drunk they'd fallen asleep with their head resting on their arms while still standing at the bar. Another rushed out of the door to vomit in the yard which could be heard by all. 'He's a tosher,' cried another. 'Stinks like the place 'e grubs about in. The sewer rats run for their lives when they see 'im comin'. Can't stand the smell comin' off 'im.'

More raucous laughter. I glanced at Stinky Ralph and decided to answer his question. I needed to gain people's trust in this dreadful, yet heart-wrenching community. I would never have surmised the person I would be making a friend of would be a sewer-grubber.

'I've bin stayin' in Spitelfields,' I said, 'but there ain't no beds. It's got too crowded and the landlord let me down. Took me money but rented me bed to someone else.'

'What a bastard. Them landlords need a good pastin'. There's a load a Irish there ain't there, come over durin' the tater famine and never went back. Them's the one's what are taking the beds.'

'Where are you?' I asked him, taking a sip from my glass. I'd already decided not to drink the jugful after seeing the cloth the barkeep had wiped it with.

'Clay Street. Bloody 'orrible it is. I shared a bed wiv two uvver men last night. I reckon one was riddled wiv lice. He kept wrigglin' around and scratchin' his arse. Kep' me awake he did.' I leant as far away as possible from Stinky Ralph. The smell of him was one thing, but the mention of lice made my flesh crawl. He glanced down at my jug of beer. 'Don't yer want that? Yer seem to be playin' around wiv it.'

I put my hand across my stomach. "Ad the bellyache. Reckon it was a pie I 'ad at dinner. Made me sick to me stomach.'

'I'll 'ave it,' said Stinky Ralph, not giving me time to agree before his arm had swiftly stretched out and taken it. He curled his filthy fingers around the handle and gulped the beer down in one. I nodded and got up to leave.

'See yer around will I?' asked Stinky Ralph as he wiped his mouth on the sleeve of his coat.

'Yeah, yer prob'erly will.'

'Where yer stayin'?'

'St Giles.'

He nodded. 'You must know someone there. They won't let yer in 'less yer do.'

'Me cousin, Bessie. She got a place for me.'

'Lucky on you then. I know these lot what live in St Giles,' he indicated the men at the bar with a nod of his head, 'but they won't gimme a place. Dunno why.'

I made for the double doors which would take me out into the relatively fresh air of Drury Lane.

'I do,' I thought with a chuckle.

Chapter 14

"Ow'dit go?' asked Bessie when I got back to the court in Charlotte Street. She was standing outside waiting for me it seemed, a shawl pulled tightly around her shoulders and tied at the waist. She was shivering and I wasn't surprised. So was I. I had discovered that being dressed as a man afforded me no more warmth than being dressed as a women, less in fact. My hands were frozen as were my toes.

By the time I had returned to Charlotte Street darkness had fallen, and the fire burned brightly in the middle of the courtyard throwing an orange glow onto Bessie's face. I went over to the flames, getting as close as I dare, and held out my hands. The warmth was like a salve on my skin. It was a cold, clear night, and stars sparkled above us. A lit candle from one of the windows threw out a yellow radiance. If I had been anywhere other than Charlotte Street I would have said it was pleasant, but there was nothing pleasant about Charlotte Street.

It had taken me some time to find my way back to the court. I'd become completely lost, finding myself in 'a right old pickle', as I've no doubt Bessie would have said, and it wasn't without a measure of anxiety. If I couldn't find my way back I would have had to return to Harley Street for the night, which would have utterly destroyed my character's story.

Edwin Smith needs to be without guile for these men to trust him. I'd also imagined that Bessie would have been asked numerous questions about me, and she would have repeated the story we had come up with between us, the one Stride had approved. If I hadn't found my way back to Charlotte Street, even if it was by way of Percy Street, Newman Street, Grafton Street and Chitty Street, my time as an undercover police agent would have been extremely short indeed. I'd even found myself on the Tottenham Court Road at one point, which meant I had gone in a complete circle. I'd never been so pleased to see the wooden sign pointing to Charlotte Street, but I couldn't help wondering what would lie in store for me once I'd got there.

'Thought you'd be back before now,' said Bessie 'It ain't safe for anyone in the streets and alleyways this time of night. Gets dark quick see. You'll find yerself garrotted if they think you've got coin.'

I shuddered at the thought. 'I got a bit lost.'

She rolled her eyes which it seemed to me she had a habit of doing whenever she thought a person was stupid, which she clearly thought I was. 'Well, don't do it again. I can't be comin' out searching for yer. You 'ave to be yer own saviour in this place. Any'ow, 'owd it go. Did yer find anythin' out?'

'I did, Bessie. Someone mentioned Smollett's name, a man called Ronnie. The others weren't happy he'd spoken so loudly in the pub. He was in the middle of a fight with his brother and he complained because he wasn't in charge. He felt most strongly he should have been, bearing in mind he found the "fings" as he put it, and he mentioned a posh geezer. I'm sure it was the man I saw in Parker Street.'

Bessie smiled. 'You've done well, Edwin. Very well indeed. We're goin' ter 'ave ter talk about what yer goin' ter do tomorrow. You'll need ter bring in some coin or the others won't let yer stay.'

'Where are they? The courtyard was full when I left.'

'They're all inside fighting over who's goin' ter sleep where. I kept a place for yer. It's next to me, I 'ope yer don't mind.'

I chuckled although it was with a feeling of nervousness. The thought of sleeping alongside strangers filled me with disquiet. 'No, I'd rather be with you, Bessie. Do the others not expect me to sleep with the men?'

'We don't do it so much in our 'ouse because there's couples what are married wiv kids. They want ter be together.' She shrugged. 'It don't bother me to be honest. I just want ter get me 'ead down. It's a luxury just to get some sleep some nights.'

'It must be so hard, Bessie.'

She nodded. 'At least you'll find out fer yerself, Edwin. I've 'eard of people bunking down in the doss 'ouses, reporters from the News of the World and such like. They write articles about it in their newspapers like they think they know what it's like. One night they stay and then they run back to their comfy 'omes and their comfy beds. They ain't got a clue what it's like 'ere.' I glanced away hoping she didn't think the same of me. 'Jeremiah reckons you're gonna give your pay to 'elp the kids round 'ere.'

'I've always wanted to help. It's just finding the right way so people don't get suspicious.'

'You just 'ave to know 'ow ter do it. Don't be rubbin' their noses in it cos it won't go down well.' I had no answer for her. Perhaps it was why I got into so much trouble before. I upset the parents because I thought I knew better. It wasn't like that as far as I was concerned. I didn't for a moment think I knew better, but of course they saw it somewhat differently.

'Come on then, Edwin, it's bitter out 'ere. Let's get inside.' I followed her to what I supposed was the front door of the house. 'You eaten?' I shook my head. 'No worries. Doris is making a stew for everyone. We share see, at teatime. During the day it's up to everyone to feed 'emselves, but at teatime we 'ave a meal what we all share in 'cos we've all very like put some money in the pot. The money you gave Sylvie would 'ave 'elped.'

I nodded smiling, wondering what on earth the food would be like. I prayed it was cooked in a salubrious way, and not like The Whistle and Flute where the cloth used to clean glasses cleaned the tables, the bar, and probably the floor. In fact I was pleasantly surprised. Doris was clearly the designated cook and took great pride in what she served. The plates were old and chipped but were clean as were the spoons. I inspected them thoroughly, hopefully without being seen, and as I was incredibly hungry, tucked into the warming stew in the same way as everyone else. It was delicious. I believed, hoped, it was mutton, and was served with potatoes, carrots and onions.

When the meal was over, some of the women and children helped Doris wash the dishes; the others helped the men pull out mattresses and palliasses that were piled high at the side of the room. The straw poked through the canvas and they smelt damp, but when it's all there is one gets on with it. All together there were ten of us sleeping on the ground floor. Six men and four women.

The first floor was the bedroom for married couples with children. There seemed to be an organisation to it, an accepted way of doing things, and although the surroundings were meagre, bitterly cold, and broken, and the facilities non-existent, I couldn't help feeling admiration for the residents. Some of the older members had lived there for many years, in fact had been born there and made their lives there.

It was hard to believe people were living in these extremes, some like myself and Violet who had a wonderful home and had never experienced a day without love or security, or a substantial meal, and here in the rookery of St Giles where home was little more than a broken down shed in which neither Violet or I would house Truffle.

My rookery fellows lived without basic human essentials...or those things I, and those like me, considered essential. There was rarely running water unless the spring was allowed to run. Apparently the landlord often turned it off when he had a mind to. The privies were shared by dozens of people day and night which meant they became full to overflowing and were rarely emptied. Who would want such a job? It was often safer, and a lot cleaner, to defecate in the corners of the court, and there were no washing facilities to speak of. If someone wanted clothes washed they were taken to a designated washerwoman who washed clothes for many of the courts, not just the one we were in, unless Bessie and Sylvie could smuggle clothes into the laundry for washing, which was a rare occurrence. If caught they would have lost their employment.

I learnt all this from Bessie before we went to sleep that night in a whispered conversation. We made sure everyone else was in the land of nod. I say...sleep. Sleep to me was an hour in bed reading, a glass of warm milk, and then a satisfied snuggle down into the soft covers. In the rookery sleep meant something entirely different.

It was a strange place to be...in the dead of night, sleeping amongst strangers, people I had never met before, yet there I was. And I had to remind myself, people made the rookeries their permanent home and considered themselves relatively better off than those who haunted the streets of Spitalfields, Seven Dials, or Dorset Street and Clay Street, those dreadful otherworld places where no one who had a choice would ever go. Hundreds of people, men, women, and children slept in the overcrowded doss houses each night, where one could not see the floor so covered with bodies was it.

Some would kill to sleep there, particularly in those bitterest of nights when the alternatives were sleeping under a bridge or on a bench in one of London's parks if they hadn't been turned out by the park keeper. Men, women...and children, slept under the bridges of London, on pieces of board, wrapped in the newspapers men of means threw away as rubbish, or rags they had found amongst the detritus on

London's filthy streets.

The sounds of the sleeping in that house on Charlotte Street was something I had not imagined and would certainly never forget. One would always expect a modicum of quiet when one went to one's bed at night, yet here there was none. Babies mewled for their mother's milk, men...and women snored throughout the night. The smells were also something to be reckoned with, and not just the sulphuric odour from the privy in the yard which had been overflowing when I visited. Men farted and snorted, scratched and coughed, belched and hiccupped. If there was a hell, surely the Charlotte Street rookery at night was the precursor of it.

The following day Bessie roused me before dawn. It was her morning for working at the laundry and she suggested I accompany her. I asked about breakfast and perhaps a wash and she snorted with derision.

'Breakfast,' she cried. 'You'll be lucky, Edwin, and don't expect a wash niver.' She leant towards me and whispered in my ear. 'If you're that bovvered you can go to the bath'ouse on the Tottenham Court Road.' I thought about it then shook my head. I was certain Bessie had asked me to accompany her to the laundry because she wanted to speak with me in private and I was curious.

Bessie wrapped herself in two heavy coats, both ill-fitting and had seen better days, then draped a shawl about her head and shoulders. I wore the same clothes I wore the day before, and was given a heavy coat from a pile of old clothes in the corner of the room. A pair of stiff fingerless gloves came from somewhere, and as loathe as I was to wear them the temperature in the house was icy, so I gritted my teeth and put them on.

Outside was worse. The wet mud and detritus in the court had hardened with ice. Water which had been dripping from the roof had formed long icicles hanging from what was left of the slates. The fire in the centre of the courtyard had long since been extinguished by the frost.

'Brr,' said Bessie into her shawl which she'd pulled up around her neck and chin. 'Gawd, it's bloody freezing. At least it's warm in the laundry.'

'What do you want me to do, Bessie? I felt there was something you wished to tell me.'

We walked apace down Charlotte Street which took us onto Rathbone Place, and then onto the Tottenham Court Road which was where the laundry was situated.

'Jeremiah's 'ad some news.'

I stared at her in astonishment. 'You've seen him?'

'I 'ave. Yest'y teatime when you was at the Whistle and Flute. The stuff what they're sellin'. It comes from the far continent. Egypt he reckons.'

I stared into the distance recalling the conversation I'd had with Mr Thomas in Parker Street regarding a big black dog he'd seen being taken into the house two doors away from his own.

'Anubis,' I said, smiling to myself. 'He was talking about Anubis.'

Bessie frowned and stared at me as though I had lost my senses. 'Who?'

'Anubis. It's the name of an Egyptian dog. Mr Thomas in Parker Street said he saw a sculpture of a dog being delivered to a house close by. I saw a delivery being made the day I'd visited, a man travelling in a carriage, not a hansom; pulling a cart on which there were various sized items wrapped in old cloths. It was clearly an illegal endeavour. As soon as I saw it I'd discerned they were stolen goods. No one in Parker Street would take deliveries of anything? In some ways it's poorer than St Giles.'

'We need to find out who they are, Edwin. And who they know at St Giles. It's the only way we'll catch 'em.'

'What about Smollett?'

Bessie shook her head. 'There's a problem with them.'

'A problem? Why?'

'The Smollett gang are notorious in Seven Dials and St Giles, and further afield. They're ruthless. They've murdered at least three people I know of who got too close to 'em. They don't like people gettin' close in case they try to take some of their income. They trust no one and would give no one the benefit of the doubt. I reckon it's a blind alley. We must find another way.'

I frowned. One of the Smolletts was involved in whatever was going on and I wondered why Bessie and Stride hadn't arrested any of them.

'Why doesn't Stride just arrest them and interview them. One of them might give something away.'

She made a scornful smile. 'Naïve, ain't yer?'

'Maybe I am, but why would one pussyfoot around. They said the name Smollett. I heard them.'

'Well, you might 'ave 'eard 'em, but I suggest you don't mention the name down at the courts. They'll be on to yer like flies on shit. They don't get arrested because there's a long game to be played and Jeremiah's playin' it.'

I sighed and shook my head. Suddenly, Bessie shoved me into a doorway and grabbed my lapels.

'Look, Edwin, the Smolletts ain't the only ones involved in this. This thing goes right to the top. They're the ones what need to be caught. We're talking high-falutin' types, people wiv real money, even more than you, and I know you've got plenty of coin.' She released my lapels and I brushed myself down, more in nervousness than anything else. She'd taken the breath out of me. 'I know you got a nice 'ouse an' all.'

I raised my eyebrows. 'How do you know that?'

'I followed yer, the day we met in the pub. Didn't even see me, did yer?'

I stared at her feeling slightly violated. 'You followed Meg and me?'

'I did. Like yer maid, don't yer? I don't know many mistresses what would take their maid's arm like what you did.'

I drew in a breath, wishing I was at home with Violet, Meg, and Truffle. 'We've known each other since we were children. Her parents were in service to my parents. We're friends as well as mistress and maid.'

'That ain't a bad fing, and it told me a lot about yer. It was what I wanted ter see...a bit of caring. I followed yer to the corner of Harley Street, then went into The Lamb and Anchor for a drink. I know some of the patrons what go in there. And some of the working gels.'

'There are working girls in Harley Street?' I cried, frowning.

Bessie threw back her head and laughed. 'There're working gels everywhere, Edwin, so don't get uppity about it. Your neighbours are likely making use of some of the services they offer. That's what they're there for. To offer services to gentlemen what can afford it. Anyway, this is what I want yer to do. I want yer to go to Parker Street and knock on the door where you saw them deliveries bein' made.'

I gasped. 'Surely not.'

Bessie stepped back and put her hands on her hips. 'And why not may I ask?'

'Won't it be rather dangerous?'

'Yes, Edwin, it will, but it's what yer 'ere for, ter do the stuff I can't.'

'And what if someone opens the door?'

She snorted with laughter again. 'It's what we want 'em ter do, yer daft cove. We want to see who's in there. You might recognise 'em and if yer don't, 'ave a good look at who's in there. And yer might see some stuff an' all. If yer do we want to know about it.'

'What should I say?'

Bessie looked exasperated. 'I dunno. Come up wiv somethin'. Use your idea of bein' taken ill. They might ask you inside. It's what yer want. Standin' on the doorstep ain't goin' ter get yer anywhere is it? You won't see nothin' like that. Come on, Edwin. We're expecting you ter do yer job.'

I walked with Bessie the rest of the way to the laundry in Tottenham Court Road. It was still dark and I was ravenous. I still had some of the money she had given me the night before, so I went to a stall selling sausages in pastry, and another selling mugs of coffee. There were queues of men at both, but I waited in line as the others were doing. Some of the men looked done for, their skin grey, their eyes ringed with the evidence of a sleepless night. I listened in to the conversations around me, mostly about lack of work and lack of money.

'Nuthin' doin' at the docks,' I heard one say. 'Weather's held up the ships. The Thames is covered in ice and they can't get in ter the docks. Comes to something when there ain't even any work at the docks. I went down there this mornin' and picked up some wood for the fire. It won't last long. When I've 'ad this I'm going to the brewery and the tannery, see if they got any porter work.'

'You'll be lucky,' said the man he was talking to who wore a jacket two sizes too small for him, and trousers tied up with string. He wore a tweed cap on top of a scarf tied around his head and knotted under his chin. 'Bin down there, ain't I? They got nuffin.' He shook his head. 'Never known it so bad.' He glanced up at me as I listened and I lowered my gaze. He began to stamp his feet on the ground. 'Bloody weather. Don't know 'ow we're s'posed to feed our young 'uns.'

I ate the sausage in pastry as I walked along the Tottenham Court Road. It was tasty, and hot, and warmed me right through. The benefit was it warmed my hands too, so I began a marching sort of walk towards Parker Street to retain the warmth it had afforded me.

As I walked towards Parker Street, my footsteps on the frost covered pavement woke some of the poor unfortunates who had spent the night in the doorways of shops which would not open until hours later. Many of them could have been taken for bundles of rags or piles of newspapers, but I discovered these piles of detritus were, in fact, men and women who had wrapped themselves in whatever was available to find some warmth on what had been one the bitterest nights.

I suddenly had a surge of gratitude for the straw palliasse on which I had slept, while trying with all I had not to think of my bedroom and the soft, beautifully appointed bed where I usually laid my head. I had been disgusted by the stiff with dirt, smelly blanket which had covered me, but it had provided warmth, as did the heat from the other bodies around me. It had enabled me to find a modicum of sleep, although the shock of waking in such surroundings is something I will no doubt remember for the rest of my days.

In some of the doorways were children, enrobed much like the men and women I had encountered. Some of them sleepily raised their tousled and lice infested heads, presumably to reassure themselves they were not in any danger from the oncoming footsteps. My heart went out to them, these poor children of the night, and I couldn't help thinking it was a damning indictment of those of us with plenty, nothing had changed since Charles Dickens had published his tales of walking through London at night.

Whilst I had stood drinking coffee at the coffee stall I had thought about what Bessie had said. She wanted me to find a way of getting into the house in Parker Street. I shook my head as I walked, passing street vendors trying to sell shrivelled vegetables to disinterested customers, pieces of china retrieved from the mudlarks, or clothes from those who had died and had been divested of their garments; the most popular stall in the sharp cold. My thoughts went back to Parker Street. What would happen if I saw Mr Thomas, although I doubted he would recognise me in my guise as Edwin. I had to find a way to get into the property which was receiving the deliveries of stolen goods.

As I turned into Parker Street, a young street vendor selling newspapers called out to passers-by, the number of which had increased a hundred fold in the last half hour.

'Man found dead in Percy Street,' he cried, his voice cracking in the cold air. 'Worst murder for many a year! Read all abaht it.'

I bought a newspaper with the last few pennies I had, hoping the boy had exaggerated the story to sell more papers, but no, there it was...a Ronnie Dines had been found murdered in a shop doorway in Percy Street.

It had been thought he was a tramper who had made his bed where many others had before him. His lifeblood, flowing off the step and into the slush which had collected on the pavement after a light snowfall, had alerted an early-morning lamp snuffer to his demise.

A gruesome caricature of the scene had been drawn by a gifted artist, showing Ronnie Dines splayed across a step, his throat cut from ear to ear, and a puddle of blood pooled around him. It was clearly the Ronnie who had been complaining the previous evening in The Whistle and Flute. A wave of fear went through me. Why had he been murdered? I could think of only one reason.

Bessie had told me in the courtyard before we bedded down for the night Ronnie was a quiet man, rather slow in his mind but quick to anger if anyone crossed him, or if he was in his cups. In The Whistle and Flute he had complained vociferously about the Smolletts taking charge of his finds, whatever they were, and of course the man he described as the "posh geezer", who I felt sure was the man I had seen when I left the Thomas's. The other men in the Whistle and Flute had clearly been displeased Ronnie had made his dissent towards the Smolletts so obvious, which was why they had told him to "pipe down". Perhaps he hadn't "piped down" quickly enough, and his murder was someone's way of piping him down. Whatever the reason it sent out a clear message. One did not mess with the Smolletts or their associates.

I walked the last few yards to the house in Parker Street. Like the previous time I walked...or ran along its fetid pavements, a freezing fog had descended on the street and those surrounding it. It felt as though the Thames had had a forewarning of my visit and had summoned a fog from its blackened waters to greet me. I wondered if it was to help or to hinder.

I reached the Thomas's house. I had an urge to look in the window. Christmas had long gone, and I wondered how the family of five were faring. I peered into the window. The fireplace had no welcoming flames crackling in the grate. It was stone cold and looked as though it had been for many a day. Where were the children? I had provided clothes for them to attend the Ragged School. Were they there or had their father sold the clothes and frittered the money away on drink? I shuddered with disappointment. I didn't know what I was expecting from this poor family, but something told me all was not well.

I took a moment to think. Perhaps I could knock on the door of number seventy-five, the house where the deliveries were made, and pretend to be looking for someone. It would look innocent enough, and if I found the courage from somewhere could claim to have become ill on the doorstep.

I stood in front of the door shaking with anticipation, lifted my hand, and knocked with my redraw knuckles. At first there was no answer. Everything in the street was as quiet as the grave, as was the house for which I was almost grateful, but at length the door was opened.

A woman stood in the doorframe. She was of middle-age with greying hair which had been loosely pinned to the top of her head, and wore a bottle-green dress of heavy cotton. She had an apron tied around her corpulent middle. The apron was brown with stains instead of the white it had probably once been. She wore a man's jacket over the top tied around her middle with string, and a shawl tied over the top of that. Plainly it was cold in the house. No rush of warmth greeted me as she held open the door.

'Yeah?' she said, folding her arms in front of her bosom. A frown crossed her face.

'I'm sorry, missus,' I said, touching the peak of my cap. 'I'm looking for someone who I've been told lives in this street.'

'Oh, yeah. Who's that then?'

I took a breath. Of course. I hadn't yet come up with a name.

'Bert.'

The frown on her face deepened. 'Bert who?'

'Bert, er...Smiff. 'E's a cousin. I was told 'e lived in Parker Street but I 'aven't got the number of the 'ouse. Fought you might know 'im.'

Her mouth turned into an upside down crescent and she shook 'er 'ead. 'Nah, never 'eard of 'im.'

I realised I wasn't getting very far. I tried to look over her shoulder while she spoke but she was tall and stout and filled the doorframe. It occurred to me I would need to resort to my extended plan.

'Oof,' I said, bending double in front of her. 'Ooh, sorry, missus, got a bit of bellyache. Do yer fink I could come into the 'all for a minute. Just to sit down and wait for it to go. I get it a lot.'

She stared at me as I glanced up at her, her eyes as hard as iron. 'You ain't got the shits 'ave yer? I don't want nuffin' in 'ere like that?'

'Oh, no, missus,' I said. 'I ain't got nuffin' like that. It's a bit of h'indigestion that's all.'

She stared at me for a moment longer then opened the door wider. 'I don't want no funny business,' she said. 'I'm only the 'ousekeeper 'ere. I don't live 'ere, and the master won't like it if 'e finks I've bin lettin' people inside.'

Still bent double I went into the hall. 'There won't be no funny business, missus, that I can promise yer. Just need a minute out'a the fog.'

She nodded, then led me into what I presumed was the front room. 'Yer can sit there,' she said, pointing to a wooden chair just inside the door, 'and don't move. D'yer need a cuppa tea or somethin'? Might it 'elp?'

I nodded. 'It might 'elp, missus. Fanks very much.' I tipped my cap to her. 'You're a very kind lady.'

This obviously pleased her. Her sour face managed to find a small smile. 'I do me best for those in need,' her face swiftly went back to its original setting, ' but I won't be taken advantage of.'

'That won't 'appen, missus. I'm very grateful.'

She left the room and went into the scullery which gave me the opportunity to look properly at the room. It was plainly not being used as a living room or sitting room. There were just three chairs, much like the one I had been directed to, all wooden, all highly uncomfortable. In the alcoves, one each side of the unlit fireplace, were wooden crates with black lettering on the sides. I tipped my head to see what was written, but the words were in a foreign language, one I could not discern. As I turned my head I startled.

Leaning up against the corner of the back wall was a tall structure wrapped in rags. Part of the rag had slipped at the top revealing a domed gold top on which was painted a large eye. It was almond-shaped and ringed with black paint. The iris of the eye was dark brown and surrounded by cream, gold-flecked paint. Next to the eye was a hieroglyph painted in black which was joined to the black paint lining the eye. It was stunningly beautiful and I assumed if I could have seen the whole thing I would have been entranced.

I stared at it for a moment longer. I knew what it was; a sarcophagus, a box for the holding of a mummy which had been entombed in an Egyptian pyramid. This is what Bessie had spoken of. Stride had been correct in his investigations. Someone, somewhere was acquiring antiques from the far continents and making a tidy sum. My stomach rolled a number of times and I wondered if the woman was aware of exactly what she was spending time with. Of course it may have been empty, but it looked heavy and I would have loved to have opened it, even though I would have been horrified to find a rag-wrapped mummy.

I heard a shuffling of old slippers in the hall and bent forward again, arranging my features into an expression of pain.

"Ow yer feeling?' she asked.

I nodded. 'It's easin' up a bit,' I said, taking the tin mug from her hand. 'It's kind of yer to let me in like this. Yer don't know me from Adam. The angels will repay yer,' I said, making a small smile and lifting the tin mug in a salute.

She threw her head back and laughed, revealing brown teeth and huge gaps where some had fallen out, clearly feeling more relaxed with me than previously. 'Angels?' she cried. 'There ain't no bleedin' angels, ducks,' she said. 'D'yer think I'd be sittin' 'ere lookin' after this lot if there was? And you wouldn't be in so much pain 'avin' to ask fer 'elp from a stranger.'

'Yer don't live 'ere then?' I asked, looking into the tea which was grey with rancid milk, thinking I'd definitely be ill if I drank such swill.

'Nah. Don't like it down 'ere. Live near Flower Street wiv me 'usband. I'm like an 'ousekeeper 'ere I am, keepin' an eye on fings.'

'What fings?' I asked as casually as I could muster.

She suddenly frowned again, her face returning to her hard expression. 'What's it ter you?'

I sighed as though I was bored. 'Ain't nuffin to me, missus. Just makin' conversation.'

'Oh,' she said, rubbing her hands down her filthy apron. 'That's alright then.'

Her attention was taken by a knock on the front door.

'I'll 'ave to answer this. Remember,' she said, pointing her finger at me. 'Don't move and don't touch nuffin.' I simply shrugged my compliance, then bent towards the doorframe so I could hear any conversation.

"E ain't 'ere,' I heard her say to the visitor. 'And 'e won't be 'ere for a day or so. 'E's got more stuff comin' from that place what 'e gets it from. Can't remember the name. We'll let yer know when we need yer, don't you worry.' I heard a mumbling answer from the visitor but couldn't make out the words. "E ain't goin' ter cut you out. 'E needs yer don't he? He's told yer that already.'

The door slammed and she came back into the room. 'Yer tea's gone all cold,' she said. I stood, wanting to leave as soon as I could. I'd seen what I was looking for and was eager to find out who the visitor was.

'Yeah, sorry,' I said. 'Was a bit worried about bringing it back up again cos of me h'indigestion. Din't want ter do that to yer.' She snatched the cup away spilling some of the tea on my hand.

'I'm glad to 'ere it.'

I wiped my hand on my coat, aware another stain on it couldn't make it look much worse. 'But fanks, though.' I went to the front door and opened it, stepping out onto the frosty pavement. I touched the rim of my cap to her. 'Thanks, missus. Like I said, you're an angel.' She slammed the door in my face.

I looked both right and left. To the right of the house a man could be seen in the distance walking through the fog. He walked in the same direction as the one in which I had arrived. I decided to follow him. I wasn't particularly familiar with the streets in the area, but he was headed for Drury Lane which I did know, and where The Whistle and Flute was situated. I didn't want to walk down that street again; it seemed every type of vagabond, vagrant, thief, and prostitute plied their particular trades there, but it was important for me to discover the identity of the man.

He was quite short and built in rather a slight way, his shoulders narrower than most men. His gait was slow and he was hunched forward somewhat, with his hands in his pockets. Was he elderly, I asked myself?

I kept my distance although I was frightened of losing him in the fog which seemed to be getting denser, and overlaid with a putrid odour which flowed into one's throat and laid on the chest. I heard him cough from time to time, but I was determined I wouldn't. It would have revealed my presence. I pulled my muffler up higher over my chin and mouth. I was quite sure he hadn't realised I was there and I wished it to be kept that way.

He turned at the corner of Parker Street and went into Drury Lane which was a different prospect entirely to Parker Street. It was thick with traffic; carts, carriages, and hansom cabs. People milled about, some on their way to work, many looking for it. I watched the man as he crossed the street, dodging a hansom as he went. The driver called out to him to get out of the bleedin' way, and the man replied with a disgusting expletive, then knocked on the double doors of The Whistle and Flute. He was quickly given admittance even though it was not yet opening time. It was then I realised who I had been following from Parker Street. The man who had called at the house was none other than Stinky Ralph, the sewer grubber I had met last evening.

Chapter 15

I didn't go into Drury Lane. There was always the danger Stinky Ralph would see me so I decided to take another route back to Charlotte Street. Instead I walked the length of Parker Street again, on the other side of the street from the house I'd just left, and made my way to Newton Street at the other end. From there I walked down the Fishguard Road and then onto Shaftesbury Avenue. It was a trek from there to St Giles, but when I saw the signpost for Rathbone Street I breathed a sigh of relief.

It wasn't a regular occurrence for me to walk alone. When I left the house in Harley Street I usually found a hansom cab, or was accompanied by Violet or Meg, but when I looked about at the women on the streets few were chaperoned, and only those who I could tell were a certain class by the way they were dressed.

The other women seemed to own far more independence. Some walked in twos; those obviously in service strolled down the streets with their fellow maids, but all in all most were alone. They clearly didn't need to be chaperoned as they went about their business. This was a world of which I knew nothing. A small part of me envied them.

When I got back to Charlotte Street it was nearly lunchtime, at least it was in my world. I had no money as I had bought breakfast at the stalls and a newspaper at the vendors. I'd folded it into a square and pushed it into the pocket of my coat and forgotten about it. My return to Charlotte Street reminded me of the murder which had taken place just a few streets away.

Bessie and Sylvie had already returned from the laundry. The fog had cleared a little, but it had begun to rain and they were sheltering inside.

When I opened the door I found them sitting around a table with Doris and a couple of men I'd seen standing around the fire in the court, and then later on in the Whistle and Flute when Ronnie Dines had been fighting with his brother. Bessie lifted her chin to me.

'You alright, Edwin? 'Ow'd it go this mornin'.'

I shrugged and shook my head. 'Nuthin' doin', Bessie. D'int make a penny. No one's goin' out 'cos of the fog. It's clearin' a bit though. I'll go out again this afternoon. Try me luck.'

'Yer want a mug o' tea, Edwin?' asked Doris, a portly woman well into her sixties.

'That would be grand, Doris,' I said, joining them at the table. 'Not nice out there terday.'

Doris got up from the table and went across to a large, enamelled urn on a settle. I pushed the newspaper across the table to Bessie and Sylvie so they could see the headline. Sylvie pushed it back to me.

'We know about it, Edwin. It's the talk of St Giles.'

'What 'appened?' I asked. "E were in the Whistle and Flute last night.'

Bessie sniffed then took a gulp of tea. Sylvie shrugged and shook her head. 'Rubbed someone up the wrong way I 'spect. It's what 'appens 'ere. Yer 'ave to keep yer nose clean, which means not asking questions. Curiosi'y killed the cat, din't it?'

'I s'pose it did.' I took my tea from Doris then buried my head in the newspaper. I'd been given the order; don't ask questions.

'Where'd you learn to read, Edwin,' Sylvie asked.

'I don't read proper like. Just some words what I learned at the Ragged School. I can get the gist of things from them, but I knew what that 'eadline said. It's big enough.'

'You givin' us any money today?'

I glanced at Bessie who widened her eyes. 'Yeah, course I am. I always pay me way. Don't 'ave it yet, but don't worry yerself. I'll 'ave some by this afternoon.'

Sylvie pushed herself up from the table. 'Glad to 'ear it. We're a mite low at present. Need all the coin we can get, and with another mouth to feed, and another bed to find...'

I put my hand up to halt her. The woman was a bully and I wouldn't accept bullying, no matter which world I was occupying.

'Like I said, Sylvie, you'll get it.' She nodded, wrapped her shawl tighter around her shoulders and went out the door into the courtyard, slamming it as she went.

Bessie glanced at Doris and the men. 'What the 'ell's eatin' 'er? She's bin like a cat on 'ot bricks all mornin'. Couldn't get a word out of 'er at the laundry. 'Ad a face as long as a fiddler's elbow.'

'I reckon it's all this business wiv Ronnie,' answered Doris. 'Fink she 'ad a soft spot for 'im on account of 'im bein' a bit slow like. They used to like talkin' to one anuvver, like friends they was. Or bruvver and sister.'

'Well, 'e must 'ave done summink. We ain't 'ad a killin' round 'ere for a long time.' Bessie looked at the men and raised her eyebrows. 'You two are quiet. 'Ain't yer got nuffink to say?'

They both shrugged and looked at one another. ''E talks out a turn,' said one. ''E was in a right two and eight last night at the pub. In 'is cups an' runnin' down the Smolletts he were...and that posh bloke what they know. Prob'ly summink to do wiv that.'

'An' they killed 'im fer that?'

'Dunno. Might 'ave bin them, or it might 'ave bin someone else. It's easy to rub someone up the wrong way, and Ronnie's mouf ran away wiv 'im 'cos 'e di'nt 'ave the sense ter keep it shut. Like Sylvie says, yer 'ave to keep yer nose out of business.' They both rose from the table and went out the door without speaking.

I remained quiet and waited for Doris to say something. I had already surmised that she saw, and heard, everything that went on in the rookery. She didn't say much; was astute enough to keep her own council.

''E won't be the last,' she said, getting up from the table and going across to the tin bowl serving as her sink.

'Who won't?' asked Bessie.

'Ronnie.'

'Why,' Bessie asked her, frowning. I hoped Doris would say a lot more, and that Bessie would gently lead her to say what she was thinking...or what she knew.

'Things always come in threes. They'll be another two what go under, you mark my words.'

'Anyone in mind?' asked Bessie as she took our empty mugs over to Doris.

'Them what don't know 'ow to keep their mouths shut. It's what 'appened to Ronnie. 'E didn't 'ave the sense yer see, to keep quiet. He fought 'e was 'ard done by cos 'e reckoned 'e was the main man in whatever they was doin'. Trouble is 'e di'nt 'ave the nous to be quiet about it. Got in 'is cups and let it all come out. Someone in the Whistle and Flute din't like what 'e was sayin'.' She glanced up at Bessie. 'Any'ow, I need the privy.' She went out of the door, pulling it to with a bang.

'Do you think she's right?' I whispered to Bessie.

'Prob'ly. There ain't much gets past Doris.' She shook her head and sat opposite. ''Ow did yer get on today?'

I explained to her what had happened in Parker Street and her eyes shone.

'So you got in there?' I nodded. 'And?'

'You mentioned Stride said he thought there was an illegal trade in antiquities.' Bessie nodded. 'They have a sarcophagus in the living room of the house. It had been leant up against the wall and some of the cloth had slipped revealing the eye of an Egyptian god.'

'Bloody 'ell.'

'In the alcoves there were wooden crates stacked up to the ceiling. I couldn't see what was in them, but there was lettering on the sides in a foreign language. Nothing I recognised I'm afraid. I tried to read them, but they weren't in French or German. It looked like a language from one of the far continents.'

'Jeremiah should know about it.'

'Yes, of course. But that's not all. While I was there the woman who let me in had a visitor who I followed when I left. I got the impression he was involved. She told him they would contact him when they needed him. She didn't say what they'd need him for unfortunately.'

'Who was it?'

'A man called Stinky Ralph. I met him last night at the Whistle and Flute.'

She gasped. 'He's the tosher, the sewer-grubber. Surely he's not involved.'

'In it up to his neck I'd say.' We glanced at each other and laughed. 'What do we do now?'

'Leave it ter me. I'll talk to one of my snouts. You've done well, Edwin, and you'll need this. She stood and put her hand in her pocket, throwing some coin onto the table. 'Sylvie won't give up until she's got yer money. And don't forget what I said, don't give up everythin'. I want yer ter go back to the Whistle and Flute tonight, so you'll need some coin. After what's 'append to Ronnie I reckon it'll be all they'll talk about. You need to get yer ears out and listen to what's said. I fink Jeremiah's goin' ter be pleased wiv what you've found out. And you'll need to find yer own coin from now on. I've only got a bit and if I keep givin' it ter you I won't be able to pay me way. I'm sure you'll come up with somethin'. Well done, Edwin.'

Bessie was right about Sylvie. As soon as I left the house that evening she collared me for money. Of course I had no proof the money I gave her would go towards my upkeep in the rookery, but she seemed to have a modicum of authority in St Giles. The other inhabitants listened to her. She was hard-bitten with a tough expression, and a voice like jagged glass that could be heard in the narrow streets and alleyways. Her attitude said she would brook no objection, so I meekly handed over half the money Bessie had given me.

'Where's this from?'

'I said I'd get some coin this afternoon. That's it.'

She nodded, looking at the money I had given her resting in the palm of her hand. 'I don't know about you, Edwin,' she said, raising her eyes to meet mine. 'Yer a strange sort. You ain't a molly are yer?'

I took a step back. 'No, I ain't a molly. What makes yer say that?'

'Yer got a look about yer. I feel you ain't quite right.'

I knew I would have to fight this accusation from Sylvie, otherwise I wouldn't hear the last of it.

'It don't matter what you feel. I ain't what yer said. If I were I wouldn't 'ave come 'ere would I? I don't wanna get beaten up, or worse. I've 'ad girlfriends, got engaged once, but she went off wiv someone else. Looks like yer not right about everythin', Sylvie.'

She pulled a grin and raised one of her eyebrows. I wasn't sure if it was in admiration or because she thought I was lying.

'I'm glad to 'ear it. I think I might like yer. Yer a good lookin' cove, but I reckon you'll 'ave to 'arden up a bit. You're a bit too quiet for round 'ere.'

'I am what I am, and as long as I ain't troublesome to yer, I don't see you've got anythin' to worry about.'

'Oh, I ain't worried, Edwin,' she said, running a finger down my cheek. She threw the coin up in the air, deftly caught it, and sashayed across the courtyard. When she got to the door she turned and winked at me before going inside. I swallowed hard and momentarily closed my eyes. I realised Sylvie could present me with a problem if I didn't keep out of her way. I wasn't sure she believed me about my engagement, but it was all I could come up with at short notice. I made a mental note to stay out of her way.

I made my way to Drury Lane. I had finally found my inner compass and had become adept at finding my way around the rookery and beyond. I was still worried about moving around the rookery in the dark. I had heard so many things about what went on there, and of course there was Ronnie's murder which made everyone anxious and apprehensive.

One didn't have to do much to upset someone in the rookery. Doris and the men in the house had been right when they said the most advantageous thing to do was to keep one's nose out of business. I would do it, to a point. I had no desire to get involved in conversations with the other men, but I could listen when they were speaking. If they thought me strange so be it.

As I got closer to the double doors leading into the Whistle and Flute I noticed there was no noise coming from the interior. Last evening one could hear the voices, chattering and catcalling from the top of Drury Lane, but that night there was nothing but the sound of hansom cabs, carriages and carts making their way through the puddles and the ordure on the cobbles. I frowned, wondering if the public house was closed, but then I saw someone go inside. I took a breath and followed him.

There was no one on the decrepit piano banging out songs for them all to sing to. The lid was firmly closed. The tables were full, but no one chatted, and the street girls were sitting in one corner, smoking cheroots. Some of the men were at the bar, but they weren't chatting or pulling each other's legs as they had been the night before. Ronnie's brother was at the bar downing whiskey as if there was no tomorrow. The air was heavy with grief.

I went to the bar and leant against it, waiting to be served. The barkeeps wife came over to me, her eyes red and swollen.

'What you 'avin?' she asked, her voice a quiet wobble.

'A beer please.'

'Quart or arf?'

'Arf.' She nodded and went over to the pumps, then pulled me a half pint. Yet again I had no desire to drink the disgusting brew, but I could hardly ask for a sherry, or a glass of wine. She brought it to me and I gave her a penny, nodding my thanks.

'Did yer know 'im?' she asked.

I shook my head. 'I 'eard 'e was well liked.'

'Oh, 'e was. Everyone loved Ronnie.' I thought not, bearing in mind his body was now lying in the morgue with huge gash across its throat, but I nodded my agreement and commiserated.

'The police 'ave been in Percy Street all day. Came 'ere an' all, though God knows what they thought they'd find 'ere.' She inclined her head to the gathering of men. 'They're a good bunch. 'Aint a bad one amongst 'em.' I raised my eyebrows, thankfully hidden under my cap, wondering if she were naïve or it was what one did...sang the praises of one's most loyal customers regardless of the type of people they were. I knew at least one of them was up to no good, and as my thoughts went to him he appeared as though by magic from the yard door.

'Get us an ale, ducks,' he said to the woman behind the bar. He threw the money onto the bar and went around the tables, shaking the hands of the men who were sitting at them, all looking morose, all with their noses stuck in their beer.

He spotted me eventually, then came to my table, the one I had sat at the previous night which had become vacant. It was by the door and I was relieved. The last thing I wanted was to navigate my way through the men sitting at the other tables. I would likely have to converse with them and the thought of it made me tremble.

"Owdy do,' Stinky Ralph said as he sat himself at my table. ''Eard the news 'ave yer? Don't s'pose yer knew 'im.'

I shook my head. 'Nah. 'Erd he were a good sort though.' I eyed him warily, wondering if he were sizing me up as I was him.

He took a long gulp of beer. 'Oh, yeah, that he were. Someone din't fink so, did they?' I shrugged not wanting to discuss it with him but, of course, he wouldn't let the subject drop. 'Got ter look after yerself round 'ere.'

'P'raps it were a mistake.'

He snorted into his beer. 'A mistake,' he cried. 'I don't fink so, Edwin. They don't make mistakes like that around 'ere. Nah, 'e rubbed somebody up the wrong way and they took an h'exception to it. Got 'iself killed.'

I wondered about pushing it further. It was what I was there for after all. 'They?'

He nodded and took another gulp of beer. 'Yeah. They.'

'Who's they?'

Ralph slowly turned his head and stared at me. 'You'd do best not to ask that question.' I lifted my head in a nod. 'There's people in St Giles and Seven Dials wants ter remain below the parapet. D'yer get my meaning?' I nodded my head again. 'And yer'd do best to do the same.'

I shrugged. 'Just makin' conversation.'

'Yeah, well, yer new 'ere ain't yer, so we don't know who yer are. I'd keep yer conversations on somethin' else if I was you.'

His eyes hardened, then just as quickly his previous expression returned. It was a look of dumb ignorance and it informed me of exactly what I wanted to know. Stinky Ralph was a big part of what was going on and he was warning me off. His demeanour of someone on the fringes of whatever was going on was a front. His changing expressions told me so. I got the message, but from what Ralph had said there was something to have a conversation about and he had simply reinforced my opinion that Ronnie had been killed because he'd been loose lipped in the Whistle and Flute the previous night. Someone with authority had given the order for him to be removed.

I waited for another fifteen minutes or so, and when Stinky Ralph went up to the bar, I left. It was a relief to leave the heavy, morose atmosphere prevailing in the pub. Along with the cloying smell of viscous beer spilt on the floor which hadn't been cleaned up, and the nicotine-heavy pall floating above the patron's heads, was the hefty blanket of grief. Ronnie had been liked, that was clear, but I also sensed an undercurrent, a feeling of fear perhaps. There was certainly no actual talk of Ronnie, no criticism, but no support for him either. Did the patrons think there was a spy in their midst? Did they think it was me?

I began to walk up Drury Lane, past the closed shops where people were making their beds for the night. No one spoke. They were not friendly towards one another. I guessed it was because they were constantly in competition with one another for the warmest place to sleep, and for whatever food they could find in the bins outside the shops and on the pavements. Even the ends of cigarettes were picked up from the gutters and torn apart, then made into rough cigarettes for them to smoke. A wave of sadness went through me. What a way to live one's life.

When I got to the Tottenham Court Road, which was still full of people going in and out of the pubs and restaurants, I felt a rather strange creeping sensation running up my back to my neck. It felt extremely uncomfortable. I looked behind me, but could see only the melee of people going about their business. I had to acknowledge I had felt it when I left the Whistle and Flute, but I had surmised it was because the area in which I found myself was not my usual neighbourhood, and I was out, alone, in the darkness.

I quickened my step. Rathbone Place was not as occupied with people and carriages as Tottenham Court Road. I almost fainted with relief when I spotted another person coming towards me, but of course they would pass me and go on their way. The closer I got to Charlotte Street the fewer people I saw. Most knew St Giles was an area to be avoided at night if one wanted to survive to see the next day.

I turned into an alleyway and began to run. My footsteps were like an echo on the damp pavement but I did not discern another set behind me. I stopped and turned. There was no one there. My heartbeat began to slow and I blew out a breath of relief. I continued to walk down the alleyway. It was not one I was familiar with in the labyrinth of the rookery, but I guessed it would lead into Charlotte Street, or at least close by.

I caught my breath and began to walk again. By now the darkness was complete. No gas lighter came down these grimy throughfares. It was too much of a risk for them. The only lights I could see was an occasional tallow candle in someone's window. Candles were expensive and a rarity in these parts.

Then I heard it. A tune. It came from behind me. In the distance. Someone was whistling.

My breath stilled in my throat. I stopped for a moment and turned, but there was no one there. It was so very dark there were no shadows to discern, so I could not see who it was, but I guessed it was from a man walking behind me, the person I had perhaps imagined as I walked down the Tottenham Court Road. Why had he followed me down the alleyway if it was not to do me harm?

As I walked the whistling continued, neither getting closer or further away. I frowned. Perhaps he was trying to frighten me. If it were the case he had succeeded. I tried to pick up the tune being whistled but it was no song I recognised.

A fog had begun to descend and I swallowed, feeling tears pricking at my eyelids. Returning to Charlotte Street with tears on my cheeks would not be the way to return. My breath came in short sharp bursts as I hurried through the alley. I was terrified I was to be killed, that Stride would find my body, battered, mutilated in a dank, dark alleyway in the fetid maze of the rookery. And then there was Violet. She would be left alone with just her memories and no one to take care of her. What had I done? How reckless I had been to think a women such as I could pass myself off as a man from the rookeries amongst these thieves and vagabonds.

Nausea swelled up into my chest and I thought I would vomit. The whistling was still there, yet the sound wasn't getting closer. I frowned and stopped running. I suddenly got a surge of courage. Who was this person to frighten me when I had done nothing wrong. I had simply gone into the Whistle and Flute. No one but Bessie knew what I was about and why I was at St Giles. No, I wanted to question this person. He had no right to follow me, and no right to frighten me out of my wits.

The whistling stopped. I waited to hear any sound. There was nothing. Had I imagined it? I turned and began to walk again. There it was. The whistling, but it was getting further away. I stopped walking again and waited. The whistling continued until it could no more be discerned. I was alone.

I walked again, slower this time, and came out of the other side of the alleyway, making my way to a wall where I stopped and bent over double. My head was buzzing with fear and my breathing was jagged and uneven. My heart thumped as though trying to make its way out of my chest. I waited a few moments to calm down, then saw a corner I recognised. It would take me back to Rathbone Place.

On the corner of Rathbone Place were a number of young women. They were sauntering along the pavement, calling out to any man who passed, even trying to grab the arms of some. There was nothing for it. I had to pass them, and after the fright I had just experienced would be nothing to me.

As I got closer one of them ran across the pavement towards me. Her face was marbled with pox scabs and her body seemed withered and spent. She wore no coat in the appalling weather, but only a low cut dress which revealed her withered breasts. Her clothes were filthy, as though she'd been rolling about in the ordure beneath our feet. It occurred to me it was probably what she had been doing bearing in mind her trade. Underneath the awfulness of her appearance I could see she was young, but had been so badly affected by her craft she resembled a much older woman.

'Rub yer tummy, guvnor,' she wheedled in a thin voice as she grabbed my arm. 'Just a penny for a glimpse of 'eaven, ducky.'

I wrenched my arm away, thinking the only place the girl would take anyone was hell, particularly if they caught the pox from her, which was likely. 'No thanks.'

'Suit yerself,' she cried. 'There's plenty who will. Yer don't know what yer missin','

'Neither do you,' I thought and I couldn't help but chuckle.

I crossed Goodge Street and turned into Charlotte Street. Never was I so grateful to see a place, a strange thing to say bearing in mind how riven with filth and danger it was.

I understood then. Charlotte Street, and St Giles in particular, may have been a den of vagabonds, thieves and illegal activity, but it was also home to many, thousands in fact. The houses were so full of people it sometimes felt difficult to breathe, but the inhabitants predicament was thanks to those who had built New Oxford Street through St Giles, their thinking utterly miscalculated. They had surmised dividing the rookery in half would break up the dealings there. Of course, it hadn't. The building of the road had simply pushed the criminals together because they had nowhere else to go, and the ordinary families had suffered because of it.

As I got closer to the court I heard screaming. I broke into a run, praying nothing had happened to Bessie. One could never know anything for certain in these environs. The unexpected and unwanted could happen. I knew this now.

I ran into the court where a fire was still burning. I was surprised. It had gone ten o'clock at night and at this time the inhabitants were usually inside. There was a group of people standing around the fire, two of them Bessie and Sylvie. The screaming had not abated and was coming from one of the houses in the court. Bessie saw me and beckoned me over.

'Wos goin' on?' I said gruffly, reverting to my new persona.

'It's Kate,' said Bessie, 'yer know, the young girl what got pregnant. It's 'er time but we fink somethin's gone wrong. She's bin like this fer hours.'

'She'll need a doctor,' I said. 'Ain't there anyone 'ere who does the midwifin' stuff?'

'Yeah,' answered Sylvie, 'but she's next to bleedin' useless. Keeps givin' 'er 'erbs or stuff, leaves, all chopped up. What bloody good's that goin' ter do? She'll pop 'er clogs, you mark my words. We'll be carryin' 'er out of 'ere in a box...an' 'er baby.'

"Ow old is she?' I asked.

'Fifteen,' answered Bessie. 'The bloke what got 'er up the duff did a runner. 'E ain't bin seen fer months.'

The screaming was getting louder and I couldn't imagine what the poor young girl was going through. I dragged Bessie away from the fire.

'I know someone,' I whispered.

Bessie frowned. 'Who?'

'A friend. He works at the apothecary in Great Russell Street.'

She pulled a face. 'Right.' She nodded and put her hands patronisingly on her hips. 'Well-thought out, Edwin. What we s'posed to do fer money? I s'pose this is one of yer 'igh-falutin' friends is it?'

'You won't need money but we need to get her there.'

Bessie shook her head and blew out a breath. 'It's all we got ain't it. She'll die if we don't do somethin.' She walked across to Sylvie who was still warming herself by the fire, and said something in her ear. Sylvie looked across at me, then called out to one of the men.

'Oi, Marcus. We need to use your barrer.'

Marcus joined Sylvie and Bessie. 'What fer?' I heard him ask. Sylvie leant up to him and whispered something in his ear. Marcus looked behind her to me, then nodded. He went out of the court and came back pushing a precarious old barrow, then called up some of the other men. Sylvie and Bessie went inside and I followed them. They went up to the first floor armed with some threadbare blankets and a cup of water. Marcus and the other men waited outside with the barrow, then at Sylvie's word they went upstairs and lifted Kate, still screaming, from a palliasse on the floor, brought her swollen body down the rickety wooden stairs and placed her as gently as they could in the barrow.

Kate was distraught. Her face was bright red and covered in sweat. She'd vomited down the front of her dress and every few minutes she screamed with pain.

'I want me Ma,' she cried. 'I want me Ma.'

'You ain't got a Ma,' said Bessie gently, 'but I'm the next best thing. 'Old onto my 'and, and squeeze it if you 'ave to. Edwin knows someone. We're takin' yer there.'

'I don't want ter go,' Kate cried.

'You ain't got a choice, darlin',' cried Bessie. 'You 'ave to go. Now try and 'ang on. We'll get yer there as soon as we can.'

Two men handled the cart, pushing it out of the court and down Charlotte Street. Bessie and I went with them while Sylvie stayed in the court, patting everyone down and explaining what was happening. The cobbles did Kate no favours. She clearly felt every bump and divot, screaming as the cart was pushed over each one.

Marcus and his men were trying to be careful, but with every scream from Kate they hastened the cart with its wooden wheels down Rathbone Street. We arrived at Bedford Square, where instead of taking the road, they pushed the cart into the square, cutting off the corners which I'm sure they hoped would shorten the journey. Gower Street was next and then, thankfully, I saw the entrance to Great Russell Street.

The shops were closed, but there were the regular prostitutes and villains haunting the pavements. We paid no mind to them. I pushed my way to the front of the little parade and knocked on the door of the apothecary. The same nurse as I had met before answered, although she would never have remembered our meeting, dressed as I was.

'Yes? Can I 'elp yer?'

'Is Mr Horrocks workin' tonight?'

'He is. Who wants 'im?'

I wanted to say Lily Pond but I stopped myself just in time. 'We've got an emergency. We need 'is 'elp.' Just as I said this Kate released another scream of pain. The nurse poked her head out of the door and raised her eyebrows.

'You'd better bring her in. I'll tell Mr Horrocks you're 'ere.'

I made a grab for her arm, then pulled my hand away at her look of disgust. 'I'm sorry,' I said, releasing her arm. 'I must speak with 'im first.' She nodded, then directed Bessie, Marcus and the others to where they should take Kate. They lifted her from the cart and laid her on the low table in the waiting room.

'Where's Mr Horrocks?' I asked her.

She pointed to a door. 'In there,' she said. 'It's where the medicines are made up, but I don't think you're allowed in there.'

'It's alright,' I replied. 'I'm a friend.'

She looked me up and down frowning as if to say, ' I don't think so,' but simply shrugged. I went to the door, opened it, and poked my head through to see Wilfred sitting at a table making up small bags of medicines. He glanced up, and when he saw me rose from his chair.

'You're not allowed in here, sir,' he said. 'My nurse at the desk will attend you.'

'Wilfred,' I said, reverting to my usual voice. I went into the room and closed the door behind me. 'Wilfred. It's Lily.'

His mouth dropped open and he staggered backwards. He came towards me and looked deep into my eyes as though this was the only thing which could convince me I was who I said I was. 'But, Lily,

...why?'

I shook my head. 'I can't explain now. It's too long a story, but I will. I promise. There's a fifteen-year-old girl in the waiting room come to her time, but there's something wrong. Can you see her?' He nodded, his eyes still on me, his eyebrows knotted into a frown. They were still on me as he went through the door. It was as though he could not believe his own eyesight.

He went out into the front office, then went into the waiting room where Kate was sobbing as though her heart would break. Wilfred nodded to the others, then got to his haunches and examined her.

'There's a room through there,' he said to Marcus and Bessie. 'Can you lift her onto the examination couch?' Marcus nodded, then waving the others away, lifted Kate into his arms as though she were a baby. One of the other men opened the door, and we watched as Marcus lay Kate onto the couch as gently as he could.

'The baby is breach,' said Wilfred. 'She won't deliver like that, not without some intervention.'

'What's that mean?' asked Bessie. I wanted to know too.

'The baby is lodged in the birth canal, bottom first. It needs to be a headfirst if the girl is to be delivered of her baby successfully.'

'Or?' asked Bessie quietly. Wilfred shrugged.

'Can yer do it?' I asked him reverting to Edwin. He looked at me and swallowed, clearly unnerved by my new persona.

He nodded. 'Yes, but it will be painful. The baby needs to be turned. There isn't room for a delivery through the normal channel if it continues to be pushed. The baby will die of lack of oxygen and the mother will certainly die. I could give her some watered down laudanum, although only a little because she'll need to deliver tonight if the turning is successful. You'll stay with her?' he asked Bessie. Bessie nodded.

Wilfred went into the surgery with Bessie while Marcus and I sat in the waiting room. The other men took the cart back to the court.

'Yer don't 'ave to stay, Marcus,' I said to him. 'I'll wait fer Bessie and walk 'er 'ome when the time comes.'

'You sure?' he asked, a look of relief passing across his face.

I nodded. 'This might take a while.'

'If yer sure,' he said. 'I ain't good in places like this. Gives me the willies it do.'

I chuckled with him. 'Go 'ome then. We don't want two of yer laid out do we?'

He smiled and got up, laying a hand on my shoulder. 'She'd be dead if it weren't fer you, Edwin. It won't be forgotten.' I shrugged and nodded.

Hours later, I don't know how many because I'd laid across the benches in the waiting room and drifted off to sleep, the door to the surgery opened and a wail of annoyance reached my ears. It was the cry of a baby who'd unceremoniously been moved from the warmth of its comfortable place in its mother's womb, and been born into the harshness of a cruel world. Wilfred was grinning broadly, and as I bent forward I could see Bessie inside the surgery cradling the babe.

'Did it go to plan, Wilfred?' I asked him, my eyes sticky from sleep. I rubbed them with the heels of my hands to get some life into them.

Wilfred rubbed his hands together. 'It did...a boy. Guess what she's called him?'

I chuckled. 'It wouldn't be Wilfred by any chance would it?'

He smiled. 'Indeed. A fine name.'

I nodded and rose from the bench. 'Thank you, Wilfred. She would have died, wouldn't she?'

'With no intervention they would have both died. You did the right thing, Li...Edwin, bringing them here.'

'I will explain,' I whispered. 'When this is all over.'

He put his hands in his pockets and stared at me. 'I expect it's complicated.'

'It is rather.'

He pursed his lips. 'You're a brave...person,' he said, shaking his head, presumably because he couldn't use my real name. 'You have my admiration. Please remember...I will always help you. If you would like I could come to St Giles with a nurse. Do you think they would accept it?'

I nodded. 'After what you've done today I should think you'll be crowned King Wilfred of St Giles. I'm sure a visit will be well received.'

He guffawed. 'King Wilfred, eh? Wait until I tell Mother. I've always been her little prince.'

I chuckled. 'Don't I know it.'

Bessie and I walked arm in arm down Great Russell Street. It was five o'clock in the morning and it was still dark. The market stalls were just being set up. Thankfully the prostitutes had gone to wherever home was, but the doorways and doorsteps were still being used as beds.

'What a night,' breathed Bessie. 'That babe did not want to be born.' She glanced up at me. 'He's a wonderful man, isn't he? One to be admired.'

'Yes, he is. I can't even think about what would have happened if we hadn't taken Kate to him. It's too awful to imagine.'

'She wouldn't be the first,' Bessie answered. 'It's 'appened before, even since I've been at St Giles. Women die in childbirth every day in London's rookeries.'

'Oh, Bessie. What kind of world is this?'

She shrugged. 'Don't ask me. From what I see the poor get poorer and the rich get richer. There's no way out of it, Edwin, not for the poor any'ow. Dunno 'ow it will ever change. There's no stairway to 'eaven from what I can see.'

'How long will you stay there? At St Giles I mean?'

'I dunno. I've bin thinking about it. I reckon once we've put away these blokes what are mixed up with this antiquities thing, I'll do somethin' else.'

'Have you anything in mind?'

She smiled up at me. 'I 'ave, Edwin.'

'Oh?' I glanced down at her.

'A detective agency, one of me own. I can do the jobs I want ter do, not the ones Jeremiah pushes me into. This one 'as been the 'ardest yet an' I don't fink I can go on much longer. I want ter go 'ome to me own bed at night, wiv me own pillows and blankets, not them what's been used by someone else. I want regular meals. I want ter keep me own pay and not 'ave to give it to the likes of Sylvie.' She looked up at me again. 'Yer do know the money what everyone gives 'er goes into 'er own pocket don't yer?'

I nodded. 'I did wonder.'

'She just 'ands over a bit of it, enough to keep Doris quiet. The rest she keeps.'

'Is that fair?'

'Nuthin's fair, ducks. No such fing as fair.'

As we went into Rathbone Street Bessie startled.

'What is it?' I asked her.

She put a finger to her lips. 'Listen,' she whispered.

We remained quiet for a moment. Then I heard it. Whistling. 'I've heard it before.' I whispered. 'Last night when I was coming back from the Whistle and Flute.'

'Everyone's 'eard it but no one knows who it is. Once 'eard never forgotten.'

'So no one has seen him?'

She shook her head. 'He's known as the Whistling Man. He always seems to be around when somethin's goin' on. It's like he can smell trouble.'

'Do you think he's dangerous? He frightened me half out of my wits last night.'

'No one seems ter know.'

'It's a man then?'

'Oh, yeah. No woman would whistle round 'ere. Yer know the sayin' don't yer?' I shook my head. 'A whistling woman and a crowin' hen, ain't no good for beast nor men.'

'Oh.'

'Superstitious, see. There's a lot of gypsies in St Giles and Seven Dials. Some of them come over from Ireland. They brought their superstitions wiv 'em.'

Bessie took my hand and we ran down Rathbone Street until we got to Charlotte Street where we bent over to relieve the stitches in our sides.

'Thank God we're 'ome. That weren't nice were it? No wonder you were scared. I feel like I've joined some sort a club. And it ain't just us. Them in the Seven Dials 'ave 'eard it as well. It's like someone's sent 'im to frighten the britches off us. As if we ain't got enough to be frightened of. I've never 'eard 'im before. D'int like it. Loads of others in the rookery 'ave.'

I stared at her in astonishment. 'Haven't you?'

She shook her head. 'Now I know what everyone's afraid of. Eerie wer'n't it?'

'It's very threatening. Like an apparition.'

'A what?'

'A ghost.'

'Oh, shut up, Edwin. I don't want ter fink about it.'

She straightened up and threw me a look which told me not to mention it again, then made her way into the court. I followed her, wondering what could possibly happen next.

Chapter 16

Sylvie ran into the house looking excited. Her eyes were bright and she clutched her shawl around her, her hands shaking with anticipation.

'The Smolletts 'ave turned up. Jim Smollett's bringin' 'is bruvvers 'ere. Early ain't they? Trouble is it's my mornin' for the laundry. I prob'ly won't 'ere what they've got to say. You can tell me after, can't yer Doris?'

Doris tutted. 'Why are we int'rested in what they've got to say? I'm more int'rested in 'ow to get the washing dry what I done yest'y. When I took it off the line it were frozen solid. Can't yer take it down the laundry, Sylvie?'

'No, I ain't taking anymore of yer stuff for yer. I've been caught once already. If they catch me again I'll be out a there for good. They've brought them new girls in from Seven Dials ter do some of our shifts an' it's gettin' worse. Tryin' to take our jobs they are. Bleedin' bitches. I'll give 'em what for, that I will.'

Doris sighed and I knew how she felt. I'd had a restless night. I had an increasing need to scratch almost every part of my body and I was certain I'd caught fleas or lice. I shuddered to think of it, but I assumed most people in the rookery were infested. Some of the children were running alive with them. They could be seen scuttling about quite clearly in their hair, but it didn't appear to bother them. The news about the Smolletts certainly bothered me, however.

'Who are they?' I asked as nonchalantly as I could.

'No one you need to worry about, Edwin,' Sylvie answered. She seemed to be almost proprietary about them.

I shrugged, making it look as though I didn't care. 'Makes no never-mind to me. Just makin' conversation. No need to get upset about it.'

Sylvie stared at me. 'I ain't getting' upset, Edwin. Yer just need to keep yer nose out of fings what don't concern yer. The Smolletts ain't to be trifled wiv, let me tell yer that. There's no int'rest there for you, mister.'

I heard Doris tut again. 'I ain't in'trested in 'em. All I'm int'rested in is 'ow I'm s'posed to get the washing dry what I did yesty.' Sylvie tutted with impatience and ran out of the door, slamming it in her wake.

A fire had been lit in the centre of the court and everyone was standing around it, rubbing their hands and stamping their feet for warmth. As I was so tired I felt colder than ever. All I could think of was home and a bath of hot, lavender water. Would I ever be clean again? I would have to scrub my skin until it was raw if I were to ever to get rid of the fleas.

Bessie wrapped two shawls around her before going outside into the icy air. I found the coat I had worn previously, thrown into a corner of the room. It smelt musty, and of something I couldn't discern, but I put it on. Someone had obviously worn it recently, but it was too cold outside to go without. At length, the Smolletts arrived in the court, striding through the ramshackle court entrance as though they owned it, stopping just inside, hands on their hips, feet apart.

I know they didn't own the court. The landlord was a Harry Andrews who owned most of Charlotte Street. I had made it my business to find out about the man before I made my home in Charlotte Street. He was a lawyer, a man of means and contacts. Extremely wealthy and not a care in the world for the people who paid for his slums.

Bessie and I stood on the edge of the gathering until we could find a path through to the fire where I stood gratefully. It was the warmest I'd felt since I'd arrived. I immediately recognised the man who had chased me down Parker Street, Jim Smollett, and the one who stood next to him was the other, his chest puffed up with importance. Behind them were other men. Each one carried a long pole. It was clear why. Any dissent and they would have used them on anyone who disagreed with them. The implied threat was plain to see. The Smollett I recognised, Jim Smollett, stepped forward.

'We've come 'ere to condole wiv yer about the loss of Ronnie. He were a good bloke. Everyone up at the Seven Dials liked 'im. We're very sorry for your loss and 'ope your grieving will be short lived.' No one said anything...just a murmur of low sound. Jim Smollett's countenance suddenly changed. 'Also, we've 'eard there's a vicious rumour bein' put about that one of us in Seven Dials is responsible for 'is murder. We don't like 'earing fings like that and we're 'oping the rumour weren't started 'ere. You wouldn't say anyfing like that about us, would yer?' he cried, his voice like gravel. Again no one answered. 'Would yer?' he said even louder, his voice carrying through the cold air.

'Nah,' someone answered. 'We wouldn't say anyfing like that, Jim,' someone at the front answered.

'Yer'd better not, cos if we 'ere about it they'll 'ave us ter deal wiv. Get it?' I looked around at the men's faces, waiting for someone to say something. 'Get it?' he cried again.

'Yeah, we get it, Jim,' someone said.

'Even though we know it were you what done 'im,' mumbled a voice behind us. Bessie and I turned and looked into the face of a big man standing behind us.

'Yer want ter keep them words in yer gob, Dennis,' Bessie said, sotto voce. 'Sayin' fings like that'll get you in ter trouble. Yer'll end up like Ronnie.'

Dennis hawked up and spat a glob of phlegm onto the filthy cobbles. 'Yeah, well, we'll see about that won't we.' Bessie stared at him for a long moment then glanced at me. I closed my eyes momentarily and she shook her head.

'An' anuvver fing,' Jim Smollett continued. 'Yer'll 'ave visitors 'ere today, one of my business associates and 'is friend, and their women.'

'Why?' asked a brave soul from the centre of the gathering.

'They want ter look at yer and this place.'

'Why?' asked another man.

'We ain't animals in a fecking zoo, Smollett,' said another.

'You're what I say you are. Don't anyone go near 'em, and don't try and speak to 'em or you'll 'ave me ter deal wiv, so stow yer tongues.' He looked round at everyone in the courtyard with narrowed eyes, hard and sharp as flint, then turned on his heel and pushed his way through his men. They in turn threw hard looks towards the crowd and followed him out.

When the Smolletts and their gang left, the courtyard was quiet. I observed the faces of the men and women, some of them hugging their children close to them in dismay. These people knew what they were, the lowest of the low, the forgotten, the disenfranchised. To be put on show like specimens to be observed and studied could only bring them down even further if it were possible, and for money; money they would certainly not see.

Some walked away shaking their heads. Others formed small groups, talking rapidly between themselves; disgruntled and gesticulating. The women huddled together around the fire, some silent, some using words I'd never heard before.

''Why, Bessie?' I asked her. We'd been left alone by the door to the house, watching as people assimilated the Smollett's plans.

'Money,' she said, rubbing a forefinger and thumb together. 'It won't go down well. Caused a load a trouble last time they tried it.'

'Do you think that's all it is? I have a feeling I know who the business associate is.'

She glanced up at me. 'The bloke from the carriage?' I nodded. 'Best wait and see. I wonder who the other one is what's coming 'ere.'

'I need to see Stride.'

She shrugged. 'Good luck with that.'

'Why?'

'He don't meet up wiv 'is agents.'

I crossed my arms in front of me. 'So I'll go to the station. He'll have to see me then won't he?'

'What d'you want to see him about?'

'I want to know why he hasn't been to the house in Parker Street and arrested the occupants.'

'He'll 'ave 'is reasons.'

'Really. Well, I want to know what they are.'

She chuckled. 'Yer plucky, ain't yer, Edwin?'

I grinned. 'When I need to be, Bessie. And this is one of those times.'

Chapter 17

A couple of hours later Jim Smollett returned with the so-called business associate and his friends. They'd paused at the entrance, their faces contorted with disgust. One of the women had a handkerchief held up to her face to prevent the miasma from the odours reaching her. I observed the men. I startled when I saw the other visitors.

Detective Superintendent Welham stood at the entrance with his hands behind his back, his face curled into an expression of disgust. The man who stood next to him was the man who had alighted the carriage in Parker Street. The other visitor was Wilfred Horrocks.

My mouth dropped open and Bessie stared at me. 'Edwin?'

I turned and faced the other direction before remembering I was not in the court dressed as Lily Pond. I was safe. Detective Superintendent Welham would not recognise me.

'What's he doing here?'

'Who? Who do you mean,' asked Bessie as she preened her neck to get a closer look at the visitors through the gathering of people in the court.

'The small man is the one from the carriage. The other is Detective Superintendent Welham...Stride's superior. Have you not met him?'

Bessie shook her head. 'Maybe it's an undercover thing? And why is your friend 'ere?'

'To give an appearance of respect I imagine.' I shook my head. 'Wilfred is a good man. He would never get involved in anything criminal. Look at his expression. He's in a state of devastation and shock.'

We turned to observe the visitors again. Where Welham, the man from the carriage, and their wives were sneering and scornful, and behaving in a condescending manner to those who lived in the court, Wilfred had his hand up to his mouth and was shaking his head in sorrow. His eyes were filled with tears and my heart went out to him. I stepped forward to make myself known to him. He saw me and shook his head, a tear rolling down his cheek. What he was observing in the court had overcome him. I shook my head in despair and he did the same. Suddenly, Jim Smollett rushed towards me, brandishing a cudgel.

'Get away,' he snarled.

I swallowed hard and stepped back. My head began to ache. Something clicked in my brain. I suddenly realised what we were up against.

'I need to see Stride. Can you organise something?' I murmured to Bessie.

Bessie pulled her shawl closer around her ample bosom. 'Only in circumstances what're extreme, 'e says.'

'I would say this is as extreme as it gets.'

The "visit" lasted just short of an hour. Welham and the others walked around the perimeter of the court, peering into the broken-down houses, shying away from children who ran about the cobbles for fear of catching something, sneering with disgust at the dead rats and nomadic dogs and cats that were part of rookery life.

I couldn't take my eyes away from Detective Superintendent Welham. Was he there simply as an interested observer? Something told me it was not the case bearing in mind the conversation we had had at the Agar Street police station. He detested these people, and had no compassion for their situation whatsoever. He had a small notebook with him and was making notes each time he looked into one of the houses.

He even attempted to go into the yards where the privies were. His wife had clawed at his arm, clearly trying to dissuade him from entering such a disease-ridden place, but he had shaken off her hand and stepped through the alleyway. Why would he go there? Why was he there at all, a policeman in the St Giles rookery? And with the Smolletts. It was unheard of. No policeman who wanted to remain in one piece ever ventured into a rookery.

It suddenly dawned on me. The people of St Giles did not know who he was. They didn't realise he was from the constabulary. I did because I had met him in the other world, the world of ownership, of control over one's life...and choices. There was no choice to be had in the rookery...and the police were hated. No policeman would ever venture into a rookery alone, not if they wanted to live.

I felt someone approach as I leant against the house, and stand by my elbow. It was Sylvie. I knew what she was after.

'You got any money for me, Edwin? Me finks you're a bit light, mate. Not going well outside the 'otels on Park Lane?'

'It's the wevver, Sylvie,' I said gruffly. 'They comes out the 'otels and gets straight in ter the carriages. Don't get a chance to get nuffin from 'em. Don't worry. I'll get some.'

'Aw,' she said, her voice gentler than before. She rubbed a finger down my cheek which made me shudder. 'Poor Edwin.' She looked about the court, presumably to make sure no one was watching, then grabbed my hand and shoved it between her legs.

'Meet me in the yard, Edwin,' she purred into my ear. 'I've fancied you from the start. We can forget all about money if you make a woman of me. You won't regret it I promise yer. I'm better than any a them prossies down on Drury Lane. Got experience see.'

I pulled my hand from where she held it between her legs and walked away. This was something I hadn't accounted for and it couldn't have happened with a more adversarial woman. Sylvie had a certain amount of authority in the Charlotte Street court. To displease her would be a mistake. Had I been a real man I likely would have known what to do, but if I had followed her into the yard she would have quickly discovered I wasn't who I said I was. The thought disgusted me.

I frowned. There was something not right about it, her sudden interest in me. The visitors were still poking their noses into life in the court. Were we to put on a sordid show for them? Was it prearranged? Something to underline the fact those in the rookeries were no worse than animals; mammals who copulated whenever desire overtook them. I took in a shuddering breath and went to find Bessie.

'I must speak to Stride and fast,' I said. 'There's something odd going on here.'

'The Amethyst Café on Percy Street. Make it just before dusk. It's rough round there, but no one will take any notice of yer. He'll meet yer in there.'

'How do you know he'll be there?'

'He'll be there.'

I loitered around Percy Street for about half an hour until I saw him go inside. Around me were small gangs of young men with nothing better to do, leaning up against lampposts, smoking, then hawking up and adding to the filth on the cobbles. Stride was wearing an old black overcoat and a less than new Homburg hat. I supposed he was trying to fit in but it wasn't quite authentic. I made a mental note to advise him.

After a few minutes I followed him inside the café. A few tables had customers sitting at them, sipping tea and making them last so they could stay in the warm. I could hardly blame them. It seemed an age since I had felt comfortably warm. My body didn't feel like my own. The tips of my ears, fingers, and toes, were permanently freezing. I sat at his table and he ran his eyes over me.

'Edwin?'

'Yes,' I said quietly. I didn't want to use my gruff voice with him. It was just too embarrassing. 'I needed to see you.'

'So I hear. Would you like some coffee, and something to eat perhaps?' I nodded and be beckoned to the waitress. 'Two large mugs of coffee and two hot meat pies please.' I almost salivated at the thought of it. 'What's the urgency? You've heard something?'

'Seen something.' He dipped his chin, encouraging me to continue. 'Detective Superintendent Welham.' Stride leant back in his chair and rubbed his chin thoughtfully. 'And...why have you not arrested Jim Smollett and his gang? He walks into the courts as though he owns them, although I know he doesn't, no matter how much money he's making from the antiquities he's stealing.'

'He's not stealing them, Edwin. He stores and fences them for someone else. Someone else steals them. We're fairly sure it's a family member of the murdered man, Ronnie Dines. We think they've got contacts.'

'It doesn't answer my question.' I frowned. 'Surely it would be worth taking him in and questioning him.'

Stride nodded. 'We've thought about it, but there are bigger fish to fry.'

'Like who? Whom is it you're waiting for? I can only guess you're hoping they'll make a mistake.' The waitress brought over the coffee and pies. I instantly grabbed one of the mugs and placed my cold hands around it. The warmth from the mug was almost too much to bear. 'Can't you tell me who you suspect? I could watch for them.' I took a sip of the hot coffee and then a bite from the pie. It tasted how

I imagined heaven to taste. I couldn't remember when I'd last eaten.

I could see Stride was arguing with himself about whether to tell me. 'I need to know more, Stride. I need to know exactly what's going on.'

Stride nodded and took a deep breath.

'At each end of this crime are people with money. First of all there are those who get the Egyptian antiquities from where they've been stored. We don't know how they're doing it. Egyptian artefacts are big business at present, the biggest, and the people involved in their acquisition and sales know it. The artefacts are brought into the country by the geologists and explorers who pay for the expeditions to Egypt. They take men with them who know what they're looking for. Once they've discovered what they want, they either pay the owners a pittance, or if they're dug up simply load them on to carts and have them transported here.'

'Where are they kept?'

'Warehouses on the docks. They're stolen then kept and stored, which is what you saw being delivered in Parker Street. The Smolletts are a gang of thugs and murderers. Their only thought is to make money and they bully people to help them, particularly those who need money and can't say no, like those in the rookeries at St Giles, Parker Street, and Seven Dials. Also, there are people involved in the operation one wouldn't expect.'

I stared at him and my heart sank. 'Not Welham?' Stride bit his lip and I gasped. 'Do you think it was why he was in Charlotte Street this morning?'

'Was he? Then I have no doubt of it.'

'So he and Smollett are in it together?'

'They're in *part* of it together. Remember I said there were people with money at both ends?' I nodded. 'At the beginning you have the aristocracy who fund the expeditions to Egypt and the transportation of artefacts to this country. In the middle you have Smollett, his gang, and the middle-class men who want more and who are willing to dabble in criminal activity to get it, like the man you saw in the carriage, and Welham. At the other end you have the men with real money, who want Egyptian artefacts at a price they're willing to pay and don't care where they get them from. As far as they're concerned they're doing nothing wrong. If we discover who they are they'll plead ignorance, say they paid what they were asked, and get away with it. In actuality they're buying stolen goods, and believe me, they know it.'

'Will they get away with it.'

'I expect so. You'd be surprised at who's willing to purchase one of these things, lawyers, judges, high-ranking policemen...the list goes on. They pay each other off because they're all in it together. If one gets caught they go to the lawyer who's already involved, and he'll use a judge who's also involved. It's just the way it works.'

'So are Welham and the other man the go-betweens, between Smollett's gang and the people who buy the goods at the other end?'

'Yep, that's about the size of it?'

'You knew about Welham?'

'Welham's been in our sights for months.' He shook his head. 'It makes me sick to my stomach to think one of our own is involved in this.'

'He's certainly an unpleasant man.'

'He's a criminal, Edwin. We must be cleverer than he is if we're to catch him...and his cohorts.'

'Do we know who the man in the carriage is?'

'We think he's Welham's lawyer, Anthony Greenwood. He works for the great and good, but he's as crooked as they come.'

'What now?'

'You've done well, Edwin. Spotting Welham at the rookery gives us a bit of evidence.'

'There's something else.'

'Go on.'

'There's a man called Stinky Ralph. He's a tosher. Grubs around in the sewers looking for lost coin and jewellery. He's involved somehow. I went back to the house in Parker Street dressed as Edwin and managed to gain admittance. Inside were wooden crates with lettering I couldn't translate. Not French, or German, or a language I recognised. Also a sarcophagus with hieroglyphics and an Egyptian eye. The rag wrapped around it had come loose. The housekeeper who had let me in wasn't thrilled I'd seen it.'

'It's a mummy,' said Stride. 'One's been reported as stolen from a warehouse on Katherine Dock.'

'I thought it might be. I wasn't sure if there was one inside. I would have loved to take a look but I didn't have time. While I was there Stinky Ralph knocked on the door. I heard the housekeeper say to him they would let him know when they needed him. What might his part be in this?'

Stride shook his head. 'I don't know, Edwin, but we've made progress. All we need to do is to join the dots. Stinky Ralph, or Ralph

Pearson, is known to us. He's a petty thief and pickpocket, although God knows why. Toshers make more money than anyone, even the mudlarks.'

I stared at him in astonishment. 'Really? I'm surprised.'

'Haven't you heard the saying, Edwin? Where's there's muck there's money.' I hadn't but it seemed rather fitting.

I took the last bite of pie and drained my coffee mug.

'How's Violet?'

'Missing you.'

My heart lurched. 'And Truffle?'

'The same.'

'You've been there?'

'I have.'

'I want to go back, just for an hour or so.'

'I don't recommend it, Edwin. If you're followed...'

'I won't be. Anyway, I need money. There's a woman at Charlotte Street who says I must pay my way if I want to be fed, or take her behind the privies and have my way with her as recompense.' Stride put his hand across his mouth and stifled a laugh. 'It's not funny, Stride. I have an admirer and not the appropriate kind for Lily. If Sylvie finds out about me goodness knows what they'll do to me. She's as hard as they come and she would let the whole world know if she discovered I was a woman. The punishment wouldn't be enjoyable I can assure you.'

'You're not Lily.'

'No. I know. At least not for now. I miss her too.'

Chapter 18

I didn't go back to Charlotte Street. I stayed in the Amethyst Café where Stride paid for another coffee and an iced bun. I sat at the table alone, nibbling and sipping as slowly as I could, so I could stay in the warmth.

I realised I must have made a rather attractive young man taking into consideration Sylvie's advances to me, and the look on the waitresses face every time I inadvertently caught her eye. She was flirting with me in a most lascivious way, fluttering her eyelashes, and occasionally pulling down the front of her dress so the top of her breasts were exposed. In the end I kept my head down while trying to keep my eye on the wall clock behind the counter.

At six-thirty I decided to leave and make my way to Harley Street. I couldn't wait to see Violet and Truffle, and Meg too, although I wasn't sure they'd feel the same way about me. They had seen me before I left when I had been dressed in the clothes Meg had procured for me, but I looked...and smelt vastly different to how I did then. It was difficult to believe it was only a few days before I had left my beloved home and met Bessie at the start of my adventure into the unknown.

When I saw the street sign for Harley Street a wave of love and excitement went through me. I sauntered down the street on the other side from the house, enjoying just looking at the houses. When I saw my home I stopped to admire it. The curtains were still drawn, and I could see Meg in the drawing room. I expected she was attending to Violet, readying her for dinner. I couldn't help but wonder what Cook had prepared for that evening's repast.

My reveries regarding my previous life had numbed my concentration. In a flash someone grabbed my arm and dragged me to a small, fenced garden at the end of the street, for the use of those who lived in Harley Street. I tried to pull away, to turn to see who it was who had taken hold of me, but whoever it was, was so much stronger than I.

'Keep still,' he growled, for it was man, of that I had no doubt. 'You'll do yerself no favours by tryin' ter get away. Keep still...Edwin.'

He knew my name. I stopped wriggling and allowed him to drag me into the garden where he threw me to the ground and stood over me, menacing and with his fists clenched. It was Jim Smollett.

'Who are yer?'

'Edwin Smith,' I answered.

'Yeah, but who are yer really?'

'I dunno what yer mean, mate. That's me name.'

'Yer new around 'ere, ain't yer?' I nodded. 'Where yer come from?'

'Spitalfields.'

'So what yer doin' around 'ere? You stayin' at St Giles?' I nodded again. 'And yer know Sylvie?'

'Not really.'

'Not really. Wos 'at mean?'

'It means I don't know 'er. Me cousin is Bessie Clacket.'

'Fancies yer though don't she?'

'Who does?'

'Sylvie.'

'Nah, yer got it wrong, mate.'

''Ave I? But you was talking to 'er, standing close like. I saw yer when I was at the court in Charlotte Street. Gettin' friendly weren't yer?'

'She was asking me fer money.'

'Why?'

'She says I'm light. If I want ter stay at Charlotte Street I've got ter give up me coin.'

Smollett grinned at this, revealing his brown and broken teeth. "At's my girl.'

His thoughts wandered off to somewhere then he looked back at me. He bent down and grabbed the front of my coat. He began to speak and his rancid breath was warm on my face. It was as much as I could do not to retch.

Now, you listen to me,' he said, his nose almost touching mine. 'Yer stay away from Sylvie,' he growled. 'She's my girl. All'us as been. Yer give 'er the coin she asks yer for then yer skedaddle, get it?' I nodded. 'And I don't want yer stayin' too long in Charlotte Street. I don't knows yer, no one does. Been asking around, see. You ain't got no truck wiv anyone apart from Bessie, and make no never mind, I'll be askin' 'er an' all. Catch my drift, Edwin?'

'Course I do. I ain't deaf and I ain't stupid.'

I don't remember anything after that. The last thing I saw was his fist coming towards me and a dreadful pain in my jaw. He had punched me with full force, knocking me out and leaving me on the ground where I lay. I woke later, who knows what time in the evening it was, with a layer of fresh snow on me, and a headache that would have felled Goliath.

I heaved, thankful there was no one else in the small garden to see, then rubbed some of the fresh snow onto my jaw and chin. It helped a little but I knew I would need more than a handful of snow to comfort me.

I pushed myself up, looking for all the world like a drunk person, straightened my back and staggered towards home. I pulled myself up the steps at the front, hanging onto the railings as I went. I reached inside my clothes and pulled out a key which I'd tied to a piece of string and fastened to the bindings around my chest, then opened the front door. I had no idea what time it was, or how long I had been unconscious in the garden, but the light was on in the drawing room, so I guessed Violet had not yet gone to bed.

I stood in the doorframe of the drawing room. Violet was doing what she always did at that time of the evening, her embroidery, her skeins of silk all around her, her forehead furrowed in concentration. Truffle sat next to her on the chaise. He lifted his head and growled, then barked. Violet glanced up and screamed.

'Oh, my God! Oh, my God. Lily! Oh, Lily, what happened to you?' She burst into tears, holding Truffle by his collar to stop him from attacking me. He didn't recognise me, not the sight of me, and certainly not the smell.

'Meg,' Violet cried. 'Quickly, Meg, we need you.' Her voice wobbled with fear and tears. I could see she wanted to come to me but of course, she couldn't. Her disability prevented it, and for the first time I was relieved. I was alive with fleas and stank like the River Thames, and I couldn't bear to think of her coming into contact with such filth.

Meg ran into the drawing room and when she saw me, screamed.

'Oh, my goodness. I'm so sorry, Miss Violet, Miss Lily. You fair put me in shock. I wasn't expectin' to see you, Miss Lily.' She shook her head and walked around me, making sure to keep her distance. She put out a hand then swiftly pulled it away again. 'You're hurt, Miss Lily. 'Ave you bin attacked?'

'I was punched. One of the men from the court thought I was trying to steal his girlfriend.'

Violet gasped. 'But you weren't?'

I chuckled then winced at the pain in my face. 'Of course not. I came to Harley Street to see you both, but I was grabbed from behind and dragged to the communal garden. He knocked me out, quite cold it would seem, although I don't know how long I was out for.'

'You mean you were unconscious, Miss Lily?' said Meg quietly. 'E could 'ave done anythin' to yer.'

'He likely would have if he'd known I was a woman under all this filth, but he thinks I'm a man which probably saved me from being violated.'

'Can you ask Dreyfus to put a bath in Miss Lily's room please, Meg?' Violet asked her. 'And ask Cook, Mildred and the others to fill it with hot water. There's some lavender oil in the cupboard under the stairs...put that in too, and we'll need a stiff hairbrush and a large piece of flannel....oh, and something for that jaw, a piece of ice wrapped in a towel, and some of the liniment I use for my back. It should help with the pain.'

'I'm not sure going back to the rookery smelling of lavender is a good idea, Violet.'

She stared at me in astonishment. 'You're going back?' she cried. 'Why? I thought you'd come home.'

'My original plan was to come here for some of the money I keep in my bedroom for emergencies. It's just coins but I'm expected to pay my way in the rookery. There's not much to eat, but when there is I must eat it, like all the others, or they'll become suspicious.'

'You'll stay here tonight.' It was a statement rather than a question. I shook my head.

'I'm afraid not. If I don't go back tonight they'll give my space to someone else, and Bessie Clacket will give up on me.'

'Space? Is it all you have there? Just a space?'

'Yes, and not a big one.'

She patted the chaise. 'Sit next to me.'

I shook my head. 'Not unless you want the chaise to run with fleas. I've become infested I'm afraid. It's impossible to avoid when one is sleeping with people who are crawling with them.'

'Do you all sleep in the same room?'

I sighed and put my hand against my jaw. The numbness had worn off and the pain was excruciating. I could feel the swelling under my palm and assumed I looked dreadful. 'The rookery is at least as awful as we always thought it would be...and I'm sad to say, much worse.'

Meg returned carrying a pile of soft towels and some bars of carbolic soap. 'I thought you might need these, Miss Lily. Cook says it's the only thing to get rid of the bugs.'

I nodded which made my head hurt. 'I'll have a bath, Violet, and perhaps something to eat, just a sandwich will suffice, then I must go.' Violet nodded, her eyes filling with tears again. 'What time is it?'

Violet looked at her watch. 'Nine o'clock.'

'I have an hour or so, then I must go back to St Giles.' I turned to Meg. 'Has Cook any of the pea and ham soup she makes. I've missed it and it would set me up for a couple of days.'

'A couple of days,' Violet exclaimed. 'Will you not eat again before then?'

I shrugged. 'I don't know, Violet. No one who lives in the rookeries knows when they'll get their next meal.'

'There is some, Miss Lily. She always makes too much. The bath is filled now. If you go upstairs and have your bath I'll come up and wash your hair, and give it a good brushing. We'll get rid of the little buggers.'

I smiled at her. 'But they'll be there next time, Meg.'

'No matter, Miss Lily. It'll make you feel better.'

I held out my hand to Violet and she took it. 'You don't mind?' I asked her.

She gave a small smile, although her eyes were filled with tears. 'You're my sister, Lily. We hold each other's hand.'

I stripped off my clothes and dropped them gratefully onto the floor. Steam from the hot water in the bath filled the room and the smell of lavender was a joy. I dipped my toe into the water. It was hotter than usual but I slipped into the bath, allowing the water to cover my head. It was almost scalding but it felt good, as though I was slaking off the filth, the ordure, the smell; every evidence of life in the St Giles rookery.

I heard the door open and I rose in the water. Meg had brought in the towels and the hairbrush.

'Let me wash your hair, Ma'am,' she said, 'then you can wash yourself with the soap before you go downstairs to eat. Cook is making up a tray for you. You can eat in the drawing room this evening, where it's comfortable, and you and Miss Violet can talk.'

I nodded and she began to lather up the carbolic soap. She scrubbed my head then, the short hair sitting upright. Lice fell into the water and I felt her hand still as she saw them, but she continued scrubbing until my scalp and hair felt new. Pouring a jug of fresh water over my hair, she wrapped it in a towel then left the room while I bathed.

Later on, when I'd dried myself and donned a thick dressing robe, I went down to the drawing room where a tray of hot pea and ham soup and thick slices of fresh bread awaited me. I ate like a woman possessed. I had eaten at the café when I had met Stride, but this was real food, good home-made fare, and I had missed it.

Part of me felt enormously guilty as I wiped the bread around my bowl, a habit I'd picked up from the hovel in Charlotte Street, but I didn't want to waste a drop. I wished all of St Giles could eat food like I had been favoured with, but it seemed an impossibility to even imagine it would ever happen. This was the life all children should have, one of good food, a mother's love, warmth and security, but there was precious little of any of it to be had in the rookeries.

'What's the time?' I asked Violet as I pushed the last piece of bread into my mouth.

She glanced at her watch again. 'Ten o'clock.'

I rose from the chaise and went to the door.

'I'll go out the garden door. At least then the neighbours won't see me. They'll not understand why a ruffian has left our home late in the evening and there will be gossip. I won't come in here again and I won't say goodbye. Not a second time.' I ruffled Truffle's ears and kissed him on the top of the head. 'Look after your mistress, Truffle. I'll be back before you know it.'

Chapter 19

I made my way down Harley Street. When I got to the corner I looked back at my home. The light was still on in the drawing room. I imagined Violet sitting there with Truffle, and she and Meg consoling with each other. It had been harder to leave a second time. I knew what was in front of me.

The snow was thick on the ground and I welcomed it. It lit the streets and the houses in a white sheen that sparkled towards me, and it meant a small amount of safety. There was no one about. I took a breath and summoned up my courage. I should not have been walking the streets after ten o'clock at night. I had already been attacked by Jim Smollett and I wondered if I would survive another assault. My jaw felt huge, and it probably was. It had swollen terribly while I had been sitting with Violet.

Some of the gas lamps had been lit by a man who clearly valued his employment, but some of them had not; left unlit by lamp lighters who wouldn't venture out into the snow. Some streets had no lighting at all.

As I got to Howland Street I realised none of the lamps had been lit and I could barely see a hand in front of me. Howland Street was one of the streets one went down before one got to the rookery. It was a dark, dank street that wasn't a pleasant journey even in daylight. The snow helped a little, but a fog had begun to fall which blunted the corners of the streets and covered the street signs.

The sound seemed far off at first, like a noise on the edge of my hearing, as though it had become part of my imagination. I walked a little faster. I looked forward to finding the turning for Charlotte Street, even though it meant an environment so very different from the one I had just left. It would mean a safety of sorts, and I imagined Bessie would have been on the lookout for me.

I walked further down Howland Street. I didn't recognise anywhere because of the fog. It had enveloped me so quickly I felt as though I were in a bubble of smog. It smelt vile and I lifted my muffler to cover my mouth. I stopped and tried to look through the fog. Where was I? Had I already passed the Charlotte Street entry?

I startled when I heard the sound. It was the whistling, the whistling Bessie and I had heard before, and the whistling when I had been alone. Why was he on the streets in the densest of fogs? Why was he abroad when I was alone? I listened intently, concentrating on the tune. I had been too frightened before; could not discern what the tune was, but now I knew. It was "My Bonnie Lies Over the Ocean". It was a recent favourite in the music halls, but whistled slowly it seemed threatening, almost malevolent.

I stood against the wall and held my breath. The whistling got closer and closer and I knew he was only a few feet away. Could he see me in the fog? Could he smell me? The lavender! I had bathed in lavender water and now I regretted it. Was it a smell he knew? Did he know I was there?

He was so close now I could feel his presence and hear his footsteps. They were louder and more pronounced. I sank to my knees. Within seconds he was in front of me. I couldn't see him...and I prayed he couldn't see me.

He stopped. The whistling stopped. A feeling of utter dread crept over me. I held my breath and closed my eyes...and waited. I prayed with all my might, asking God to protect me from this nightmare, the terror of which alone I thought would end me. I could see nothing of him and it was entirely unnerving. He was there. I knew he was there.

Moments later, the whistling began again, a slow, laborious whistled rendition of, "Oh, Where, Oh Where Has My Little Dog Gone?" I felt movement in front of me rather than saw it. The fog swirled around the creature who had seemingly turned around, walking back the way he came. His footsteps slowly made their way past me, and by the sound of his whistling was moving further and further away from me, down Howland Street and back to the crossroads.

As a small fissure opened up in the fog I saw the crumpled top of a tall hat. It was The Whistling Man who had stalked me that night, and I had never felt fear so intense or so numbing.

I decided to walk further up Howland Street hoping to see some sort of landmark I recognised. Suddenly, the other side of Hog's Yard came into view and at last I felt secure. I ran the rest of the way, into the fog, not knowing if there was anyone else out on such a night, past the yard, and into Charlotte Street. From the entrance to Charlotte Street I could get to the court with my eyes closed, which was as well as the fog here was just as dense.

I pushed open the door and almost fell into the house. Most of the floor was taken up by palliasses, the inhabitants readying themselves for sleep.

'Where the 'ell you been?' whispered Bessie as I settled down next to her. 'I'd almost given up on yer. Surely you ain't bin wiv Jeremiah this long?'

I shook my head. 'I went home,' I said sotto voce, pushing my chin and mouth under the blanket

"Ome!' She looked around to make sure no one was listening, then gazed at me in astonishment. 'What the 'ell for? Did Jeremiah know you was goin' 'ome?' I nodded. Bessie pulled the blanket over her shaking her head.

'You take some risks, Edwin. You might 'ave been seen.'

'I was.' I told her what happened with Jim Smollett.

'Did 'e know you was going into one of the 'ouses?'

'No. It was before I went inside.'

'Did 'e give yer that jaw?'

I nodded again. 'Do you want to know why?'

'Course I do.'

'He and Sylvie,' I whispered, then made the sign I'd seen many of them make when they were discussing a couple...crossed fingers.

'Nah, yer got that wrong.'

'He was seeing me off her, Bessie. He said he'd seen us speaking and accused me of fancying her.'

'And do yer?' I gave her a look.

'She asked me for money then said I could pay in kind, 'Bessie raised her eyebrows, 'which was why I went home, to get some money. I can't afford for it to happen again. Next time I might not be able to fend her off.'

'That girl. She's a right trollop she is, but I never thought she'd 'ave any truck with the Smolletts.'

'You need to get a message to Stride. I think it's significant, Bessie.'

'You think she might be in on things?'

'I do. Unfortunately we don't know what part she's playing, but I'll try to find out. Perhaps you could do the same'

Bessie nodded. 'I'll 'ave a word. And just one fing, Edwin,' she said, pulling the blanket up to her chin and laying her head on the palliasse.

'What's that?'

'Use rose oil in yer bath next time. Prefer it ter lavender.'

Chapter 20

We were woken by a commotion in the courtyard. Bessie crawled out of bed and went to the door.

There were cries of, 'Close the feckin' door, Bessie. I'm freezin' me clods off 'ere", and 'For Chris' sakes, who let Jack Frost in?'.' She went outside and closed the door after her. I followed.

'What is it?'

'They're bringing stuff into the courtyard.'

'What stuff?'

She inclined her head to the court entrance where two men from the Smollett gang were carrying a large crate into the court. They took it into one of the houses where people were just getting out of bed. There were cries of derision, but they were told to keep their mouths shut. One of the men got a backhander from one of Smollett's men, bloodying his lip. It did the trick. No one questioned them afterwards.

'Why are they bringing the stuff here?'

'No more space in their safe house. Prob'ly planning to deliver some of it. They know the police won't come 'ere, too bloody scared. Smollett already did for one police officer when he got too close.'

'You mean, killed him?'

'Yeah. Got away wiv it too.'

'How?'

'No evidence. Cut his throat and dragged 'im out of the court. Left his body in the Tottenham Court Road. 'Ad 'is minions get rid of the blood.'

I winced. 'How do you know?' I whispered.

She turned and looked at me. 'We all know, but we know what would 'appen if we talked.' She turned to go back into the house. 'Anyway, we've got more important things to think about. I'll get word to Jeremiah about you know who, and about what's 'appened this mornin'. I reckon they're about to move the stuff.'

'Will he act now?' She shook her head. 'Why not? He seems to be holding back.'

'Yeah, he is. He knows what 'e's doin'. We want the end game. Don't forget that, Edwin. It's them at the end we want. When we get them we'll get the rest of 'em.'

The crates continued to be brought in, along with huge structures which looked very much like Anubis, the dog Mr Thomas saw in Parker Street, and others which were clearly sarcophaguses, very much like the one I saw.

'There's uproar in the courts,' said Bessie as we stood in the doorway, entranced by what was going on. 'These fings are bein' 'idden in their 'omes, in their yards, even in the privies if yer can imagine it. Some are sayin' they can't even go in an' 'ave a shit 'cos there's somethin' in the way.' She shook her head. 'I'm worried.'

'Are you?' I asked her 'Why?'

'Look at their faces.'

The inhabitants of the Charlotte Street rookery stood around the edge of the court, their faces like stone. Life was increasingly hard in the rookeries. They had so much to cope with, lack of food, no water when it was needed, filth and ordure beneath their feet and in their homes every day. With it being winter life was doubly hard. Now even their homes were being taken from them, homes they paid money for, as ramshackle and polluted as they were. And any money was hard to come by. Smollett and his associates were using their homes to store the goods from their criminal activities and they were not permitted to object. They all knew what would happen if any of them showed signs of dissent. The knife in Jim Smollett's belt told them quite plainly.

He glanced across to Bessie and me, grinning, no doubt at the huge, black and purple bruise on my jaw. My eye had swollen almost shut.

'That man needs takin' down,' said Bessie under her breath.

Just as we were about to be pushed aside so the men could get into the house with a dozen or more crates, Sylvie turned into the court.

'Not in there,' she cried. 'We don't want none in there.' She turned to Jim Smollett and put her hands on her hips in a confronting stance. 'Not in there, Jim,' she said. 'There ain't enough room as it is.'

'There ain't enough room in any of the 'ouses,' someone called out. 'We pay rent for 'em. Why do we 'ave to put up wiv this? What's 'Arry Andrews goin' ter say?'

Jim Smollett threw his head back and laughed. 'He'll say bring more in, mate. And yer can mind yer own feckin' business. I know you're be'ind wiv yer rent so I don't reckon yer've got much to say.' The owner of the voice shrank back into the gathering of people standing around him and turned his face to the cobbles. 'If anyone else feels the same they can come and see me,' he said, resting his hand on the hilt of the knife. Quiet descended on the crowd.

Sylvie walked across to Smollett and whispered something in his ear. He turned towards her, grinning again, revealing his brown, uneven teeth. He nodded and my stomach churned with disgust.

'She's in on this,' murmured Bessie under her breath. 'Can 'ardly believe it of 'er. Fought she was one of the good 'uns.'

I blew out a breath. 'Nothing is as it seems.'

'Yer can say that again.'

Sylvie wandered up to us and stood next to Bessie. 'That told 'im.'

'Promise 'im somethin' did yer?' Bessie asked her.

Sylvie chuckled. 'Funny what the promise of a bit of kitty'll do fer a man.'

'Ain't you got any standards?'

Sylvie threw back her head and laughed. 'Standards? In this place? You takin' somefin', Bessie. Who are we to 'ave standards?'

She sashayed past Bessie and me and made to go into the house. She paused holding out her hand. 'Coin, Edwin.' I put my hand in my pocket and pulled out a few coins, decanting them into her palm. She looked down at her hand and sneered.

'S'pose that'll 'ave ter do, lover.' She winked at me and went through the door, shutting it with a back-kick.

'Jesus,' said Bessie, sotto voce. 'What's comin' next?'

'Something I've been waiting for,' I answered.

'What's that?' I inclined my head towards the entrance. 'Stinky Ralph!' Bessie nodded. 'You were right, Edwin.'

'He's in on this too.' I turned to face her, 'but we must find out how.' I glanced at him again hoping he wouldn't come over. I couldn't help feeling Ralph thought we had a sort of friendship which repelled me, but then logic kicked in and I realised I could use it to my advantage. 'He's the one who will give it away.'

'Ralph? I wouldn't bet on it.'

'I think he likes me. We drank together in the Whistle and Flute. What if I were to get him in his cups and gently steer him towards it?'

'Yer need coin fer that. And 'e likes yer because no one else'll go near 'im.'

'I have coin.'

Bessie raised her eyebrows, then nodded. 'I'll leave it ter you then, Edwin.'

'Can you get a message to Stride about what's happening in Charlotte Street? And tell him again about Ralph. My instinct tells me he has an important part to play in what's going on. As soon as I know anything I'll need to see him.'

'Fancy 'im do yer?' She looked a little jealous I thought.

Jonathan's face loomed up in my mind's eye. I shook my head. 'No, Bessie. He's not for me.'

She pursed her lips and looked contrite. "Ad a fiancé din't yer?' I nodded. 'Yer got jilted I 'eard.' I said nothing and blinked away the tears gathering under my eyelids. If Jonathan and I had married, would I have accepted Stride's proposal to be a police agent in the Charlotte Street court? Bessie patted my shoulder. 'Life's 'ard, innit, Edwin, but I don't need to tell yer that, do I?'

Later that evening I braved the cold and fog and went to Drury Lane. I more or less knew Stinky Ralph would be in the pub because I gathered it was the first place he went after a day of sewer grubbing, rather like his second home. Or maybe his first.

I had a good supply of money with me. My aim was to get him drunk and lead him to speak to me about his role in the stealing, storing, and selling of the Egyptian artefacts. It crossed my mind he might even know who was buying them, but if I could get some information about how the artefacts were delivered we could work out everything else with logic.

The atmosphere in the pub was how it was the first evening I had visited there; rowdy, with lots of catcalling, ribbing, beer being spilt by men already in their cups, even though it was still only seven o'clock.

The night-time women had returned, and there was someone on the piano who, because of being drunk, kept playing the wrong notes, which had everyone in fits of laughter. Each time they laughed he hawked up and spat phlegm onto the floor. I winced every time he went off key. I was an experienced pianist, and if I'd thought it would not have given me away, I would have pushed the repugnant drunk off the piano stool and played the piano myself.

Stinky Ralph was sitting at the table by the door which pleased me more than I can say. I had yet to venture right into the public house where the other men were punching each other on the arms, in a friendly way they would say, and calling each other unpleasant names which they found amusing. I dreaded when it might become necessary for me to join in. Ralph had joined me when I had sat at the table without even a gentle request, so I assumed the same would be acceptable for me.

'Whad'yer want? he snarled at me. In truth Ralph was not looking happy

'Will yer not let me buy yer a drink, Ralph?' I asked him. 'I 'ad a good day today.'

His face brightened. 'Go on then,' he said, holding out his glass. 'And a whiskey to go wiv it if yer so well orf.'

I clapped him on the shoulder and went to the bar, ordering his quart and whiskey, and a half for me, which I wouldn't drink for fear of catching something unspeakable.

"Ad a bad day, Ralph?' I asked him.

He sniffed and wiped his nose on the sleeve of his jacket. 'Jus' wish people would do what they say they're goin' ter do.'

'Women trouble?'

'Nah, nuffin like that.' He glanced at me. 'I fancy that Bessie though. Fine figure of a woman ain't she? You sniffing round 'er yerself?'

I frowned. 'She's me cousin.'

He shrugged. 'So? Couldn't put a word in for me then could yer? I could show 'er a good time. I ain't poor.'

I made a small smile and nodded, wondering how Bessie would take it when she knew Stinky Ralph had designs on her. I couldn't imagine any woman being flattered by his interest. He was well-named. The stink of the sewers followed him wherever he went.

'Another?' I asked him.

'You must a made a bit today if yer buying.'

"Ad a win on the dogs. Illegal like but I weren't asking no questions. It weren't a fortune but it'll stand us a few drinks.' I looked down and softened my voice. 'I don't know many people round 'ere niver.'

He feigned a punch to my arm. 'Well I liked yer soon as I laid eyes on yer. I'm a good judge a character. Yeah, I'll 'ave anuvver drink wiv yer.' I bet you will, I thought.

Seven rounds of whiskey later and Stinky Ralph was well into his cups. He clearly wasn't used to it. His cheeks had turned blush pink and he slurred his words. I felt it was the best time to pry. I opened up the questioning.

'So, who let yer down, Ralph?'

He sniffed. 'Thems over there.' He inclined his head to a group of Smollett's men who were standing at the bar. They were the rowdiest of the lot, bullish and loud.

I took a pretend swig of my beer. 'Them?' I frowned. 'D'yer know 'em then. Yer need to be careful, Ralph. It's what everyone says.'

'Well, everyone's wrong,' he slurred. 'They're alright. They know me talents well enough.'

'Your talents? I don't know your talents and I thought I were a mate.'

'You are a mate,' he said, giving my arm a weak punch. 'Only one I got round 'ere. I's a tosher, ain't I? They need me talents, but they won't pay me what they promised. They're offering me 'alf now of what they said, and I'll ave ter do it 'cos if I don't you'll likely find me floating in the Thames. Bastards they are. Feckin' bastards.'

I so much wanted to ask him a straight question about what he'd been asked to do, but I knew I should proceed carefully. 'Ope it ain't dangerous, Ralph.'

'Nah, it ain't dangerous. I know what I'm doin' dun I? Just gotta get the stuff through the sewers to where they got ter go. No one,' he thumped the table, 'no one knows them sewers like I do. Knows 'em like the back of me 'and I do. They're me second 'ome.

'I'm the best tosher in London. Some a these fellas thinks there's easy pickin's down there, so they go in ter the sewers wiv out knowing nuffin' about 'em. Do yer want ter know what 'appens to 'em?' I nod. 'They take a little lamp wiv 'em and when it goes out they can't find their way out. They panic and start sloshing around in the sewage cos they've lost their way. They die, Edwin, drown most of 'em.' My stomach rolled. 'I find the bodies sometimes. I don't tell no one when I find one. It's their bloody fault ain't it. Greedy, see. They got greedy and they paid the price.'

'So where will yer be goin'? D'yer need any 'elp?'

He looked at me, his head swaying on his shoulders, his eyes barely able to keep focus. 'You'll want payin' though, won't yer? It'll 'arv me money again.' He shook his head. 'I dunno. Wish I'd never got involved. The stuff they want me to move is 'eavy, some of it bigger 'an you. I'd make more money on one of me trips.'

'Yer don't 'ave ter pay me, mate. We're mates ain't we? Don't like ter see a mate lookin' so rotten. I'll 'elp. Yer can do *me* a favour one day.'

He glanced up at me and after a few moments, narrowing his eyes, then nodded. 'Alright, Edwin, yer on. I'll buy you a quart of ale, will that do?'

'Yeah. That'll do.'

He finished his whiskey and got up. 'Need the privy. See yer around, Edwin. I'll let yer know.'

He staggered through the public house, bumping into some of the men at the bar who jeered at him and pushed him away. He wasn't a popular figure that was certain. I waited for him to disappear out of the yard door and left. It was a relief to get out into the fresh air.

I sniffed at my clothing and grimaced. Some of Ralph's stink had transferred to me, or at least it's what it smelt like. Or I just couldn't get the smell of him out of my nose. I could almost taste it and I heaved into the gutter.

I made it back to Charlotte Street in record time, mindful of my last experience with The Whistling Man. I had never been more terrified, more frightened than when Jim Smollett grabbed me in the dark and punched me insensible. He was solid, more apparent. The Whistling Man.... in truth I didn't know what he was. I shivered involuntarily.

When I turned into Charlotte Street I noticed Bessie and a group of women standing outside the court. I could hear their chatter, but it wasn't the usual loud twittering, the raucous, gravelly laughter. They spoke in low voices, murmuring to each other, some not saying anything, preferring to keep their own council. Bessie turned when she heard my footsteps on the cobbles and walked towards me, her expression one of cold stone.

'Bessie?'

'There's bin another murder.' My mouth dropped open.

'Close your mouth, Edwin. Yer look like yer catching flies.' I closed it.

'Who?'

'She put an arm through one of mine and walked me into the court. 'Well, there's the thing. It's one of the Smolletts, Jim Smollett's younger brother, Dan.'

'Why would someone murder him?'

She shook her head and widened her eyes. 'No idea, but 'e was left in Percy Street.'

I frowned. 'But isn't that where Ronnie Dines body was found?'

'It were.'

'Retaliation?'

She shrugged. 'Maybe. People ain't liking what's goin' on 'ere.'

'But why him?'

'Dunno, Edwin. The Smolletts ain't popular wiv anyone, so it could be anyone what did 'im. Any'ow, 'ow d'yer get on?'

I looked around us, wary someone might be listening to our conversation.

'Can we go somewhere else, Bessie? Somewhere private?'

'Can it wait 'til mornin'? We can go to the Amethyst Café. It's far enough out the rookery to be safe. I'll get a message to Jeremiah. Yer don't want ter be tellin' the story twice.'

'I was followed from there by Jim Smollett, Bessie. It's how he found me in Harley Street. I'm not sure it's safe anymore.'

She nodded. 'I'll find somewhere.'

The following morning Bessie and I left the court. The weather wasn't as cold as it had been on the previous days. Bessie had donned only one shawl and left her hair uncovered. I could see what Stride had seen in her. Her curly, blonde hair hung down her back like a curtain, and she was younger than I'd first thought. Her skin was unblemished, a surprise bearing in mind how much time she'd spent in the rookery.

'Have you washed this morning, Bessie?' I asked, grinning

She looked up at me, frowning. 'I always wash.' Of course I knew it to be a lie. Most mornings there was no water for something as dispensable with as washing. We were meeting Stride. Something told me he was still in her heart.

'You look very nice.'

'Are yer making some sort of proposal, Edwin?'

I pushed my lips together in a stifled laugh. 'No, but there's someone who'd like to get to know you better. He says,' I put a finger on my chin and stared up at the sky with a squint, pretending to think, 'he says...he'll show you a good time and he isn't poor.'

'Oh.' She smiled, looking flattered. 'And who might that be, pray?'

'Stinky Ralph.'

Her face went dark and she gritted her teeth. 'I'm fed up not 'ard up, Edwin. God, yer couldn't get near 'im. And while we're on the subject, you're beginning to smell like 'im.' I buttoned my lip thinking Bessie was not someone to take on lightly. She always made sure she had the last word.

'So, where are we going.'

'The Tambourine in Beak Street. Them new Salvationists have set up a stall there where they serve soup to the 'omeless. Don't worry you'll fit in...more 'n me at the moment.'

'What about Stride?'

"E knows what ter do.'

We walked for about twenty minutes until we reached Beak Street. Dare I say it was a pleasant walk. The sun had broken through and it warmed me to my bones, so much so I removed my outer garments. Bessie took off her shawl and held it over her arm. She began to fuss with her hair. She turned from me and pinched her cheeks to give them some colour. I smiled.

'It's unseasonably warm,' said a voice behind us. It was Stride, unrecognisable in the clothes of a costermonger.

'Hello, Jeremiah,' said Bessie. 'What d'yer look like?'

He raised his eyebrows. 'Like a costermonger, I hope.' He nodded to me. 'Edwin.' I nodded back. 'I hope you've something to tell me. I'd like the shortened version if you will.'

We went to the coffee stall and Stride bought three coffees. I drank mine with relish. Coffee wasn't easy to come by in the courts.

'What's so urgent?'

'Edwin's got some news,' Bessie said, blowing on her coffee.

Stride glanced up at me.' Go on.'

'They're moving the artefacts through the sewers,' I said, lowering my voice to a murmur. 'Stinky Ralph...or Ralph Pearson you said he's called. He's a tosher as you know, and he's helping the Smolletts get the artefacts to the buyers, but they don't want to move them where they can be seen so they're using the sewers. I'm guessing they'll go at night and take them through the sewers to the nearest manhole to the street where they need to be delivered.'

Stride frowned. 'Ralph Pearson's going to move the stuff by himself? And you're right, we do know him as I said. Rich as Croesus and shifty with it. He makes a mint out of the sewers, but he's had his fingers in more criminal pies than you've had dinner parties.'

'He won't be by himself, Stride. I'll be with him.' Both Bessie and Stride stared at me in horror.

'No, Edwin. It's much too dangerous. Do you know how many bodies wash up in the Thames that have come through the sewers?'

'Only when they don't know what they're doing. Ralph told me it was because people thought it was easy. They would take a small lamp with them and then the lamp would go out and they would lose their way, get completely lost, and drown because they were overcome by the fumes. He knows what he's doing. He says he's the best tosher in London and I believe him. You said he was wealthy. It must be because he's good at what he does. He seems to be the only one who has made a real living from it. The Smolletts have decided the best way to get the artefacts to their customers is through the sewage system, and the only tosher they trust is Ralph. That says something to me.'

'So how did they get it from Parker Street to Charlotte Street?'

'They took a risk I grant you, but it's a stone's throw from Parker Street to Charlotte Street. In a peasouper no one would see them. I should think no one batted an eyelid. I had a look out of the entrance while they were storing the crates in the houses. It was the carriage again, the one I saw in Parker Street, pulling a cart behind it, but clearly they wouldn't dare risk going into Bayswater, or Covent Garden, or Westminster by a carriage pulling an old cart. It would draw too much attention, which is why they've elected to deliver to their customers by using the sewers, underground and out of sight.

'Also, I can only imagine their customers wouldn't appreciate crates being delivered to their esteemed addresses by anyone other than Fortnum and Mason, or Harrods, and preferably in huge wicker baskets, not in wooden crates, and certainly not by ragamuffins from the rookeries.'

Stride nodded. 'When will it happen?'

'When Ralph tells me. I think he was worried about it. He's one man and those crates and sarcophaguses looked heavy. Even for two it will be a struggle.'

'He'll float them,' said Bessie. 'In the sludge at the bottom of the sewer.'

'And you're not a man,' said Stride, quietly.

'Someone must go with him,' I said. 'It's the only way we'll find out who the antiquities are going to.'

Bessie and Stride stared at each other. 'Are you determined to go?' asked Stride.

'Who else will do it?' It went quiet again. 'And he trusts me. Please don't misunderstand, this doesn't come easy to me. Apart from anything else, going down into the maze of London's sewers is repugnant to me. I could catch all manner of filthy illnesses, and the thought of rats...' I shivered. 'I am unable to think of anything more disgusting. Also, I'm not used to pulling the wool over someone's eyes no matter how objectionable they are. It doesn't sit well with me, but I'm here to do a job and I will see it through. I want the money I'll earn from this to send the Thomas children to school. Their father isn't up to the job, and if I can change the lives of just those five children in the whole of my life, all of this will be worthwhile. I can certainly afford to pay for their schooling myself, but you were adamant Stride, I should not give them money. This is the perfect answer.'

Bessie gazed at me; her eyes full of tears. 'Well, Jeremiah. What have yer to say ter that.'

He inhaled a deep breath. 'If anything happens to you your sister will never forgive me.'

'If anything happens to me, I won't forgive you either, Stride. I will haunt you for the duration of your life. You can depend on it.'

'Do you trust 'im?' asked Bessie as we made the walk back to Charlotte Street from Beak Street.

'Stinky Ralph?'

She shook her head. 'Stride.'

I frowned at her. 'Shouldn't I?'

She smiled, then sighed. 'He's one of the most trustworthy men I've ever met.'

'But you're asking me if I trust him. Why would you unless you did not?'

'It's not that I don't. 'Course I do, but for this to work he needs to be on his metal, just as you do. There's a lot at stake, not least, your life, Edwin. I'm guessing as soon as you're given the nod, Ralph will expect you to go into the sewers with him. Jeremiah and his men will follow the Smolletts because they'll want to make sure the stuff gets to where it's intended. Should anything go wrong...if the Smolletts find out they've been rumbled, I don't fancy your chances. Ralph will drown you in them sewers as good as look at yer.' My stomach rolled and I realised talking about doing something was easier than actually doing it.

'You'll have to trust that Jeremiah knows what 'e's doin'. This isn't just about how you play your part. Jeremiah must play 'is part too. I'll make it clear for yer, cos 'e didn't. You're the one in danger. Not Ralph, not the Smolletts, unless we can catch 'em in the act, and not Jeremiah and his men. They can ride off into the fog in their carriages if they get nobbled. You'll be stuck down a sewer with Stinky Ralph who would top 'is own grandmother if she fell foul of 'im. Don't forget, I know these people. You don't. Are yer listening?' I nodded, swallowing hard. 'Yer can back out at any time, Edwin. Yer can say yer don't want ter do it and no one will think any the worse of yer.'

'Would you do it?'

'Would I 'ell, but I ain't you. I've got ter hand it to yer, Edwin. I thought you would be a mill stone round my bloody neck, that I did, but yer plucky, more than plucky really. Yer downright brave. I'm proud of yer too. You ain't a man. You're a woman, a woman like me in a strange world, one what found love and lost it again....just like me.' I stared at her. 'But you've seen life in these parts and you want to make it better, do something about the imbalance. I admire yer for that, but you won't lose my admiration if you change your mind, or Jeremiah's come to that. Once you've agreed to go with Stinky Ralph, it's game on.'

'You still love him don't you?'

Bessie gazed ahead as we walked. 'I never stopped.'

'So what happened?' She glanced up at me. 'You don't have to tell me. It's none of my business.'

"E's got two kids, did yer know that?' I nodded. 'I would 'ave taken 'em on but 'e said 'e wasn't sure it was right. Their ma died and they were 'eartbroken; too young to deal with their grief and too old not to know what it meant when someone yer love dies. I know they went through an 'ard time. 'E told me about their nightmares and the sobbing. 'E said 'e thought it would never end, but gradually it got better. Then 'e and I met up, and well, we got close. It got a bit too hot for 'im 'cos 'e said if we didn't stay together for the duration they would 'ave ter deal with it all over again and 'e couldn't risk it, so we broke up. I didn't want to. I told 'im I was in it fer the long 'aul but 'e wouldn't be persuaded. It near broke my 'eart.'

'So why are you working as an agent in the rookeries, Bessie? Surely there's something else you could have done?'

'To forget, Edwin. Same as you.'

Chapter 21

I slept badly for two nights...partly because I dreaded Ralph giving me the nod, as he put it, and partly because of what Bessie had said to me after we'd seen Stride. It wasn't the fleas keeping me awake, it was the thought of being down in the sewers with Ralph amongst the rats and effluent.

I didn't know anything about the sewers, only that they were the bowels of London, carrying the daily waste of the population which was finally emitted into the Thames. The Thames smelt like a bilge tank, the miasma carrying far and wide. London's daily influx of waste was the reason why.

'Can yer not keep still?' Bessie had said to me on the second night. 'It's like bein' in the middle of the sea on a raft lyin' next ter you. What's the matter wiv yer?' Of course, I knew what the matter was with me. I was frightened. Had I miscalculated? Had I not put enough thought into it? When Ralph had agreed for me to help him I had silently cheered. I was not cheering now.

On the third day Bessie advised me to go to the Whistle and Flute that evening.

'You've decided to go then, 'ave yer, Edwin?' I nodded miserably. I wanted to tell her in truth I hadn't made a hard and fast decision. I was allowing events to dictate what I did. Part of me hoped it had already taken place and that Ralph had decided not to include me. 'We need to get this thing over and done wiv. Go ter the pub and find out what's 'appening.'

The Whistle and Flute was busy, busier than I had seen it. There was no sign of Ralph so I ordered a half and sat in the usual place. I kept my eyes on the yard door and my ears tuned to the double doors at the front. I would know instantly should he enter the pub. I waited for half an hour and was almost about to leave when the yard door swung open and he came in. He was already drunk, and I wondered if it was because he'd been paid for the job.

He went to the bar and ordered a quart and a double whiskey. The barman was more than happy to serve him, even though he was already deep into his cups. Then he espied me.

'Want a drink, Edwin? he shouted across the pub. I shook my head and lifted my still full glass. He collected his beer and whiskey from the bar and came over to the table. 'You still ailing?' he asked me. 'How's yer gut?'

'Not so good,' I said.

'Oh, well,' he said, knocking back the beer as though he was dying of thirst.' You'll be in the right place if yer need to make a run for it,' he murmured under his breath. 'It's on fer tomorrow night,' he said sotto voce. My heart sank like a stone. 'I'm celebratin'. The Smolletts 'ave put me money up a bit. I can afford to 'ave a few tonight. You stoppin'?'

'Not fer long, mate. I was wondering when it were about to go off.'

'Yeah? Glad I've seen yer then. Fought it might be a bit rich fer yer. Meet me on the corner of Charlotte Street and Percy Street. We've a long way ter go, Edwin.'

'Where?'

He tapped the side of his nose with a filthy finger ending in a yellow fingernail. 'Yer don't need ter know that. Just be there at nine o'clock. Got any boots?' I shook my head. 'I'll bring yer some. Yer'll need 'em 'cos you'll be walking through the sewers for a long while.'

I arrived at Percy Street on time. The bells of St Giles in the Fields church mournfully rang out nine tolls in the tower. It had turned cold again, but I assumed the weather outside would not dictate the temperature in the sewers. It would be cold, freezing Bessie had said. Thankfully no one needed the old coat I wore from time to time so I was able to wear it that night. Bessie had leant me her gloves so I pulled them over the ones Meg had found for me. I was worried about my feet. I had only two pairs of socks to wear and I was sure they wouldn't be enough, but where does one get socks in a rookery? Some people had none. Some of the children didn't have shoes or boots. I quietened my mind on the subject.

It had begun to rain by the time Ralph appeared. He looked inordinately happy and wasn't drunk which was a relief.

'Yer 'ere then?' I nodded. 'Ere's yer boots. Yer can put 'em over yer shoes. They should stop the muck getting to yer, but sometimes, if it's deep, it'll slop over yer boots. Yer'll get used to it.' I wanted to assure him I wouldn't ever get used to it and had no intention of doing so. The smell from the boots alone was enough to make me nauseous and I prayed I wouldn't retch.

'Where we goin',' I asked him.

'Westminster Bridge. There's a culvert there I use sometimes what leads into the main sewer. It's 'ow we'll get the stuff to where it's goin'.'

'D'yer know what it is? The stuff, I mean.'

'No idea. I don't ask questions.' he glanced at me. 'I never ask questions and niver should you.' I felt roundly chastised.

It took about three-quarters of an hour to get to Westminster Bridge. We crossed Shaftesbury Avenue and Leicester Square, and made our way down Whitehall until we got to Great George Street. From there the Palace of Westminster could clearly be seen. Ralph shuddered.

'I 'ate that bloody place,' he said, his voice a snarl.

'Do yer?'

"Ain't done nuffin fer me 'ave they. Bloody toffs all decked out in their suits and toppers while the rest of us 'ave to scrape a livin' togevver. Make me sick, that they do.' I knew that successful toshers earnt more money than other people, but I had to acknowledge most people would not want to do what Ralph did to come by it.

He led the way, moving like an animal ferreting about in the undergrowth. I chuckled to myself. Ferret was good name for him.

'Wassat?' he asked me. 'Yer made a noise.'

'Yeah, got stomach-ache.'

'Ain't goin' ter be a problem is it?'

'Nah, got it all the time.'

He led me down some steps which disappeared into a mound of bushes. I followed, pushing the branches aside, hanging onto some of them for dear life. There was no handrail and the steps were glossy with slime.

"Ang on, Edwin. We're nearly there,' Ralph murmured over his shoulder. I heard his footsteps stop at the bottom of the flight of steps. 'Urry up,' he whispered. 'Don't want the mudlarks to see us.'

'When will the stuff be delivered?' I asked him.

'Already 'as,' he said, walking across the mud to the gulley. 'Look.' He pointed to an archway leading to a gulley underneath Westminster Bridge. 'There it is.'

My breath caught up in my throat. If the artefacts were already there it meant the carriage and cart carrying Jim Smollett and his men would not be joining us. There would be no one for Stride and the police officers to follow. I was on my own with no one knowing where I was.

'We'll carry the stuff down to the sewer. This lot's goin' to a bloke in Westminster. 'E's an 'igh-up in somefink. Got money to burn. Bloody 'ell I could shop the lot if I wanted, but what good would that do me. At least this way I'm making some coin. If yer do a good job yer can join me next time, Edwin, an' I might see fit to give yer a reward. Yer don't seem to 'ave much, not as much as me any'ow.' I shrugged, wondering who it was the artefacts would be going to.

'I've never 'ad nuffin,' I said. 'A bit more wouldn't go amiss.'

He nodded then began to walk to the entrance of the culvert, an arch constructed of brick. The bricks were covered in green slime and smelt appalling, an odour which got more pungent the closer we got to it.

I could hear running water, a sound which sent shivers down my spine. I chided myself. It was only water I could hear, but the Thames was a just a blink away from the gulley and my imagination began to run wild. What would happen if the Thames broke through the old walls? How would I get out if something happened to Ralph? I stopped myself. I could run. This was my last chance. I could escape and no one would blame me.

'Come on, Edwin. Nuffin to be scared of. I'm down 'ere every day. Pull your scarf up over yer nose. It'll make fings better for yer.'

I nodded and did as he advised me. 'How will we get the stuff through the sewers?' I asked him.

'I got a raft,' he said proudly. 'It's what I been doin' for the last week, making a raft to carry the stuff through the sewer to the man'ole.'

I frowned. 'But 'ow will we get it out the uvver side?'

He touched his nose to his finger as he was wont to do. 'That's a secret. You'll see, Edwin. Don't worry, mate. We got everythin' covered.' I nodded miserably.

He instructed me to help him get the crates and a sarcophagus onto the raft.

'Some of the sewage ain't as deep as the rest. It goes up and down in places. We'll 'ave to use our muscle to get it across.' He grinned at me. 'Well, you will. I ain't got much muscle.' I realised I had been duped. Stinky Ralph could never have moved the raft on his own. I guessed he had always planned to ask me to help him, but he'd used his wiles to encourage me to agree to help him for no reward. The man was a charlatan, amongst other things.

We pushed the raft into the sewer. I stared into the blackness. It was gloomy even though Ralph had a lantern. I turned to look behind me. The entrance to the gulley got smaller and smaller, the daylight dimmer and dimmer as we walked through the slime and detritus under our feet, the odour getting more and more cloying. The smell made me sick to my stomach and I retched.

'That's it, Edwin. Get it out mate.' I wiped my mouth on my glove and took one last look at the entrance, my only escape to the life I had known before.

We followed a bend in the sewer, and it was gone.

Chapter 22

We'd entered a cavernous space made from Portland stone, Ralph at the front with one hand on the raft, me at the back steering. I knew what the stone was because our neighbours in Harley Street had built a folly in their garden from the same stone. The stone of their folly was pristine and white. The stone in the sewers most certainly was not. The curved walls were now covered with every detritus, and their accompanying stenches.

Below our feet water flowed, much like a stream or river, but the water was thick with sludge, dark brown, lumpy, the most disgusting occurrence I had ever seen. Our feet sloshing through the brown soupy fluid echoed off the walls. Our shadows, thrown by Ralph's lantern seemed other-worldly. Every so often one could hear more water coming into the sewers. Sometimes it sounded like a waterfall, sometimes just a trickle.

The tops of the tunnels were low, which suited Ralph admirably, he was a short man with bowed legs. It suited me less. Some of the tunnels were so low they required me to bend from the waist, bringing my face closer to the sludge I waded through. I pulled my scarf even tighter across my face, glad I had worn two pairs of gloves, although I doubted they would protect me from the filth seeping through the wool. Ralph stopped suddenly.

'What is it, Ralph?' I asked him.

'Up ahead in the curve of the tunnel. Looks like a body but I can't see too well. Me eyesight ain't what it was. 'Ere, you 'ave a look.' He stood aside and I made my way past the raft and stood next to him. There was something big floating in the sludge with some movement around it. 'Rats,' he said, 'eatin' what's left of the poor sod. Bet he was toshing. It's the only reason someone would come down 'ere on their own. I do 'cos I know the sewers like the back of me 'and, but a lot of 'em don't 'ave a clue. Bloody stupid they are. Think it's easy but it ain't. Yer 'ave ter know what yer doin.' I nodded and returned to the back of the raft.

'We'll 'ave to go by it?' I asked, my stomach churning at the thought.

Ralph nodded. 'No uvver way, mate.'

'Ow much further?'

'As the crow flies it's about ten minutes, but there ain't no crows dahn 'ere.' He let out a laugh which echoed around the walls. It made him sound like a madman and I shivered. 'Nah, we're lookin' at 'arf an hour or more. The sewers don't run in straight lines, Edwin. We 'ave to follow 'em where they go. The sewers is a fickle mistress, leading yer this way and that, just like a bloody women leading yer on, but I love 'er. It's where I make me money, and where I feel at 'ome. There ain't nowhere like it. Don't 'ave to talk to no one see. No one to answer to. I'm me own boss.'

'We ain't tonight though is we?'

'We are while we're dahn 'ere. When we get the uvver side and they take over it's up to them ain't it? I don't care. As long as I get me money. That's all I care about.'

We floated the raft further into the sewers. It was beyond anything I could have imagined; a place of nightmares, of wild imaginings, the most putrid of odours, and a graveyard for some.

The body we passed had been mutilated beyond recognition. Only the hair had been left by the rats. I tried not to look, but curiosity got the better of me. I could not avert my eyes. I screwed them up to stop tears from forming. Sadness overwhelmed me. Perhaps he had thought he could feed his family by coming down into the depths of the sewers full of hope of finding things he could sell. How mistaken he had been. Now his family had no one to care for them. A woman was at a disadvantage without an earning man in the house. How would she cope? She had no husband and the children had no father. It near broke my heart.

'You still there, Edwin,' called Ralph over his shoulder.

'Still 'ere, Ralph.'

'Yer a good 'un you are. There ain't many I know what are brave enough to come down 'ere.' Or stupid enough, I thought. 'Five more minutes, son. Tha's all. Just annuver five minutes and we'll be where we're meant to be.' I didn't answer. I was overwhelmed by what was happening; where I was. My face was numb because I'd pulled the scarf so tightly around my face to stop the stench. My hands and feet were frozen, and my eyes were sore and watery because of the putrid air. There was nothing for me to say.

A while later Ralph held up his hand.

'We're 'ere, Edwin,' he shouted. 'We made it, wiv all the stuff kept on the raft. We done a good job.'

Anxiety suddenly swept over me. This was the part I didn't know about, the element of which I had no knowledge. I wondered who would be waiting the other side. Reason told me one of them at least would be Jim Smollett. I could only imagine what he would say when he saw me with Ralph. He wouldn't be alone; of that I was certain.

My thoughts went to Stride. How would he know he needed to be in Westminster to arrest and charge Jim Smollett and his men? That part of the plan had gone badly wrong. We had surmised the Smolletts would have waited until much later that night to deliver the artefacts, to meet Ralph and I at the point of departure into the sewers, but they had been transported earlier in the evening, presumably when the fog had been at its densest.

'What now?' I asked him.

'We stay 'ere.'

'For 'ow long?'

"Til the mornin'.'

My mouth dropped open. It was an annoying habit of mine I had promised myself I would get out of. 'The mornin'? Where we goin' ter go til the mornin'?'

'We ain't goin' nowhere, Edwin. We got ter stay 'ere until Jim opens the man'ole. 'E can't deliver stuff this time a night. Wouldn't look good would it? The customer said tomorrow mornin' and tomorrow mornin' it must be.'

I looked around the stained walls of the sewer, stunned. The filth, the miasma which would surely kill me. The rats. We were to stay in the sewers until the morning amongst all the detritus and effluent the people of London would jettison into their cesspools? I had seen dead dogs and cats floating in the sludge, rodents of indeterminate species, two dead bodies, spiders and slugs. How could we be expected to sleep there.

'I won't sleep 'ere, Ralph,' I said firmly.

'Yer don't 'ave ter. I've slep' down 'ere afore. It don't bovver me. I do it all the time when I can't be bovvered to go 'ome.' That he would prefer to stay in the sewers overnight instead of going to his lodgings said everything.

'Where will yer sleep?'

'On the raft.'

'But yer might fall in.'

'Nah, not me. Done it too often.'

I shook my head. 'I can't do that, Ralph. I'll stay awake.'

'Suit yerself.' He pulled the raft towards him and knelt on it, then stretched his body across the length of it where there was a small gap in between the crates. Moments later he was snoring.

Tears began to fall then and I didn't try to stop them. I was in a nightmare of my own making. I hadn't been forced to help Ralph. No one said I had to join him, in fact it was obvious to me Stride and Bessie would have preferred it if I hadn't.

Stride hadn't forced me to go to the St Giles rookery either, yet I had convinced him, and myself, I was more than up to the task. What I wouldn't have given to close my eyes then, open them once more, and find myself back at Harley Street, sitting on the chaise opposite Violet and Truffle after eating a good dinner prepared by Cook, with Meg fussing that my bathing water would be getting cold in my room if I didn't take my bath soon. I cursed myself for my stupidity. I had always been the same; brave to a fault, determined to not be dissuaded from anything simply because I was a woman, and thoughtless to boot. If I had put myself in danger because of my ignorance there was no one to blame but me, but it would be Violet who would suffer from my foolhardiness.

Jonathan's face loomed before me again and I found myself cursing him too. If he had only thought well enough of me to turn up on our wedding day I would be anywhere but spending the night in the sewers of Victorian London with Stinky Ralph. I shook my head. The tears came again and I swept them away with the end of my scarf. It wasn't Jonathan's fault, it was mine. I prayed I would not pay the ultimate price.

I sat on the raft all night. Stinky Ralph's snores accompanied me as I thought about the decisions I'd made and how I could avoid some of the situations I often seemed to find myself in. I had to think about something, anything, so I could stop ruminating on what I considered to be a self-inflicted prison and what was happening around me.

It was without doubt the longest night of my life. The sounds of the sewer were horrifying in the extreme, the rushing water, the rats scuttling through the sludge and over the walls; and other sounds I could not discern, perhaps would rather not discern. The time stretched out before me like the black caverns we had come through. I pulled my feet up onto the raft, rested my head on my knees, and waited.

I jolted awake. I stared into the gloom in front of me. I had fallen asleep, my head still rested on my knees, my arms wrapped around them. I was so stiff and so cold I thought my limbs would never hold me again.

'You're awake then?' came a gravelly voice behind me. 'Fought you said you wouldn't sleep.'

'I don't remember trying ter sleep,' I said. 'I s'pose I must've bin tired.'

'When you're tired yer sleep. Don't matter where you are.'

'Is it time?' I prayed with everything I had it was.

'It's time.' We moved the raft forward to where a few stripes of light dappled the sludge and the walls. 'Look up.'

We were standing in a square of bricks which denoted the end of the particular branch of the sewer. Above me was a large square manhole. Within seconds the manhole had disappeared and four faces stared down at us from above.

'Yer made it then, Ralph?' said a voice I recognised. It was Jim Smollett and my stomach rolled with fear. With him were two men who I believed were his brothers.

'Yeah,' replied Ralph. 'Told yer we would.'

'We?'

'Me and Edwin.'

'Yer brought that git wiv yer?'

'He ain't a git. He's a good 'un, 'e is. 'As the mortar been dug out?'

'Yeah, we're ready.'

Cobble by cobble the area around the manhole was dismantled until it was big enough to get the sarcophagus through. 'Get the crates through first, then the bigger one.'

'We'll need someone else down 'ere, Jim,' said Ralph. 'The big one's bloody 'eavy.'

'I know 'ow 'eavy it is, yer dim wit. I 'elped to carry it off the cart to get it under the bridge. Just do as I say. Push the crates up first.'

Ralph nodded to me and I made my way to the front of the raft. One by one we pushed the crates up to Smollett and his men. Then it was the turn of the sarcophagus. Jim came down the concrete steps leading from the manhole then jumped down the rest of the way. Between the three of us we managed to lever the sarcophagus up to the hole above us. The men above got hold of it and pulled it clear of the hole.

Jim turned to us rubbing his hands together, grimaced at the place we were standing in then pulled himself up to the steps. When he got to the manhole he knelt down and glared at me.

'Ralph, take the raft back to Westminster Bridge. Edwin you're up 'ere wiv me.'

'Why? asked Ralph, frowning. 'Why can't he come wiv me?'

'Yer want yer money don't yer Ralph?' Ralph nodded. 'Then do as I fecking say. 'E's wiv me.'

Ralph shrugged and glanced at me. 'Yer'd better go wiv 'im, Edwin,' he said, his voice low with anger. I felt this was confirmation Jim Smollett didn't trust me. Crossing him would have been a stupid thing to do, so I obeyed his instructions. I began to climb the steps up to the street. What greeted me there was something I could never have imagined.

The manhole came out into a cobbled alleyway just off Caxton Street. The buildings in Caxton Street were quite magnificent, and I imagined inhabited by doctors, and politicians whose daily bread was earnt in the exalted halls of The Houses of Parliament, but it was not this which surprised me.

In the alleyway was a pile of baskets. Sylvie, dressed in finery I am sure did not belong to her, was wrapping the artefacts in fine cloth and placing them into the baskets, I suspected for delivery to the customer. It looked like a cottage industry.

'Yer can get yer eyes off 'er,' said Smollett to me. 'She don't want no truck wiv yer, understand?' I nodded. Smollett then turned and disappeared around a corner at the end of the alleyway, only to return minutes later dressed in a suit, a pristine shirt and cravat, and an embroidered waistcoat. I was sure the suit didn't belong to him either. No one in the rookery could afford clothes such as they wore, and they would not have worn them even if they could. It would have made them stand out and it was the one thing one did not do in the rookeries. One did not stand out. Then the penny dropped making quite a clang.

Sylvie had clearly taken the outfits from the laundry in which she worked. They couldn't be seen in Caxton Street dressed like rookery dwellers, and the buyer of the artefacts would not have wanted such people asking for admittance to his home.

'Are yer nearly done, Sylvie?' Jim Smollett asked her.

'Yeah, all done. What time do we 'ave ter deliver 'em?'

'About now.' He looked around at the others. 'We need two more ter 'elp. You Jed, you look the cleanest. You can stand be'ind Sylvie and me. He looked me up and down and I begged all that was Holy he wouldn't choose me. His eyes went to one of the other men. 'And you, Sid. You can carry the goods. I'll speak to the customer, alright?' Everyone nodded. He grabbed Sylvie by the arm. 'There ain't no need fer yer to say anything, Sylvie. Just keep yer mouth shut and make eyes at the man what opens the door. Prob'ly be a butler or someone like that. Understand?'

She nodded and stared up at him adoringly. 'A course Jim. Whatever you say, darlin'. You're the boss.' He leered at her, his teeth brown and broken. Then his glance landed on me.

'Yer the look out, Edwin. Anyone you see what's dodgy you whistle, right, wiv two fingers. You can do it, can't yer?'

I was elated. I had taught myself to whistle when I was a girl. Mother had said it was unseemly, but Papa had simply laughed. 'I can do it.'

'Go on then.' I stuck two fingers in my mouth and produced a piercing whistle. Smollett just nodded.

'Let's get the stuff there then. You two,' he pointed to Jed and Sid. 'Go an' get the big one.

They hurried to the end of the alley where the sarcophagus was leaning up against the wall. Sylvie had wrapped it in cloth and tied a bow around the middle which I thought was completely unnecessary. It looked like a Christmas present. Smollett and Sylvie picked up one of the baskets, carrying it between them with the handles. Jed and Sid followed, carrying the sarcophagus. I followed behind.

I trailed them out of the alley and down Caxton Street to a smart house with a recently painted front door finished with shiny brass door furniture. The windows were similar to my home in Harley Street, tall with small panes of glass and smart white frames. Smollett and Sylvie placed the basket on the ground and Smollett knocked on the door. I surreptitiously looked up and down the street. Would Stride arrive, or had he been thrown off the scent simply because of one seemingly small thing we hadn't bargained for, which had made the difference between failure and success; the delivery of the goods earlier than expected the day before. I felt anxious and could hardly stop myself from shaking. On one hand it was imperative that Stride was in the area; on the other I wondered what would happen if he were. I was worried, and incredibly frightened. How could Stride possibly know about this morning's delivery or where it was taking place?

The door was answered by a butler dressed in a morning suit; black long-tailed jacket and pinstripe trousers.

'Yes, sir,' he said, rather pompously. I'd vowed never to have a butler. They were always so self-important.

'We've got a delivery for Mr Welham,' said Jim in a pretend posh voice that was less than successful.

I gaped. Welham? Surely not. How on earth could Detective Superintendent Welham afford to live in such a house? And in Westminster too. It was beyond ridiculous. I wondered if our illustrious politicians were aware they had a lowly police officer living amongst them. This beautiful house was not one any police officer would afford, no matter how high up in the police hierarchy they were.

The butler nodded and asked them to wait while he got the footmen to take in the baskets and the sarcophagus. Jim looked at his men, grinning. 'This is where we get the dosh, mates. We'll be quids in when this lot is delivered, and we got anuvver one tomorrow night.'

As he rubbed his hands together, I noticed Sylvie wasn't looking so jubilant. I frowned. The one thing I knew about Sylvie was she liked money and I should know. Every time she caught me she would ask for coin. Then she turned towards me and grinned, looking over my shoulder. I frowned, wondering why. I felt the hairs rise on the back of my neck and I glanced over my shoulder. I gasped with astonishment.

From Dacre Street to Palmer Street was a line of men. I narrowed my eyes, thinking Stride must have discovered the address of where the antiquities were to be delivered. Had someone informed him of their destination? But then... I frowned, recognising Marcus whose barrow we had used to push Kate to Wilfred Horrocks's apothecary. He grinned at me and nodded, and Dennis, who had been in the courtyard when Jim Smollett and his men had threatened the inhabitants should they accuse them of murdering Jonnie Dines. I shook my head and tried to organise my sensibilities. Why were they here?

I looked further down the line. All were men from the Charlotte Street Court, and all were armed, with knives, cudgels, chains, and all manner of other implements they clearly meant to use as weapons. They had quietly positioned themselves in Caxton Street. They made no sound and it astonished me. Sylvie caught my eye and nodded, then made a gesture of putting two fingers in her mouth. I understood immediately, placed two fingers in my mouth, and gave the loudest whistle I could muster. The door to Welham's house slammed shut.

Jim Smollett turned at my whistle. When he saw the men in the street he paled. He knew why they were there. They were ready for a fight. He turned to look for Sylvie but she had long gone. I'd seen her scuttle away, down Caxton Street to the alleyway where she had wrapped the antiquities.

I waited to see who would make the first move. It was clear that Jim Smollett and his men were outnumbered, a rare occurrence for them I would imagine. He cowed the people of the courts by taking his gang with him wherever he went, but on this occasion he had only three other men with him, including me. There could not be a happy outcome for Jim Smollett.

The men from the court began stamping their feet on the cobbles. It was a frightening sound, one to make one's blood run cold. Jim Smollett backed against the wall, then tried to mollify the angry men in front of him.

'Come on now, Marcus. Dennis. We've supped down the Whistle and Flute together afore. There's no need fer this is there? If yer not 'appy we'll make it up ter yer. We'll move the stuff out of yer 'omes, ow's that.' Neither Marcus or Dennis answered him, but simply continued to stamp their feet.

These men, the downtrodden of the rookeries, had had enough of being crushed and vilified. It was bad enough indeed the upper classes should look down on them so, people who neither thought of them or cared to make their lives better. To have people who lived the same way, who knew and had experienced the terrible life one had if one was a rookery dweller who thought it was acceptable to use their poverty against those in the same situation, yes, it would have been impossible to swallow. These men who were not without dignity had decided to accept it no more.

'We're not all 'ere to give yer a pastin',' said Marcus. 'We'll play fair, Jim. Three against three. The others'll watch you gettin' what you deserve.' Smollett glanced at me.

'Not 'im,' said Dennis. "E's one of us. We knowd you give 'im a pastin' fer nuffin. Bessie told us. 'E ain't part a this, and 'e surely ain't one a yourn.'

I tried to make my feet move but they would not. I was standing in between the two lines of men, Jim Smollett's short one, and the men from the court. I knew I must get out of the way, but fear overtook me.

'Over 'ere, Edwin.' A voice came from the alleyway. I recognised it belonging to Bessie. The relief at hearing her voice was like a warm bath. I turned to see her standing at the entrance with Sylvie. Suddenly I was able to move and I made my way through the men from the court and walked towards them.

'You alright, Edwin?' she asked, putting a hand on my arm.

'I am now,' I answered, looking at Sylvie who had changed out of the clothes she had been wearing and was back in her usual attire. 'I thought I was done for.' She nodded. 'How did this come about?'

'Sylvie organised it.' I glanced at Sylvie and she made a small smile. I noticed there were tears in her eyes and she looked away. I frowned. 'She's got 'er reasons,' said Bessie.

Suddenly, Marcus and Dennis ran towards Jim and his men, along with another from the court. It was the one who Jim had shown up in front of the others regarding the non-payment of his rent. I assumed the poor devil hadn't had the wherewithal to pay it.

The fight began. Jim and his men had seemed to be at a distinct advantage until they pulled out their knives from their belts and began slashing the air in front of them.

'Come on then,' Jim snarled. 'Let's be 'avin yer. Yourn bastards ain't no match fer me an' my men.' Marcus and Dennis waded in with their cudgels and knives. Jim Smollett took on Marcus who was built like a brick outhouse. It made him slower, but he was far stronger than Smollett. One punch and Smollett was on the ground, reeling from a punch to the face. Dennis took on one of the brothers. Dennis was a big man also and he landed a crack on the Smollett brother's head with his cudgel. It was chaos and I was sure it would erupt into carnage if it wasn't stopped.

'Where's Stride?' I asked Bessie.

'On his way. Proper put out 'e was. 'E'd been followin' Smollett for days but some'ow he threw Stride and 'is men off the scent. I sent a snout to 'im when I 'eard about today.'

'Who told you?'

'Sylvie.'

'It's not as we thought then?' I said sotto voce. Bessie shook her head.

Suddenly Sylvie broke away from us and ran into the melee. She stood over Jim Smollett, looking down on him with a sneer on her face.

'Ain't such an 'ero know are yer, yer bastard.' She spat in his face. Before anyone could stop her she pulled a knife from a pocket in her skirt and brought it down into Jim Smollett's chest. Bessie grabbed my arm, her mouth open in a silent scream.

'That's fer Ronnie,' Sylvie screamed at Smollett as he flailed on the cobbles. 'An if yer wanna know 'oo done fer yer bruvver, it were me. It were bofe of yer what done 'im. Now yer've bofe 'ad yer comeuppance.' She put the knife in her pocket and ran.

The fighting suddenly stopped. Both Smollett's men were lying on the cobbles, bloodied and heaving up their guts. A police whistle sounded in the distance. The men from the Charlotte Street court began to run, down the cobbled back alleyway, across the parks, making their way back to St Giles. All that was left was Smollett's dead body, and the almost comatose men who had been defeated by the men of the court.

'We'd best go,' said Bessie. 'If we're found 'ere we'll be the ones who'll 'ave to answer questions. I'd rather they didn't find us 'ere.'

'But whose side are we on?' I asked her. 'Sylvie's, and the men from the court, or the police?'

'We're on our own side, Edwin,' she said, pulling me away. 'Yer don't need ter be on anyone else's side.'

Back at the court there was jubilation. A huge fire had been built in the centre of the yard, and Doris had put together a huge stew which she was dishing out to everyone in the courtyard. I couldn't tell what meat she'd used and I didn't like to ask, but it was hot and tasty. It was all that seemed to matter.

Children ran around the fire yelping and whooping, enjoying a day of happiness, something so rare in their lives. Someone brought out an old violin, someone else a penny whistle, and they played through the night. I watched my fellow rookery-dwellers as they danced, men and women together. They were laughing and drinking ale from the taverns. Even Marcus and Dennis joined in, limping through the dances after their fight with the Smolletts. They were having a party and I couldn't help smiling.

Bessie came over to me, nursing a glass of ale.

'I think you're done here, Edwin,' she said. 'You can go 'ome.' I nodded and she nudged me in the ribs. 'Don't tell me yer sad.'

'Maybe a little. I can't say it's been enjoyable, but I feel it's done me a service to see how other people live, to be a part of it rather than simply listening to hearsay, or reading articles written by journalists who don't really know how it is.'

'This life was never meant for anyone, Edwin. It just 'appened. There will always be those who 'ave more than other people, but I think you understand better now.'

'I do. I'm just worried about the police. They'll want to know who stabbed Smollett won't they?'

'Of course they will, but I can assure you that every last person here will deny knowing anything about it.'

'Will you?'

'She's gone, Edwin. We'll never see Sylvie again. There could 've been any number of witnesses looking out of their windows at what was goin' on in Caxton Street. Someone would 'ave seen her stab 'im.' She looked hard at me. 'The police don't need us to tell 'em, and if Welham wants to make life easy for 'imself, 'e'll prob'ly tell 'em. I've no doubt 'e was 'iding in 'is 'ouse watching the fight from somewhere. It don't need to be us do it?' I nodded. She was right as she seemed so often to be. 'Anyway,' she said. 'Stride wants ter see yer.'

'Where?'

'Usual place...The Amethyst Café.'

'When?'

'No time like the present, Edwin.'

'We did it, Edwin. We got them, all of them, Welham too. He's in this up to his neck and it's not the first time. We've been trying to nab him for years but he's always been too slippery for us. There's nothing so bad as a bent copper, and he's as bent as they come.'

'And Anthony Greenwood, the lawyer?'

'His body was found in the Thames last night.'

'I heard Jim Smollett say he was going to kill him, the day I was hiding from him in Parker Street.'

'You'll likely be called as a witness.' I nodded, thinking it wouldn't be the worst thing I'd ever been through.

'I'm not sure what to do now, Stride.'

He chuckled. 'You can go home now, Lily,' he said gently. 'You can go home and carry on with the life you had before any of this happened.'

I shook my head. 'I'm not sure my life will ever be the same again. And I'd like to say a proper goodbye to someone, someone without whom I would never have got through this.'

'Bessie?' I nodded. 'Give her my best regards.'

'I don't think it's your best regards she wants, Stride. Think you were a bit previous there if you don't mind my saying.'

He blushed bright crimson which made me smile. 'I had to do what I thought was right.'

'For your children?'

'Exactly.'

'So they'll grow up without a woman's love.' He bit his lip. 'I'm sure you're the best father a child could have, Stride. You were putting their welfare front and centre, but Bessie loves you, and your children.'

He looked surprised. 'Still?'

'Still.'

We left the Amethyst Café and stood outside for a moment.

'I should speak with her perhaps.' He swallowed hard then began to walk away, his hands dug deep into his pockets. 'Are you alright to get wherever you're going?'

'I spent the night in the sewers, Stride,' I called to him. 'I think I can get home by myself.' He smiled then lifted his hand in farewell.

Chapter 23

I didn't need to go back into the court at Charlotte Street. On my journey back to Harley Street I saw Bessie sitting in the little park where Jim Smollett had knocked me cold. She didn't look up when I approached. She was resting her chin on her hand, one of her elbows on the arm of the bench, looking rather glum. I sat down quietly.

'I forgot to ask yer. Yer di'nt come 'ome last night. I was worried. Fought somethin' 'ad 'appened to yer?'

'I slept in the sewers with Stinky Ralph.' Her eyes widened. 'It was as much a surprise to me as it is to you. I thought he was joking when he suggested it. He wasn't.'

'Did it all work?'

I nodded. 'I've just spoken with Stride. There's so much to tell you. Suffice to say Chief Inspector Welham is now in custody as are the rest of Smollett's men. Jim Smollett's body was taken to the morgue.'

'She loved Ronnie Dines. Loved 'im like a brother. He were a bit slow like, and she took care of 'im. She hurt bad when he was murdered. Didn't speak of it though. Some people don't do they?'

'I have a feeling it's why she was cosying up to Smollett. It was so she could get near to him...be part of his criminal dealings. Pretended to be keen on him. My best guess is she planned it all along. He murdered Ronnie and she wanted revenge. Well, she got it.'

'What'll yer do now?'

'I'm going home, Bessie, just as you said.'

She put out a hand and placed it on one of mine. 'I'm goin' 'ome too. I've 'ad enough of the rookeries, the filth and the squalor. I've done me best. And you, Edwin. You did a good job. Changed everythin' yer did.'

I squeezed her hand. 'It's been an experience. Something to tell the grandchildren if I ever have any.' I pulled a face, then smiled. 'What will you do now? You said you had the makings of a plan.'

She sat back in her chair and sighed, grinning.

'There's something I would talk to yer about, Edwin. Yer know I said I'm thinkin' of starting a little detective agency of me own.' I nodded. 'Nothin' too complicated, 'usbands out on the town when they shouldn't be if yer get my meaning, lost dogs, stolen goods, that kind of thing.' She sat forward and looked me in the eye. 'I was wonderin'....., she nervously licked her lips, 'I was wonderin' if you'd like ter join me, as a partner. I've got a bit of money put aside for rent and that. We work well together you and me. I've enjoyed yer company. It's bin a bit lonely at times to be honest...in the rookery, and I reckon we'd 'ave a bit of a laugh too...and make some money at the same time. What d'yer say? We could be Clacket and Smith...or Smith and Clacket. I don't mind either way.'

I smiled widely at her. 'Not Pond?'

'Fing is, Edwin, I think we'd do better if we 'ad a bloke in the mix.'

'And I would be that bloke?'

'Yer would. And would yer want your associates in your society to know you're a woman what works? Don't go down too well wiv the likes of them do it?' She inclined her head to one side as I considered her proposal. 'Yer can take yer time to think about it if yer want.'

I shook my head. 'I don't need to. The answer's yes...I would love to work with you.' I rose from the bench, eager to get home. 'Come and see me at Harley Street tomorrow. I know you know which house it is. For dinner. We can talk long into the night and make plans. You can stay if you will.'

'Thank you, Edwin. You don't know 'ow 'appy you've made me.'

I bent and kissed her on the cheek. 'See you tomorrow.'

I stood on the corner of Great Cavendish Street and Harley Street and just stared. This was the place I knew. This was the place where my heart was. A thrill went through me.

I turned into Harley Street and walked towards the house, then stood on the pavement across the street and looked into the drawing room. Violet was sitting in her bath chair, sewing by the long window. Then I heard barking and Truffle jumped up at the window, yapping for all he was worth. He knew. He knew I was coming home.

Violet looked up, and when she saw me her face broke into a broad smile. I smiled and waved. I saw her call to someone behind her, and Meg appeared in the window, her hand over her mouth. 'Miss Lily,' I saw her say.'

I crossed the street and went up the front steps, my key in my hand. The door flew open and there was Meg, her eyes bright with tears.

'Are you 'ome, Miss Lily?' she asked.

I nodded and smiled. 'Yes, Meg. I'm home.'

THE END

NOTES FROM THE AUTHOR

Hello,

Just a brief note to thank you for choosing THE CURIOUS LIFE OF LILY POND. I'm honoured you have chosen it and I hope you will come to love Lily as I have.

I have always been attracted to anything concerning Victorian England; I find the way the Victorians lived endlessly fascinating and I scoop up every book written about the era I find on my travels, whether it be fiction, or non-fiction. I am constantly learning new information about them, and endeavour to include as much about their lives as I can in my books. There was such a disparity between peoples' lives; some lived in splendour while others in dreadful circumstances, and I endeavour to document the imbalance in my writing.

THE CURIOUS LIFE OF LILY POND is the first book in a new series. The next story in the series is the beginning of Lily and Bessie's new venture, a Victorian detective agency known as Clacket and Smith Private Detective Agency. Lily will remain in her persona as Edwin Smith, for as Bessie says, 'We need to show we've got muscle.' I hope you'll be as excited as I am about their new adventures and where those adventures take our intrepid girls. Be assured, the very darkest places of Victorian London will be explored. Nothing will escape the astute observations of Clacket and Smith, Private Investigators.

I hope you will join them on their next adventure.

Fondest regards,

Andrea

More books by Andrea Hicks...

Books in the Camille Divine Murder Mysteries Series
THE CHRISTMAS TREE MURDERS
MURDER ON THE DANCEFLOOR
THE BRIGHTON MURDERS
MURDER AT THE CHRISTMAS GROTTO
MURDER IN PARIS
MURDER AT THE CAFÉ BONBON

Books in the Lily Pond Victorian Murder Mysteries Series
THE CURIOUS LIFE OF LILY POND

Books in the 99 Nightingale Lane Series
PART 1   (Free)
PART 2
PART 3
PART 4
PART 5 – CHRISTMAS
PART 6 – 1918
PART 7 – THE HOTEL

MRS COYLE'S COOKBOOK
INSPIRED BY STORIES FROM 99 NIGHTINGALE LANE and to accompany the popular series.

Stories and recipes from 99 Nightingale Lane from Ida Coyle I do believe I was born thinking about food, which didn't do me much good seeing as we didn't have much of it. I know I'm lucky compared to many who had it harder than me…I've worked at 99 Nightingale Lane for most of my life, taken in by the family who lived there before the Sterns when my Ma was killed by The Ripper. They were an old London family, not that I would have taken any notice then. I was just a smidgen of a girl, one of many who worked here, nearly as many as the fleas on a dog's tail. And…this is one of the things I learned from Mrs Brimble, the cook who taught me everything I know.

'When I think about where I was born, where we lived over the tanners shop, and what my Ma had to do to put food on the table,' I shook my head, 'she wouldn't believe that I stood there in that grand room, amongst all those beautiful things. And now I'm here in this kitchen with you, cooking the Hamilton's luncheon. I so wish she could see me now.' Mrs Brimble put a hand on my arm. 'She is watching, Ida, and I know she'd be proud of how well you've done and how hardworking you are, but not because of who you work for. She'd be proud because of who you are, the type of person you've become. That's what's important, ducky, not money and things what can be bought. Not tables of silverware and fruits from the continents or gowns from the salons of Bond Street. You're just a little'un really, still young, but you will learn about what's important, and there will be more laughter and smiles and happiness below stairs around our simple table when we have our Christmas dinner than there will be in that beautiful room, you mark my words.' She lowered her voice. 'Y'see, Ida, they haven't learned how to count their blessings. This is just another day to them. They see rooms like that all the time so they've forgotten how to be swept away by it. Do you think Lady Davinia will go into that room and widen her eyes in wonder like you did? Do you think Mr and Mrs Hamilton will take much notice of the table that the upstairs maids and the footman worked so hard to make look lovely? They'll give it a glance only to find an imperfection. It's how they are. They have plenty, they definitely do, but none of them appreciate it.' She stared at me. 'And that's for your ears only,' she whispered.

You see. I had the best teacher. This is my story, of when I was a girl starting work at the age of thirteen and how I fought my way through the ranks below stairs to become cook at 99 Nightingale Lane. And I've brought my favourite recipes with me, documented in MRS COYLE'S COOKBOOK for you to make yourself for you and your family to enjoy.

I hope you love my story and my recipes. It means so much to me that I've been given the opportunity to share them with you.

Warmest wishes from your friend, Ida Coyle, Cook at 99 Nightingale Lane

THE DANDELION CLOCK

Sixteen-year-old Kate McGuire has a secret. Her father, Joe has disappeared, and Kate, her mother, Stella and sister, Emma are left to fend for themselves with little income and no one to turn to. For two years they are heartbroken, wondering why he left, or whether he is still alive. Kate decides she must take on a role she never wanted; as carer for her abusive alcoholic mother, and guardian of her sister who seems intent on finding the solace she needs her own way, a decision that leaves Kate almost unable to continue because of the hurt she causes. Kate is devastated because in her heart she is almost certain she will never see her father again, and wishes for his return on the dandelion clock he gave her years before, the seed heads of a flower she wrapped

in a piece of pink fabric and placed in her memory box as a lucky charm. Kate wonders if she will ever find the love and affection she craves and whether her dad loves her enough to return to them and the place they call home.

CHRISTMAS AT MISTLETOE ABBEY

Review: *A charming-to-read Christmas romance novella to snuggle up with under a tartan blanket, sipping a glass of spicy mulled wine. Enjoy! 'An enjoyable read that was entertaining from start to finish. It was simply delightful, and I highly recommend Christmas at Mistletoe Abbey.'*
'From the first page to the last, this fun romance novel kept me hooked. A real page-turner I couldn't put down!'

THE CHOCOLATE SHOP ON CHRISTMAS STREET

The sweetest Christmas Romance to cuddle up with!

THE GIRL WITH THE RED SCARF

Tom Alexander has no memory of his life at House in the Hills orphanage on the outskirts of Sarajevo, or of his birth parents, the ones whose faces he wants to see, but doesn't remember. When he receives a letter from ChildAbroad, the agency that arranged his adoption in 1994, he is offered the opportunity to search for the boy he once was,

Andreij Kurik—if he returns to Sarajevo. With Sulio Divjak, the driver and interpreter Tom befriends, he searches the derelict orphanage and discovers he has two siblings, one who was also at House in the Hills. Sulio uncovers a faded photograph in Andreij's file of a girl wearing a red scarf. She looks like Ellie; the girl Tom fell in love with at first sight in a café in Regent's Park. Devastated when he realises what it could mean, Tom goes back to the UK to get some answers. Accompanied by Ellie he returns to Sarajevo to find his birth parents, only to receive news that destroys everything he thought he knew about Tom Alexander—and Andreij Kurik.

A young love forged at the height of war, a chance meeting, and a collision of faded memories and half-truths, The Girl with the Red Scarf will appeal to fans of historical, women's and romantic fiction. From the author of The Other Boy, shortlisted for the Richard & Judy Search for a Bestseller

THE OTHER BOY

Their new home promises so much, an idyllic life in the countryside, a peaceful existence outside the busyness of London. She'd dreamt of it. A forever home. But something happened there, a heart-breaking tragedy infused in its walls. The history of the old house returns to haunt her, and when the memories she had buried return she isn't the only one who fears them.

Before you hide the truth, make sure the dead can't give up your secrets. If you love gripping, ghostly psychological thrillers that you can't forget, make a big pot of coffee - THE OTHER BOY won't let you go.

Find out why Amazon reviewers are saying, "Unputdownable and heart-breaking. Not just a psychological thriller, not just a ghost story, but so much more"...*Birdie Advanced Copy Reviewer*